"Here," Wolf said, holding his hand out and asking for the comb.

Serena hesitated, then gave it to him. Wolf slowly moved his hand toward her hair, aching to touch the burnished strands. He realized that her breasts were still very sore, preventing her from lifting her arms high enough to comb her tangled hair on top of her head. He would do it for her.

"Safe," he told her as his fingers barely touched the crown of her head.

Serena winced and cowered.

Wolf froze. She was acting like a beaten dog. His heart bled for her, and he again murmured, "Safe." With each stroke of the comb, she began to relax.

Serena closed her eyes, relenting in degrees. Each time his fingers barely grazed her scalp, her skin tingled wildly in response. She had never been touched by a man until Blackjack had raped her. Wild, confusing emotions began bubbling up through Serena, and she could do nothing but sit there and hungrily absorb Wolf's tender touch.

Dear Reader,

Welcome to Harlequin Historicals. We hope you will enjoy this month's selection.

From Lindsay McKenna comes *Brave Heart,* the story of Serena Rogan, a deeply troubled young woman who discovers a world of love and respect under the gentle care of a Lakota medicine man.

In *Destiny's Promise* by Laurel Pace, Lucinda Chandler hides away on a remote Georgian plantation, but must face her past when she falls in love with her new employer's son.

Ana Seymour's first book, *The Bandit's Bride,* was one of our 1992 March Madness titles. We are very pleased this month to be able to bring you her second book, *Angel of the Lake,* set in Wisconsin in the mid-1800s.

Last, but not least, *Spindrift* by Miranda Jarrett. This captivating romance features the younger Sparhawk brother, Jonathan, from *Columbine* (HH #144), as a shipwrecked seaman determined to unravel the lovely widow Allyn's carefully guarded secrets.

Next month, keep an eye out for *A Warrior's Quest,* the next book in Margaret Moore's Warrior series.

Sincerely,

Tracy Farrell
Senior Editor

Brave Heart

LINDSAY McKENNA

Harlequin Books

TORONTO • NEW YORK • LONDON
AMSTERDAM • PARIS • SYDNEY • HAMBURG
STOCKHOLM • ATHENS • TOKYO • MILAN
MADRID • WARSAW • BUDAPEST • AUCKLAND

Harlequin Historicals first edition May 1993

ISBN 0-373-28771-2

BRAVE HEART

Books by Lindsay McKenna

Harlequin Historicals

Sun Woman #71
Lord of Shadowhawk #108
King of Swords #125
Brave Heart #171

LINDSAY McKENNA's

Native American background spurred her interest in history, which she feels is a reflection of what goes on in the present and an indication of what the future will be like. Most interesting to Lindsay are the women of history. She feels their strength of spirit can be an inspiration to the women of today. Her three favorite historical periods are the Old West, the medieval times and the Roman era.

Lindsay, an avid rock hound and hiker, lives with her husband of fifteen years in Arizona.

Chapter One

They've left me to die.... Serena barely lifted her head from the coarse bulrushes that crowded the banks of the shallow river. It hurt to breathe, but she took in a deep, quivering breath, pushing herself upward on unsteady arms. Dawn was peeling back the inky coverlet of the September night. A shiver wound up her spine. It was a night she'd never forget. Blackjack Kingston's narrow, mustached face leered through the fog of her pain.

Shaking her head as if to banish thought of the rich gold miner, Serena forced herself to think beyond the open wounds on her breasts. Green eyes narrowed with agony, she stared groggily at the peaceful river that flowed through the Black Hills of South Dakota. Steam rose in wavering fingers off the surface, creating fog across the river and surrounding marsh. Her home, Wexford, Ireland, was so far away. She was halfway around the world, abused by a depraved man and then thrown away to die.

"No," she muttered, gritting her teeth. She looked down at her thin blue calico dress. The bodice was stained with blood and seepage from the wounds Kingston had inflicted upon her, and the material stuck to her flesh. His last words haunted her: "I'll make damn sure no man wants to lay a hand on you again, you redheaded witch."

Lifting her fingers to her bodice, Serena closed her eyes, her emotional pain overwhelming her physical pain. It was impossible to erase the memory of Kingston stalking across the polished wooden floor from the fireplace with the red-hot poker in his hand. A sob escaped from her constricted throat. There was no way to halt the forthcoming terror as she replayed the scene in her mind. Because she refused to submit to the miner's demands, he'd repeatedly raped her, taking her virginity, and with it her dignity.

Serena hung her head, gently placing her fingers against her aching right breast. She came from a poor family of Catholic farmers in Ireland. Perhaps her flaming red hair, which now hung matted and unkempt, was a banner heralding her unbreakable spirit, and Kingston had sought to break her because of it. Her spirit was all she had left, Serena thought, dazed by the sudden turn of events. Last night she had tried to escape, not eating the drugged food. The fight to elude Blackjack had turned into a violent confrontation. She had almost made it past the door to freedom, but he had wrapped his hand into her waist-length red hair and yanked her off her feet.

Serena reached out, sliding her fingers into the clear, quiet water. Serena longed to wash away the terror she tasted in her bloodied mouth. Slowly she crawled into a kneeling position, the dress hampering her efforts. The water was so clear and inviting in comparison to how she felt inwardly. Dirty. Filthy.

Scooping up a handful of water, Serena allowed the cooling liquid to sluice across her face. Blackjack had always talked of how pretty she was: the tilt of her forest-green eyes, her generous lips and her thick, red hair.

nstead of using the hot poker to scar her face, he'd
carred her breasts.

She knelt on the bank, hands in her lap, watching the
ed ribbon across the horizon. Around her, the world was
wakening, birds heralding the arrival of the dawn with
heir melodic chorus. *I'm alive. I can make it. Some-
ow, I can make it.* The water was clearing her senses.
erena leaned down, scooping one handful after an-
ther onto her mouth drinking deeply of the life-giving
vater. After ripping a piece of the calico material from
he hem of the dress, she dipped it into the water. She
ried to scrub away from her face, neck and hands the
dor of Blackjack and of the last terrible months of im-
risonment.

As she sat there, hidden among the tall reeds and
ushes, Serena watched the red dawn turn gold, and then
fragile pink color. The world around her was pristine,
ntouched and heart-stoppingly beautiful—all the things
he would never be again. Kingston had robbed her of her
irginity, the only thing she had left to give the man who
night be her husband. Worse, he'd claimed her self-
ood, leaving her stripped and humiliated. Tears
queezed into Serena's eyes, but she froze them in place,
efusing to cry, to give in to them.

Throughout the months that she'd been a prisoner of
Kingston, Serena had never shown fear or cried. Black-
ack had taken her bravery as his personal challenge to
reak her spirit, to make her cry out in pain, or at least
o bring her to a state of tears. He'd accused her of being
witch, of having no heart or feelings because he hadn't
ccomplished his goal. Serena hung her head, staring at
he young grass shoots. Gently, she touched them with
er muddied fingers. Once she'd been like them—vul-
erable to the ever-changing world around her.

"Never again..." she whispered hoarsely. Men meant nothing but pain, degradation and humility. Her spirit, her ability to fight back for what she felt was rightfully hers, had been a beacon to men who disagreed with her. They tried to break or kill her. The hatred that welled up in Serena took her by surprise. It was murderous, and she had never contemplated hurting anyone in her eighteen years of life. But that was before she had tapped the rage suppressed deep within her heart.

Men. She closed her eyes, wincing. Men scared her now. Kingston didn't have to worry about her wanting a husband. She wanted *no* man! Serena slowly opened her eyes, staring at the unsullied water. If God would answer her prayers and help her survive this latest twist in her life, she swore she would *never* marry. Better to eke out an existence alone than to bow to a man and become his slave again. Men meant nothing but pain and agony, capable only of hurting, maiming and raping a woman.

The braying of a mule jerked Serena out of the hatred in which she was wallowing. She flattened out among the bulrushes, remaining well hidden. Within minutes, six burly miners with mules loaded down with gold-mining tools moved past her on the bank above. They were looking for gold, no doubt, trying to strike and claim another mother lode. Heart beating wildly in her throat, Serena pressed her face to the cooling, abrasive texture of the reeds. *Don't let them see me.... God, please don't let them discover me....*

Just the nearness of the hulking, bearded men made her tremble with fear. They passed her, unaware of her presence. Barely breathing, Serena closed her eyes and dug her fingers into the mud. Blackjack had dumped her somewhere west of the town of Kingston. How far she was from the outpost that served as a gold-mining camp for miners such as these, she had no idea. For two months, he'd had her cuffed and chained to a bed. That one room of his large, two-story cabin had been her cage, her only existence.

If these men discovered her, they would capture and rape her—just as Blackjack had done. They had greedy faces and hard eyes. From the maid, Lucinda, a black slave from the south who would sometimes keep her company when Blackjack was out of town, Serena had heard that the miners often ruthlessly slaughtered the Sioux Indians who lived on these gold-strewn Black Hills of the Dakota Territory. In her heart, she felt sorry for the Sioux.

Serena had learned that Blackjack hated anyone who wasn't male and white. Often, he'd whipped Lucinda for the slightest infraction of the strict rules he'd laid down. And too many times Serena had heard of Blackjack's notorious gang of miners, who rode into Sioux villages killing men, women and children just to get a new gold claim. Children... Her stomach rolled and she swallowed hard, fighting the urge to vomit. Children, no matter what their color or religion, were helpless. In her eyes they were precious, and deserved protection. But Blackjack called the Sioux little more than animals that deserved to be trapped and slaughtered, just like foxes or wolves. They didn't have hide like animals, but their scalps were worth upward of ten dollars apiece at his trading post, he'd boast.

The last of the miners disappeared around the curve of the river. Serena dragged in a shaky breath, lifting her head. Looking down at herself, she realized her dress was not only in dire need of a washing, but damp and muddied. So were the thick, twisted strands of her red hair that hung against her aching breasts.

After waiting another five minutes, Serena was convinced the miners were gone. She tested her legs, finding them rubbery but willing to sustain her weight. Getting up, she planted her bare feet apart to steady herself. A cutting smile crossed her lips. Blackjack had forced her to wear shoes, but every time, she would get rid of them. All her life she'd gone barefoot, the thick calluses on the bottoms of her feet tougher than any shoe leather. Digging her toes into the mud reminded her that there was life despite the feelings of numbness within her.

I'm free. Blackjack thinks I'll die. But I won't. Somehow, I'll survive. Just like I did before. Serena picked up the folds of her skirt and lifted her head. In front of her was a small knoll with several large oaks upon the crown. If the miners were heading north, she'd go south, following the river. In Ireland, she'd eaten roots, grubs and anything else in order to survive. Standing at the river's edge, she could see mussels in the shallows, and a fish peeking out between rocks. There was food to survive upon.

Just as Serena turned to begin her trek south, she heard a woman's piercing scream slice open the dawn. Jerking around, she nearly fell, dizzy from the sudden movement. Another scream, this time from a different woman, split the air. Children began to shriek in alarm. She heard a baby crying. Then, a gun went off, shattering the calm for miles around.

The cries of the women triggered something primal within Serena. Gripping her skirts, she moved clumsily up the riverbank. The bulrushes slowed her momentum, but after she reached the halfway point, the land smoothed out into velvet-green grass. Panting from the sudden exertion, Serena staggered to a halt at the top of the bank, leaning heavily against one of the rough-barked oak trees.

Her eyes widened. First terror struck her, and then revulsion. Below, the six gold miners had discovered a group of unarmed Indian women, with their babies lying in cradleboards nearby. Roots that had been gathered from the river's bank lay scattered around the area as the miners attacked the women. Mules brayed and danced nervously. Gasping for breath, Serena gave a low cry of anguish. The miners had chased down the women and were in the process of raping them. One child, barely four years old, lay dead. Serena saw another woman holding her baby to her breast as a black-bearded miner ran after her, hunting her as if she were little more than a game animal. *The children!*

Hatred spurred Serena into action. For two months she'd been tortured by a white man. She'd endured rape and incredible pain from the constant beatings. And now these filthily clad miners were going to rape these innocent, unarmed women. Without thinking, Serena grabbed a long oak limb. Her hands were small but her fingers were long, and she wrapped them around the huge club.

"No!" she shrieked, flying down the bank, her hair streaming like a red banner behind her. "You won't hurt them! You won't!" Lifting the club above her head, Serena allowed the momentum of the slope to carry her into the fray, surprising the miners, who had dropped their guns to rape the Indian women.

Evening Star, mother of a two-month-old baby boy, gripped the cradleboard to her breast. Her eyes widened enormously as she saw a white woman with red hair flying down the hill, screeching at the top of her lungs. The miner who had been chasing her jerked to a halt, equally surprised. He had no time to yell a warning to his busy comrades. Evening Star saw the wildness in the white woman's green eyes as she brought the oak branch down hard on the miner's head. The black-bearded one fell with a grunt, unconscious.

Before Evening Star could say anything, she saw the white woman whirl around, leaping toward another miner who had taken down her older sister, Redwing. Sobbing, she gripped her baby, realizing that Redwing was dead. Satisfaction soared through her as the red-haired woman brought down the club on the murderer's neck. A crack split the air. The second miner toppled like a felled ox, his back broken. Just reward for killing her sister!

Placing her baby beneath the protection of a clump of willows, Evening Star ran back to help defend the women of her village. She, too, picked up a dead tree limb. Then, noticing the red-haired woman was in danger, Evening Star cried out a warning.

Serena saw a brown-bearded miner hesitate, his pants down. An Indian woman lay unconscious beneath him. Mules were braying and stampeding in all directions, mud being kicked up everywhere. The miner fumbled toward his holster, but it lay too far away from him to retrieve before Serena got to him. At the last second before she charged him, a crazed mule began kicking out viciously with his rear feet. The second kick caught the miner in the head just as he stretched across the muddy earth to reach the gun. In seconds, he was dead.

"Bitch!" a blond-bearded miner roared at Serena. "You're gonna die!" And he jerked up his trousers.

Serena saw the miner lunge for the closest weapon—a limb of a tree that was twice as long and thick as the one she carried. A baby, no more than three months old, lay in a cradleboard on the ground between the miner and herself. The baby was in danger if she charged the miner.

The blonde scooped up the limb, his blue eyes gleaming with hatred as he whirled back upon the red-haired woman. "You're dead, bitch!" he roared.

Unleashing further rage, Serena threw her weapon as hard as she could at the miner, and ran forward to pick up the child. *Escape! We have to escape!* The miner ducked her poorly aimed tree limb and scrambled after her. Her legs rubbery from fatigue, Serena tripped over the hem of her long skirt. Holding the baby to her breast, she fell forward. At the last moment, she twisted to her side. Her shoulder and hip took most of the impact, absorbing the shock of the fall instead of the baby.

"No!" Evening Star shrieked, running toward the miner who stalked the red-haired one and Redwing's infant daughter. She lifted the branch, hoping to frighten away the half-dressed miner. It was no use! Despair filled Evening Star. She increased her forward speed, hoping to protect the white woman and her sister's daughter. Too late! Too late! Evening Star saw the miner raise the limb like a mighty sledgehammer above his head as he loomed over the crouching white woman. As she struggled closer, Evening Star could see the defiance and hatred in the white woman's eyes as she faced her enemy, unafraid. To her bosom she clutched the cradleboard, protecting Redwing's daughter.

Serena stared up into the blond miner's angry blue eyes. Her hatred of him as a man knew no bounds. His arms were thick and hairy, looking more like oak than human appendages. He was built like a bull. As he raised the limb that would strike and probably kill her, Serena no longer cared. What mattered was the tiny baby clinging to her breast. It was a good trade, she thought in those seconds that slowed to a crawl as she saw him lift the club to kill her. Her life wasn't worth living. But the baby had a chance, undefiled and untouched by whites.

Something commanded Serena to look beyond the miner who would take her life. An eerie calm filled her as she lifted her eyes to a hill not far away from where she knelt. An Indian warrior on a black horse appeared at the top, his bow drawn back, the arrow pointed down at her. At that moment, the sun brimmed the horizon, sending blinding shafts of light across the land, illuminating the warrior in blinding radiance. Serena had expected herself to feel revulsion and hatred for the Sioux warrior because he was a man. She felt anything but that. There was a calmness about him, an energy that radiated from him just as the sun's rays enveloped him and his horse. He was dressed in buckskin, his thick black hair in two braids, with brown and white golden eagle feathers attached to his head.

Serena watched the limb coming down to strike her. She saw the warrior draw back the bow to release the arrow. Who would kill her first? Suddenly, she felt acceptance of her death. Her eyes never left the warrior's grim, chiseled features. His face was as hard and rugged as the cliffs along the Irish Sea. There was no forgiveness in the lines around his broad, generous mouth or in the narrowness of his sable eyes that glittered like those of a barely tamed wild animal. The look in those eyes, in that split second, when they made direct contact with her, changed. No longer were they hard. Instead she not only saw, but felt his concern and anguish over her predicament. A shaft of warmth, of hope, shot through her. *Why would he care? I'm a stranger. A white woman.* Confused, Serena's last conscious thoughts revolved around that feeling that gave her hope and courage when she had none left herself.

Black Wolf released the arrow. With a grunt of satisfaction, he saw it strike the miner in the back of the neck. But not before the miner had struck the white woman who protected Redwing's child. Angry that he'd not arrived moments sooner, Black Wolf sank his heels into his mount and galloped down the hill, while loading another arrow into his bow. In twenty-five years of hunting, Black Wolf had never missed a target from the back of his favorite buffalo runner, Wiyaka. Squeezing his long, curved thighs against the ebony mare, he guided her with astonishing precision between the women and children, his targets the last two miners.

Satisfaction soared through Wolf as his arrows struck their targets cleanly and with deadly accuracy. He pulled on the rawhide jaw cord of the mare, whirling her around. What greeted his eyes broke his pounding heart. His oldest sister, Redwing, lay unmoving, a red stain eating up the front of her buckskin dress. The miner who lay dead at her side had a broken neck.

As he dismounted, Black Wolf heard another cry. He saw his sister Evening Star drop a tree limb and race toward him, arms outstretched.

"Wolf! They attacked us out of nowhere!" she sobbed, throwing her arms around him. "We never heard them coming."

Wolf held his youngest sister of seventeen. They were surrounded by carnage. Six women and four children had gone out to hunt roots along the river. Something they did once a week to help feed the village. His eyes grew stormy as he swept his gaze across the inert bodies of the miners. "Why did they do this?" he croaked.

"It's always the same," Evening Star wept. "Why can't the *wasicun,* the white man, leave us in peace? Redwing!" she wailed. "They killed her!"

Bile crawled up into Wolf's mouth. His lips thinned. Redwing's throat had been slit and she had been raped. Squeezing Evening Star gently, he whispered hoarsely, "Come, we must get help. You must mount Wiyaka, and ride to the village. Get five warriors and extra horses."

Wiping tears from her round face, Evening Star pointed to the left. "She saved us, Wolf. The white woman charged the miners like ten warriors. She was swinging that oak limb as if it were a war club. If not for her, Redwing's baby would have been killed. I don't know if she was a member of their party or not. She struck like a thunder being, surprising all of them."

Wolf stood there looking at the white woman, who lay unmoving, the cradleboard beneath her body. "Ride for help, Evening Star," he commanded. "I will do what I can until they arrive." Boosting her onto the black mare, he took his medicine parfleche from the rear of his cottonwood saddle. "Hurry!" he ordered, slapping the horse on the rump.

As soon as Evening Star disappeared over the hill, Wolf turned to those who needed him. As medicine man, his life revolved around the well-being of his people. Little Swallow, his twenty-six-year-old sister, limped toward him, her face etched in pain. She too, had been raped.

"Wolf," she pleaded, "see to Redwing first."

"She's dead."

Little Swallow winced as if struck. At her side was her daughter of three. "Then take care of the others first. I will be fine."

Wolf reached out. "Your daughter?"

Little Swallow knelt down, examining her distraught daughter. "She is all right. She ran and hid in that bank of willows when the miners attacked us. All she has are some scrapes and bruises."

Nodding, Wolf turned his attention to the other two Indian women. One had a broken arm, the other suffered a broken jaw. Swallowing his hatred of the *wasicun,* Wolf couldn't erase his curiosity about the woman with the red hair. She was a warrioress, challenging her own kind. Why? Weren't all whites like these miners?

He placed the broken arm between willow bark and then wrapped it with rawhide thongs to keep the bone in place. For the woman with the broken jaw, there was little he could do but give her herb to hold between her teeth to minimize the pain. And there was even less he could do for Little Swallow, who suffered without tears or complaining.

"Cleanse yourself down at the river," Wolf told her in a voice strangled with emotion.

"What about the red-haired one? She bleeds heavily from the head." Little Swallow's brown eyes narrowed. "She saved us from sure death, Wolf. Does she not deserve our help?"

He scowled.

"You are a *wapiya,* a healer," Little Swallow began in a pleading tone, "and you're bound by vows to save another's life. Do that much for her. She saved Redwing's baby, your niece."

Moved by Little Swallow's impassioned words, Wolf nodded. The healer in him wanted to go to the white woman. But part of him, the part that had had so many of his family members murdered by the *wasicun,* wanted to leave her to die. Another part of him was afraid of her. Afraid! Why should he be afraid of a mere white

woman? As he approached her, Wolf realized that she
was anything but "mere." Her red hair lay about her face
like a blazing halo of light from Father Sun. Crouching,
he moved her arm aside to see if Redwing's baby was
unharmed. Relief fled across his hardened features as the
baby, who had been named Dawn Sky, slowly opened her
eyes, staring up at him.

"Little one," he soothed, setting aside the parfleche
and carefully removing the cradleboard from the white
woman's arms. To his surprise and relief, Dawn Sky was
uninjured. And like all good Lakota children, the baby
hadn't whimpered one cry during the battle. Straighten-
ing up, Wolf took the child in the cradleboard to the bank
of willows, placing her with Little Swallow's daughter.
Making sure both children were well, Wolf walked back
to the white woman.

As he placed her on her back, he admitted in some
small part of himself that she had been braver than any
five warriors he'd ever known. Attacking six armed
miners with nothing more than a tree limb was a great
coup. For that, he would name her Cante Tinza, Brave
Heart, even if it went against his beliefs.

Hesitating in his examination of her, Wolf had never
seen red hair before. It was thick like a horse's mane and
heavily matted with mud. His thoughts shifted to the
women who sat wearily nearby. If they saw him vacillate
in attending to her injuries, they would surely laugh at his
unexplained cowardice. Picking up a thick strand of red
hair, Wolf removed it from the region of her breasts.
Blood had congealed across her bosom as well as on her
right temple. Where to begin? The scowl on his broad
brow deepened as he unbuttoned the front of her dress.
His fingers trembled as he lifted away the thin material.
An ivory chemise crossed her breasts, and that too was

soaked with fluids from the injury. With an oath under his breath, Wolf pulled the knife from the scabbard at his side. Placing the point in the material, he slit it upward.

A grunt of surprise escaped him as he pulled the chemise aside. The woman's breasts bore deep, fresh burns. He hunched over, perplexed by the unusual wounds. She had small, firm breasts, their ivory roundness crowned with pink-tipped nipples. The urge to touch them, to see if they were as velvety soft as they appeared, moved through Wolf. Disgusted with his physical reaction to Cante Tinza, he turned his thoughts back to healing. He took a special powder ground from comfrey root and sprinkled it across the terrible scars on her breasts.

"Who has done this to her?" Little Swallow demanded, leaning over his shoulder. She jabbed her finger downward. "This woman has been hurt by *wasicuns.*"

Wolf gave her a bare glance. "It could be the Crow who did this, too. They are known to burn great scars on the bodies of their enemies."

"Perhaps," Little Swallow muttered, coming around to kneel at the woman's head. Taking a cloth wet from the river, she pressed it against the head wound. "Has someone whipped her, also?"

Glancing up from his work, he saw that Little Swallow was pointing to some fresh, pink scars that lay like ribbons across the white woman's small, proud shoulders. "Let me dress these wounds first, and then we will find out," he muttered.

"She saved us, Wolf. Do not be bitter about trying to save her."

Compressing his lips, he held on to his anger. Little Swallow had been raped, and she was unraveling emotionally before him, her hands shaking as she daubed the blood away from Cante Tinza's head wound. "I will do what I can," he promised quietly.

"I saw the hatred in her eyes," Little Swallow whispered, tears beginning to stream down her cheeks. "She hated these miners. Perhaps they tortured or abused her—like they abused us...."

"If that is so, then she has an even braver heart than I first thought," he admitted as he carefully closed her chemise and rebuttoned her dress.

"I have never seen someone fight with such fury, such anger," Little Swallow continued.

Wolf reached over, placing his hand on Little Swallow's slumped shoulder. "*Tanksi*, sister, go and sit down. You are shaking like a young leaf in a storm."

Managing a wobbly smile, Little Swallow nodded. "You are right, *tiblo*, brother." Patting the woman's shoulder, she whispered, "This one is special. I do not care if she has white skin—her heart is Lakota."

"You have always had an eye on those who are good and kind," Wolf agreed. "Now, go. Sit and rest. The warriors will be here shortly to take everyone back to the village." It felt as if a hand were squeezing his heart. Wolf acknowledged his younger sister's words of wisdom. No longer did he try to hold his hatred as a barrier toward Cante Tinza as he moved to dress her head wound. If not for her courage, he could have lost the last of his once large family. He owed her much.

His mind moved forward. Many things would have to be done. Once the bodies of the miners were found, the Lakota would be held responsible for their deaths by the *wasicun* whether they deserved it or not. Chief Badger Mouth would have to move the village; otherwise fort soldiers would kill all of them, swooping down upon them like hawks from the sky. Right now, there was an unstable peace between all Lakota and the *wasicun*.

There were Lakotas who wouldn't like the fact that he was going to take the red-haired woman into his tepee, Black Wolf thought. Badger Mouth would oppose it. Every family in the village of one hundred people had lost someone to the guns of the *wasicun*. They bore hatred toward the miners, who continued to steal their ancestral lands. With a sigh, Wolf gently ran his hand across her dirty forehead. She needed to be bathed, and her hair needed to be unknotted, washed and combed. Despite the torture Cante Tinza had undergone, there was still beauty in her face. As Wolf heard the sound of hoofbeats reverberating through the foggy dawn air that told the warriors were approaching, he wondered what color Cante Tinza's eyes were.

Chapter Two

"You are not going to take her with you."

Wolf looked up from where he knelt at Cante Tinza's side, now acutely aware of his hand on her shoulder. He held it there in a protective gesture when he saw the chief, Badger Mouth, approach him with a disapproving look on his face. The chief, more than sixty seasons in age, halted and glowered at him, hardening his weathered face. His words were an order, not a question. Around them, the warriors were helping the injured women and children to mount the extra horses, and none seemed interested in coming to Black Wolf's aid.

"She saved the lives of our women," Wolf countered in an equally authoritative tone.

"So Evening Star says," the chief groused. He stood with the lance in his left hand, staring toward the south. "That sister of yours is like a blue jay, constantly chattering. All I heard riding here is that the red-haired *wasicun* saved our women and children from sure death."

"She is a warrioress." Wolf grew sure of that as he had time to study her thin, bony features. Her forehead was broad and unmarred, her eyebrows arched like the curve of a hawk's wing, and she had a small, dainty nose with flaring nostrils. Although she was unconscious, her lovely mouth was pulled in at the corners, indicating the level of pain she suffered even now. There was a vulnerability to Cante Tinza, and Wolf found himself wanting to draw her from the darkness she resided within and bring her into light. Each moment he spent with her increased his questions as to who she was and what she was doing with the miners. She couldn't have been friends with the miners if she defended the Lakota women against them, he guessed. In his heart, he sensed that she'd been injured by them. Why? He had to have time to find out after she regained consciousness.

Badger Mouth snorted, watching through squinted eyes as the last of his warriors mounted. "You ought to leave her for buzzard bait just as we leave the other *wasicun* to them."

"Even our enemy, the Crow, would not leave a woman to die in this manner." Women were held sacred in the eyes of the Indians, no matter what their tribe.

The chief glared at Wolf, his hand tightening on the staff topped with the skin of a badger. "It would go better in the village if she *was* Crow."

That was true, Wolf acknowledged. They had captured Crow women who, over the years, had decided to stay in their village and not return to their home. The Lakota women had come to accept them as their own, with time. "Little Swallow feels she has been tortured at the hands of these miners."

"She is *wasicun*, Black Wolf."

Slowly lifting his hooded eyes, Wolf held the chief's challenging stare. "No," he whispered, "first, she is woman. We Lakota recognize the strength and courage of our women. She is one who gives us birth, who gives us life through the milk that flows from her breast, and who is able to give her blood back to Mother Earth every moon. As men, we can do none of these things, making us less important. We have nothing to compare to a woman's sacredness.''

Irritated knowing that Wolf spoke the truth, Badger Mouth muttered, ''Do what you want. You will anyway. But remember this, she is *wasicun* and, therefore, trouble. What of Deer Woman?''

''She lays claim to my heart, but I have told her that she pines for the wrong warrior. She does not hold my heart.'' Wolf slid his hands beneath Cante Tinza's small shoulders and long, curved thighs, lifting her upward. As her head lolled against her chest, something old and hurting broke loose in Wolf's chest. In the past four seasons, his heart had been cruelly torn with the loss of half his family at the hands of the greedy *wasicuns* who killed for the gold metal that peppered the Black Hills. As Cante Tinza's cheek pressed against the region of his aching heart, he felt comfort for the first time since then.

''Ho! You make yourself twice as much trouble, Black Wolf. Deer Woman won't take kindly to this *wasicun* sharing your robes and tepee,'' Badger Mouth scolded.

Walking carefully toward his ebony mare, Wolf ignored the chief's warning. Deer Woman was an eighteen-year-old maiden who had fallen madly in love with him years ago. He'd never invited her affections, yet she constantly hinted that she'd like to be his wife. He wanted a mature woman for a wife—not a child in a woman's body. Swift Elk, a brave who had yet to count coup, could marry her, he told himself. He was as young as she, and pined equally to have Deer Woman for his wife, yet she foolishly spurned his advances.

''I will take this woman as I would any injured person into my lodge for care,'' Wolf reminded the chief sharply. One of the older warriors, Tall Crane, held the woman as

Black Wolf mounted Wiyaka. Wolf saw Tall Crane's reaction to Cante Tinza as he patiently held her, waiting to transfer her to Wolfe's arms once again. Did she have the ability to break down hated barriers with just her small form and fiery hair? Taking the woman from Tall Crane, Wolf settled her across his thighs, her body leaning against his.

"Who is she?" Tall Crane wanted to know.

"A stranger." *In more ways than one,* Wolf thought wryly.

"Do you intend to keep her?"

"As a prize of war?"

"Yes."

Wolf saw Tall Crane's unbridled interest in the woman. Less than two seasons ago, he had lost his wife and son to an attack by the Crow. Since then, the warrior had been lonely, and in need of a family again. Although Tall Crane was well thought of in the village, and a good hunter, Wolf felt suddenly protective of Cante Tinza. "She is mine."

A sly smile crossed Tall Crane's ample features, his chocolate eyes dancing with amusement. "Ah, so the *wapiya* finally takes a woman. Many maids will have their hearts broken to see you ride into the village with this red-haired one in your arms as your chosen mate. No doubt you will train her in the medicine ways to help our people?"

Uncomfortable at the prospect of all the problems Cante Tinza would cause him because of his unexpected decision, Wolf glanced over at the gangling warrior, who rode a bay gelding. "If her hair is any sign, she will do exactly as she wants."

Laughing heartily, Tall Crane slapped Wolf on the back. "Well stated, my friend. A woman with hair the color of fire. Are you blessed or cursed, I wonder?"

Wolf wasn't sure. "She may not live long enough for either of us to know that answer."

Sobering, Tall Crane nodded. "Evening Star said she is a warrioress. I honor her for that. I do not care if she has white skin. If she helped save our women and children, then I consider her one of us."

Wolf glanced over at him. "Half the village will hate and distrust her. The other half will be wooed by her red hair, just as you have been."

"I cannot deny it." Tall Crane frowned. "Deer Woman will take your decision with great sorrow."

The sweet, innocent face of Deer Woman danced before Wolf's eyes. "She is a child."

"But with the body and desires of a woman."

Grimacing, Wolf said, "I have laid no claim to her. I have made that clear to the chief, and to her family."

Picking at the bay's black mane disinterestedly, Tall Crane said, "Sometimes our heart chooses of its own accord, despite what our head tells us."

In that moment, Wolf hurt for his friend. Tall Crane deeply loved his wife and daughter. In a Crow attack by One Feather, ten Lakota had been slaughtered. Even now, he could see the grief in Tall Crane's dark eyes. "There are four maids who look for husbands now in our village. Can you not soothe your heart with one of them?" Wolf asked quietly.

Patting his mount's neck, Tall Crane shrugged. "None stirs my heart. I would do these fine maids an injustice by pretending otherwise." A sparkle came to his eyes. "Now, this red-haired one stirs me. She interests me."

A slight smile softened the line of Wolf's thinned mouth. "There is spirit and courage in this one," he agreed.

"I honor your choice, my friend." And then the spark died in Tall Crane's eyes. "But be careful. There are many who will hate her if she survives."

"If you speak of Deer Woman's reaction . . . I find her incapable of hurting anything or anyone."

"She is as gentle as a butterfly," Tall Crane agreed, "but do not be dissuaded by her demeanor. Thus far, no one has challenged her claim on you."

"Deer Woman will be disappointed, but she would never lift a hand in anger toward me or this red-haired one." There were too many other concerns for Wolf to think about. The village had to be moved immediately. The women and children injured in the attack would need continued care and attention.

"I do not envy your position, Wolf. Your responsibilities are many besides having a heartbroken maid plus an enemy sleeping in your tepee. Be on guard."

Secretly, Wolf acknowledged Tall Crane's wisdom. Looking down at Cante Tinza, he prayed to White Buffalo Calf Woman to spare her life, to bring her back to the realm of the living. Then, another thought struck him. When she did regain consciousness, how would she react to being taken in by him and his people?

A low, gentle chant filled with emotion rippled through Serena's awareness. The throbbing in her head gradually faded as she focused on the man's voice. He sang in a language she'd never heard before, and yet the very tone wove a fragile web around her groggy state, holding her, comforting her.

She struggled to awaken, to pull from the darkness holding her captive. There was light in his song, and more important, her heart revolved toward him, toward the gentle, soothing tones. Gradually Serena became aware of her fingers. She flexed first one, and then another, realizing she was still alive. Flashes of the miners attacking the women and children surfaced. Each time a flash of memory hit her, her stomach knotted in unadulterated fear. And then she would cling wildly to the chanting song, finding a haven of calm within the melody.

Wolf smiled down at his three-month-old niece as he placed her into the beautifully beaded cradleboard. Softening the lullaby he sang to Dawn Sky, he watched as the baby's eyes drooped until they closed. The darkness within the tepee was alleviated by a small fire in the center. Smoke rose in lazy wisps toward the opening at the top of the huge lodge. Something prompted Wolf to look across the expanse to where Cante Tinza lay beneath the buffalo robe.

Rising silently, he covered Dawn Sky with a small deerskin blanket and made his way to the red-haired one's side. Four days she'd been unconscious. Would she awaken, or die soon? He wasn't sure. Placing his broad palm against her cheek, he noticed her brow was marred with a frown. Easing the frown from her flesh with his fingers, he lightly caressed the rich crown of her copper and gold hair.

"Come back, Cante Tinza," he called softly in his own language. Picking up one of Dawn Sky's deer rattles, he shook it gently. He moved it from the top of her head slowly toward her feet. Although a child's toy, it was also used to heal a baby or an adult from grievous emotional wounds. Black Wolf placed his palm inches above the region of her heart and felt heat. That meant she carried terrible wounds to her emotional spirit, which had to be healed in order to make her want to live and not walk across the Rainbow Bridge.

The flickering fire bathed her face in shadow and light. Wolf brought the rattle full circle over her, singing a chant that invited her broken spirit back to this realm. The song came from his heart, and he allowed all his tightly suppressed emotions for his dead family to surface. Closing his eyes, he visualized himself pulling Cante Tinza back from the Rainbow Bridge, pleading with her to return to the here and now.

Serena focused on the man's voice, which wrapped itself around her heart and soul. The emotion wrenched at her, and she felt herself moving toward some indistinct golden light that seemed so far away to her. The chant was filled with hope, and she felt her heart burst open, spilling out all of its deeply hidden misery. She felt her eyes fill with the warmth and life of tears, which then spilled silently down her cheeks. Serena struggled, fighting to surface, to pull away from the darkness.

"Ah, so you hear me, Cante Tinza." Wolf placed the rattle aside and touched the tears that shimmered like molten silver down her waxen cheeks. Smoothing them away beneath his thumbs, he smiled for the first time. This was a good sign. His heart told him she lay between light and darkness now. That she wanted to return to the land of the living but was not ready to cross the Rainbow Bridge yet. Her face was tense and small beads of sweat formed on her brow.

"Don't struggle so much, my Brave Heart," he coaxed, taking a cloth and dipping it in a wooden bowl filled with fresh river water. "You will come back to me. I will sing you songs filled with hope and strength—a beacon in your darkness." Daubing her brow, he smiled as he saw the corners of her mouth begin to ease, the stress disappearing with each ministration to her forehead. The deer rattle had worked its magic, allowing Cante Tinza to begin to release her hurt and fear.

There was a scratch on the tepee. Wolf placed the cloth on her forehead and moved to the opening. It was late at night, and he wondered who it might be. Pulling the skin aside, he motioned for the visitor to step inside.

Deer Woman blushed deeply as she entered. "Black Wolf, I have come to offer my services to you," she stammered softly, clasping her hands nervously in front of her.

Wolf sat back on his haunches, knowing that this confrontation had been long in coming. The morning he'd ridden into the village with Cante Tinza in his arms, Deer Woman had covered her mouth with a cry and fled to sob her heart out somewhere in the surrounding forest. He'd felt badly, but there was nothing he could do. If only Deer Woman would realize that he didn't love her, that she must walk her path with another man.

"Sit," he invited, gesturing toward a nearby buffalo robe.

Unobtrusively, Deer Woman sat, her eyes downcast. "I did not mean to disturb you, Black Wolf, but so many have needed your help in the past five days, I wanted to wait."

Sighing, Wolf pulled up one leg, encircling it with both arms. At this time of night, he was dressed only in a breechclout. "I thank you for your sensitivity, Deer Woman. Now, what is it you wished to see me about?"

Her rounded face was softened by the firelight as she raised her black lashes and studied him nervously. "How is the red-haired one? I hear so much gossip. Is it true? Is she dying?"

Wolf shook his head. "There are signs she is ready to awaken any time now."

It was true, rumors about Cante Tinza had abounded like wildfire. The reaction within the village had been sharp and divided. A number of warriors and wives had come to him directly, telling him that a *wasicun* was evil and bad luck to all of them. And quietly, as was his demeanor, Wolf acknowledged their concerns and then tried to convince them that Cante Tinza was not a threat. They'd leave, shaking their heads, still in disagreement with him but powerless to make him change his mind.

"Oh . . ." Deer Woman unclasped her hands, resting them on the thighs of her deerskin dress. "Well, then, I come to offer you help."

Surprised, Wolf ruthlessly assessed her. "What kind of help?"

"When Redwing was alive, she and her daughter lived with you. She cared for your needs while you supplied her with food and shelter." She motioned to the baby. "Now, you must raise and tend a baby daily without a woman's help. And this red-haired one demands equal attention, plus our people look to you daily for healing. I can care for your niece as well as tend to this *wasicun.*" Eagerly, she leaned forward, her topaz eyes wide and begging. "I can cook and sew for you. I can ease the many burdens you must carry, Black Wolf. And before you say no, I have already gone to your sisters, Evening Star and Little Swallow. Neither can help you because of their own families and responsibilities, even though they may want to."

Scowling, Wolf realized the wisdom of her words. "Deer Woman, if I accept your services, understand that it does not mean you become my wife." He bored a look into her golden eyes. She lived in a world of fantasy and hope, too young and unwilling to see the reality that he did not love her.

A hesitant, hopeful smile touched her bowlike lips. "I—yes, of course, I understand that. But the Lakota way is to aid those in need of help. My mother does not require me, and my hands are idle. Dawn Sky's needs are many. Although my breasts do not carry milk, I can become her mother in all other ways. I know that Dove That Flies nourishes her along with her own child. I would gladly take over Redwing's duties for you." Her voice trailed off and she looked longingly at Wolf's set features.

Glancing at Cante Tinza, Wolf knew Deer Woman was right. The baby demanded full-time care. She had stood back and assessed the situation, showing him that she was capable of common sense. For that, Wolf was grateful. "Very well," he said gruffly. He pointed to the buffalo robe that had been Redwing's pallet. "You will stay with me until I ask you to leave. Until then, you will tend Dawn Sky and cook and sew for all of us." He made a point of gesturing to Cante Tinza. "For her, too."

Deer Woman's eyes widened. "But—I heard that you intended to keep her as a slave if she recovered. I would not be expected to sew or—"

"Cante Tinza deserves our help, not our placing her in a position of humility," Wolf growled. "Do you reward bravery with slavery?"

Tears sprang to Deer Woman's huge eyes. "Then— then you intend to take her as a...wife when she is well?"

"I intend," Wolf snapped, "to allow her to make her own decisions. She is not our prisoner. We do not own her." Anger simmered deeply within him as he watched Deer Woman struggle with the all too vulnerable emotions that crossed her face.

"But—Tall Crane said you claimed her for your own."
Her voice was strained and subservient.

"I claimed her so that she would be allowed the freedom that she has won by defending our women. Whether
she stays or goes is up to her. By claiming her as my
woman, I make sure no one challenges her on that is-
sue."

Gulping unsteadily, Deer Woman stared at the woman.
"She is *wasicun!*"

Reaching over, Wolf gripped the maid by her arm. "In
my eyes, she is a woman, sacred and deserving our
goodwill, not our prejudice."

Trying to master her unraveling emotions, Deer
Woman pulled her arm away. Wolf had not hurt her. Instead, he'd merely made physical contact with her to em-
phasize his words. "So, if she wants to leave, you'll let
her?" Hope rose once again in Deer Woman's heart.
Perhaps, if she could prove how good a mother she could
be to Dawn Sky and could show him her sewing and
cooking talents, Wolf would finally realize that she was
the right woman to be his wife.

Harried, Wolf nodded. "I won't force her to stay once
she is well enough to go." Besides, she probably has a
family and husband anxiously waiting for her, he
thought.

Casting her eyes back to the robe she kneeled upon,
Deer Woman whispered, "You called her Brave Heart.
This is a special name, one that the *wapiya* of our village
has chosen to give her."

Smarting beneath the problems already surfacing,
Wolf got up. He went over and arranged Deer Woman's
pallet. "She has earned the right to be called that," he
parried grimly. "And she has paid dearly for it."

Chastised, Deer Woman nodded and scrambled to her feet. "Your wisdom has always been correct in such matters. Who am I to question the name you give her? The mighty spirits you work with know better. I am sorry."

Throwing back one robe, Wolf rose slowly to his full height of six feet three inches. Deer Woman was small-boned, like a bird. And just as fragile emotionally, in his opinion. "Sleep with Dawn Sky in your arms. She won't wake until Father Sun comes up. Then, take her over to Dove That Flies to be fed."

Joy bubbled within Deer Woman as she looked up at Wolf's harsh features. A smile of gratitude crossed her lips. "I will serve you well, Black Wolf. Soon you will see how good a mother and caretaker I am for you and yours."

Disgruntled, and having no choice in the matter, Wolf went over to Cante Tinza to check on her one last time before going to sleep. "I am grateful for your help, but do not place any more importance than that to it," he warned her darkly.

Drawing Dawn Sky's cradleboard down beside where she would lie, Deer Woman nodded. She watched as Wolf's set features melted with an undeniable concern as he crouched over the red-haired *wasicun*. Her heart ached because she saw Black Wolf's gentle manner as he leaned over and touched the woman's damp, wrinkled brow with a cloth. If only he would touch her in such a way. Sighing softly, Deer Woman lay down and closed her eyes so that she would not have to watch. Instead, she cuddled the cradleboard next to her, in which the baby slept soundly. Tomorrow was another day, a new day. One that brought promise that she could show Black Wolf how indispensable she was to his life.

* * *

The same soft, haunting chant began again in Serena's head. Time had no meaning as she struggled upward, longing to hold on to each low note that the man sang. Each tone swept through her like a gentle wind, evoking and releasing emotions. Fighting as never before, Serena concentrated on opening and closing each of her fingers. As she did, her body became heavier and heavier until she felt as if it weighed hundreds of pounds.

The chant continued, interspersed with the gurgling sound of what could only be a tiny baby. Serena felt the pain leave her head as she heard the baby's cooing and the deep, quiet laughter of a man nearby. Was she dreaming? Men did not sing like this. Men did not laugh. It must be some wild fabrication of her own, she thought, focusing now on opening her eyes. In her heart, Serena mused, she must have made up this man and his haunting voice that played her like an Irish harp. The baby was easily explained: she loved children. Especially the little ones.

Wolf laughed again, watching Dawn Sky's dark brown eyes widen upon him. He sat cross-legged on the buffalo robe, holding his niece above him, smiling into her delighted features. Another day had slipped by quickly, and Father Sun had set hours ago. Deer Woman had excused herself earlier to wash some clothes down at the river, so he'd taken the opportunity to play with his niece.

With a monumental effort, Serena dragged open her eyes. At first, all she could see was a gray fog. Eventually, her eyesight began to clear and she realized it was dark except for the flickering of a small fire nearby. Weakly, she ran her hand against the buffalo robe, perplexed as to where she was. Visions of the river and miners struck her, and she winced with inward pain. Fear overtook her. Fear of men—of what they were capable of doing to her.

The sound of a man singing quieted the raging terror she felt within herself. Looking up, Serena saw huge tanned skins supported on long, thick poles, coming to an apex far above where she lay. Where was she? Forcing her head to move to the left, she focused her eyes.

An array of emotions battered Serena in those seconds after her gaze halted on him. It was a man, an Indian, she guessed, sitting across the way holding a small baby of the same skin color. Her eyes widened as she watched the dancing flickers of firelight bathe his large copper body. His face, despite its harsh lines and grooves, was filled with kindness. A smile eased those hard features as the baby cooed.

There was so much power waiting in coiled anticipation within the man. Serena sensed it, and tasted the fear of what he was capable of doing to her. The fact that he was naked with the exception of a breechclout frightened her. His shoulders were broad and capable, his chest powerful and his arms tightly muscled. The flatness of his belly, narrowness of his hips and muscularity of his thighs brought added terror to Serena. She'd never seen a man of such terrible beauty in her life. Kingston was flabby and weak in comparison. Her dread grew. Who was he? Was he Sioux? Serena, never having seen a Sioux, could only go on Lucinda's description of their red color and their dress.

Her head pounded in agony. She tried to lift her hand, finding herself incredibly weak. Sweet Mary, how was she going to get out of this? Had Indians found her after she attacked the miners? They must have. A ragged sigh escaped Serena's lips.

Wolf's sharpened hearing heard the sigh. Could it be? Was Cante Tinza finally becoming conscious? Fighting back his sudden elation, Wolf turned his head, hoping against hope. It was then that he felt as if someone had knocked the air from his chest. Emerald eyes framed with thick red lashes stared back at him. His lips parted as he drowned in them in those sweet seconds afterward. Never had he seen such green and glorious eyes, so wide and filled with such intelligence.

Something was wrong. Wolf's arms tightened momentarily around the baby in reaction. Plumbing the depths of those eyes, he felt her pain—her revulsion and fear. Yet, before he saw the shadow drown out all he'd fathomed, he'd seen her vulnerability, her gentleness. Holding on to that knowledge, Wolf carefully placed his niece back into the cradleboard and covered her up.

Serena gasped as she watched the man uncoil like a huge wild animal from where he sat. Desperation filled her, and she struggled to rise.

"No..." Wolf cautioned, holding out his hand to her. His English was poor at best, having been taught by traders who used to visit the village when he was much younger. From halfway across the floor of the tepee, he could see the revulsion come to Cante Tinza's eyes. "No harm... I mean you no harm. Understand?"

He was coming to get her. Memories of Kingston flashed before Serena's eyes. One moment the face of this man stared at her, the next, the leering sneer of Kingston's. Heart leaping to a rapid pound, throat constricted with a scream, Serena tried with all her will to move. It was impossible!

"No!" she cried, her voice cracking with weakness.

Panic struck Wolf. He watched the woman try to escape—to no avail. She was too weak from nearly a week with very little water and virtually no food. Her mewing plea shattered his heart and he crouched down on his heels, watching her. The language barrier was frustrating. Holding up both his hands in a sign of friendship, he waited to see if she would stop trying to escape.

"Friend," he pleaded, "friend, do not hurt self."

"You," Serena shrieked, hysterical, "get away from me! I hate you! I *hate* you!"

Stunned by her screams, Wolf got up. He turned his back to her, stalking over to his pallet and his niece, where he sat down. What had he expected? She was *wasicun* and, therefore, hated all Indians. Angry, he glared at her as she struggled without reason. Sweat stood out on the woman's face, her eyes large and filled with unadulterated hatred.

Why was he so stung by her denial of him? Wolf sat there, trying to digest his reaction. What was it about this red-haired one that tugged at his heart, making it feel more alive and more anguished than ever before? Her face was contorted with many emotions, and each one of them struck Wolf full force. Tasting bile in his mouth, he turned away, staring into the darkness of the tepee. Who did this woman think she was, anyway? Did red hair make her unreasonable? Couldn't she see that he'd doctored her wounds, made her as comfortable as possible and given her shelter? What kind of rudeness pervaded women with red hair? Obviously, she was spoiled and deserved some stern measures. He'd tried to converse with her, to tell her that she was a friend, not an enemy—and certainly not a slave.

Disgusted, Wolf jerked his head up, glaring across the way at Cante Tinza. He laughed harshly at himself for giving her such a name. This kind of behavior wasn't becoming to someone who carried such an honored name.

Perhaps Little Swallow and Evening Star were wrong about her. In the heat of the attack, their imaginations might have made this red-haired one larger than life. Girding himself for another of her revilements of him, Wolf slowly unwound and got to his feet, holding her fearful look. Whether she liked it or not, he was going to tend and nurse her back to health. Walling off the disappointment in his heart, he strode purposefully toward her. As he drew closer, her shrieks got louder and louder. Crouching down, Wolf leaned forward. Just then, he saw her clawlike fingers come up, slashing out toward him as if she were a cornered cougar.

Chapter Three

Wolf grunted, feeling the razor slash of her fingernails sink deep into his left cheek. Throwing himself backward to avoid her second slash, he fell close to the small altar and fire in the center of the tepee.

Serena dragged herself up to a sitting position, breathing harshly through her mouth. The Indian raised his hand, his large palm pressed against his bloody cheek. His eyes grew thundercloud black as the silence around them became palpable. It was only a matter of minutes before he'd attack her just as Kingston had, she feared. Was there no end to her suffering?

Pain throbbed through his cheek, and Wolf felt his anger soar upward like a mighty golden eagle taking flight. The woman was shaking so badly that he wondered how long she could sustain her own weight. Her emerald eyes were glazed with darkness and fear.

A frantic scratching at the door caused Wolf to look toward the entrance. "Come!" he muttered.

Little Swallow quickly came inside, her square face filled with concern. Her mouth dropped open as she stared at Wolf. Then she looked over at the red-haired woman.

"Wolf," she called softly, moving toward the *wasicun*, "do not move. She's frightened. Can't you see that?"

Hiding his bruised pride, Wolf leaped to his feet. He savagely rubbed his bloody palm down his left thigh. "I see that she is wilder than any animal."

Serena's gaze went between the man and the woman. Despite her fear, she instinctively realized that the younger woman who was now holding her hand out toward her meant protection. Her arms collapsed, and Serena fell back on the robe. Exhausted beyond her last reserve, she sank back, helplessly watching the woman approach her.

"*Tiblo*, do not be angry. I told you before, she has been hurt by men." Little Swallow slowly approached the pallet and then knelt down. Although she had suffered rape, she ignored her own discomfort and turned all her attention to the *wasicun*. Her hair was unbraided because she had been preparing for bed when she heard the screams coming from Wolf's tepee. "Let me talk with her. Perhaps I can calm her."

Rubbing his square jaw, Wolf stalked over to his pallet. "I do not care what you do." He opened the medicine parfleche to look for a powder to place upon the four deep scratches on his cheek.

Little Swallow gave her brother an understanding look. "She is like any mistreated animal, *tiblo*. You must be gentle around her and not cause her more fear. Of all people, you can sense fear around someone. She smells of it. I think I know how she feels. Patience . . . let me speak with her."

Serena watched the Indian woman extend her hand as if in friendship. "H-help me," she rasped. "I must escape. I—I can't—won't—allow him to touch me. . . ."

"Sshh," Little Swallow soothed. "Friends," she began awkwardly, always finding English an unwieldy tongue. "You, me, friends. Yes?"

Friends. Was the woman telling the truth? "Please, help me. Don't let him touch me."

"No one hurt you. Name is Little Swallow. Yours?"

"Serena."

"Suna?"

Her head ached so badly that she closed her eyes. "Serena. Little Swallow, where am I?"

Picking up the small wooden bowl, Little Swallow slipped it into a larger vessel filled with water. "We are Lakota. Remember river? You helped us?" She moved slowly so as not to frighten the *wasicun*. "Thirsty?"

The promise of water made Serena open her eyes. She recalled Little Swallow's face and the fact that she had been raped. Her heart went out to the Lakota woman. "Yes, I remember the river." She reached out for the bowl. "P-please..."

Smiling gently, Little Swallow slipped her arm beneath Serena's shoulders. "Friends," she repeated softly, placing the bowl against her trembling lower lip. "Friends."

Wolf, now holding a cloth against his smarting cheek, watched Little Swallow treat Cante Tinza as if she were one of her own children. The exertion and combat had left the red-haired one fragile, her skin stretched taut against the bones of her face. He smarted with guilt, realizing he'd caused that reaction within her. *Wapiya* were healers, not destroyers. She tried to hold the bowl, but couldn't, so his sister held it for her. Patiently, Little Swallow filled the bowl again and again until her thirst was sated.

"Thank you," Serena whispered, grateful to be laid back down on the robe. The effort to keep her eyes open drained her.

"Sleep now. You with friends." Little Swallow pulled the robe across her shoulders, tucking her in. "A warrioress should long rest after hard battle. Wolf is right— you a brave heart."

Wolf watched Little Swallow hold the woman's hand until she fell into a deep sleep. Then his sister placed the bowl next to the water gourd and got up, walking to where he sat.

"How badly did she scratch you?" she asked, removing the cloth from his cheek to examine the injuries.

"She hurt my pride more than anything," Wolf grumped. "I was playing with Dawn Sky when she awoke."

Cleaning the wounds, Little Swallow sighed. "And she was confused, no doubt."

"Fear," he muttered, "I saw nothing but fear in her eyes. It was as if I were some hated, ugly thing to her. I tried to speak in her language to tell her I was her friend, but she became *heyoka,* crazy."

"Well," Little Swallow replied, making Wolf tip his head to one side while she applied the powder to stop the bleeding, "I don't think her reaction is to you personally."

He slid his sister a wry glance. "That makes me feel better."

Giggling softly, Little Swallow patted his shoulder. "Her fear is of men. All men."

"Because of the torture she has endured?"

"Exactly."

Wolf managed a lopsided smile of thanks when Little Swallow completed her task. He motioned toward the woman. "What am I going to do with her, then? How can I treat her wounds if she fears me?"

"Let Deer Woman help Serena. You can see she does not fear her own kind."

Grimacing, Wolf rubbed his brow. Where was Deer Woman? She ought to be in by now and sleeping. Was she out with Swift Elk, the brave who wanted her hand in marriage? Wolf shifted his thoughts back to his patient. "Is that her name? Suna?"

"Yes. I wonder if it means anything?"

Wolf shook his head. "The traders said their names meant nothing. The names are hollow, like all *wasicuns.*"

"Most *wasicuns,*" Little Swallow corrected, "but not her."

The fire was dying and Wolf got up, moving over to the small stack of wood just inside the tepee door. He placed a few sticks on it and came back to sit down with his sister. "I worry that Deer Woman may become jealous and mistreat Cante Tinza...I mean, Suna."

"Then I will care for her."

Placing his arm around Little Swallow, he shook his head. "You do too much for all others, *tanksi.*" And then Wolf looked at her closely, seeing the ravages of the attack she had suffered hidden in her brown eyes. Little Swallow was just as upset as the red-haired one, yet coping with it better. "And what of you?" he asked, squeezing her shoulders. "Have you rested this day after the attack? Or did you allow your husband and all your children to make their usual requests upon you?"

She rested her head on Wolf's shoulder for a moment. "My way of dealing with the attack is to remain busy, *tiblo.* That way, my head and feelings won't overwhelm me." Little Swallow gestured wearily to Serena. "This one mirrors what I feel inside, only she wears it on the outside. A while ago, my husband came over to hold me, and I shrank from him. I was shocked at my actions, and so was he. I told him how I felt inside, that I feared the touch of any man since the miner had his way with me...."

Wolf wrapped his other arm around his sister. "Do you feel fear now?" he asked, his voice laden with emotion over her suffering.

Sighing, Little Swallow shook her head. "With you, I only feel peace and protection, *tiblo*." And then she laughed. "But I have always felt that with you. Cante Tinza is fortunate."

Snorting, Wolf muttered, "Why?"

"Because she has you. When she realizes that you are as gentle as a mother with her newborn foal, she will no longer fight you. She will cease to see that you are a man who might hurt her once again and begin to respond to you on a deeper, more important level—from her heart. I know you are a brave warrior who has counted coup many times, but in your heart you are a gentle man. Cante Tinza will sense that. She is a woman, and her heart will eventually outweigh her fear."

Wolf wasn't so sure, but his worry right now was Little Swallow. In the dim firelight he could see how washed out her skin had become. He loved his sister fiercely because she embodied all that was good in a woman. Little Swallow was unselfish and generous with others. Sometimes to her own detriment, he thought. Giving her another affectionate hug, he helped her to her feet.

"Come, I will walk you back to your lodge. Is there anything I can do for you?"

Reaching up, Little Swallow pressed a chaste kiss on his uninjured cheek. "You are a healer by simply holding me, *tiblo*. I feel better already. And no, do not walk with me. Stay with Cante Tinza. She needs you...."

"I must try and find a way to get her to trust me enough to help her."

Little Swallow rolled her eyes. "Ho, *tiblo,* you are a great *wapiya*, but surely you realize your limitations. Give Deer Woman a chance to help Cante Tinza get used to us and our way of life. Deer Woman is a child not given to envy and jealousy."

"No, just dreams that will never be," Wolf muttered unhappily.

Patting his hand, Little Swallow moved toward the entrance. "I saw Deer Woman speaking with Swift Elk earlier. Perhaps he courts her more strongly than ever now that she lives with you. Call me if you need help with Cante Tinza."

"I hope Deer Woman comes to her senses and marries the brave. If Cante Tinza refuses my help, I will call you," he promised gloomily.

Little Swallow turned, a wistful expression on her face. "She is like a hurt child, Wolf, this red-haired one of yours. Your greatest gift as a *wapiya* is placing yourself within another person's moccasins. Understand her fear and pain." Her eyes grew misty with love for him. "If anyone can earn her trust, it is you."

Wolf wasn't so sure of Little Swallow's parting words. Getting up, he carried his parfleche across the tepee to where Serena now slept. Kneeling at her side, he carefully moved several strands of clean red hair away from her right temple. The injury was healing well. White Buffalo Calf Woman had answered his prayers.

But what had he prayed for? As he rested his hands on the hard surface of his thighs, he studied her face. The face of a proud woman. Just the angular shape of her features told him she was a spirited warrioress. Her cleft chin did nothing but confirm that even more. But it was the softness of her parted mouth that drew his attention. Wolf felt the heat within his loins stir as he stared in fascination at her lips. Despite the pallor of her flesh, they were the color of ripe red raspberries in season. The brown spots that dotted her skin across her cheeks and nose made her look childlike.

Pulling the robe down to her waist, Wolf took the risk of waking her. The dressings on the burns that scarred her lovely breasts had to be changed three times daily. Thanks to the comfrey root powder the injuries were making miraculous progress, but they needed constant attention.

Serena lay in a cotton gown that Wolf had traded for years before. His gut tightened as he carefully lifted away the dressings. Wolf laughed at himself. A part of him expected her to draw from sleep and explode into the fury of a cornered cougar again. But she slept deeply, unaware of his cautious ministrations.

Halfway through the changing of dressings, Deer Woman slipped into the tepee.

"Where have you been?" he demanded in a low voice, not wanting to awaken Cante Tinza.

Deer Woman moved to her pallet, taking Dawn Sky from the cradleboard to check the wetness of the dried moss that was used to soak up the baby's urine.

"I was out for a walk."

"Little Swallow says that Swift Elk was with you."

Shaken by Wolf's growling demeanor, she reached for the soft, dry cattail mixture and placed it within Dawn Sky's fawnskin diaper. "I—yes, he wanted to see me. I came back when I heard screams."

Wolf kept his attention on Serena. He didn't speak again until he'd completed the dressings and moved back to his pallet. Sitting cross-legged, he watched Deer Woman gently care for his niece.

"The screams came from the one called Cante Tinza. Little Swallow came to help me with her because you weren't here."

Deer Woman heard the censure in his voice and chose to ignore it. "She screamed because she is with us?"

Wolf stared down at the altar, which contained a golden eagle feather and a bear fetish carved out of red pipestone. "No," he muttered, "she is afraid of men. All men."

Giggling, Deer Woman replaced the coverlet over the baby and began unbraiding her hair. "That is silly."

Snapping his head in her direction, Wolf nailed her with a blazing look. "Foolish child! How can I count on you to help her if you laugh at her fears?"

Hands frozen on her braid, Deer Woman stared hurtfully across the way at him. "Why do you chide me, Black Wolf? Are you angry that I left the tepee for a while? I have been stuck in here all day without rest. I have cooked and sewn. And then I picked up and folded the robes and cleaned the tepee. After all that, I went down to the bank to gather willows for new baskets that you need. Am I not allowed a few moments of rest?"

Grimly, Wolf shook his head. His gut instinct had been correct: Deer Woman could not deal with Cante Tinza. She wasn't envious or jealous of the *wasicun,* but simply lacked the experience or skills necessary to deal with her wild, fluctuating emotions. Further, a woman took pride in the work she had to do around a tepee and for others. Little Swallow or Evening Star would *never* complain over such tasks. Deer Woman was a spoiled and lazy girl, little more. Exhaling forcefully, Wolf lay down and jerked the buffalo robe across him.

"From now on," he muttered, "you are to care for Dawn Sky only. I will tend to Cante Tinza."

Blinking, Deer Woman began once again to unbraid her hair. "Well, of course, if that's what you want, Black Wolf."

She knew he was angry at her. Why? Was he jealous now that she had told him that Swift Elk had met with her? Hope mushroomed within her heart once again. Spirits lifting, Deer Woman began to hum a lullaby. This was the first inkling she had had that Wolf really cared for her. And what of Serena? Well, he was the *wapiya*, so naturally, he would want to care for her himself.

The next time Serena awoke, her vision cleared immediately. She saw sunlight lancing through the opening in the hides of the lodge where she lay. Hearing the gurgle and laughter of a baby, she moved her aching head to the left. Her eyes widened immediately. There he was, the same Indian man. This time, he was dressed in buckskin leggings; his powerful chest was bare except for a claw necklace that hung from his thickly corded neck.

It hurt to breathe as Serena forced herself to watch him. He was playing with the baby once again, his face not harsh but gentle this time. She recalled the anger and hardness in his features after she'd slashed at him. As he turned his face, she saw four deep scratches on his cheek. They were welted, and the side of his face was swollen. And yet he hadn't beat her as Blackjack had done for the same thing. Why?

How could a man who played so lovingly with a baby hurt her? Serena's heart asked. But her head was screaming another message. She lay very still, barely breathing because she didn't want to be discovered awake by him. What of the woman she had seen? Little Swallow? Was that her name? Or was it all a dream fabricated by her fear of *him?*

Wolf sensed Cante Tinza was awake. He was careful not to let her know that. Instead, he played with Dawn Sky, nuzzling the baby affectionately, listening to her delighted laughter. Taking one of the baby's tiny hands, he marveled at the beauty of how a woman could create such perfect life within her body. Surely, there was nothing more sacred than a woman.

Wolf feared Cante Tinza's revulsion from him once again, which caused his heart to beat harder inside his chest. Trying to remember Little Swallow's observations, he searched for ways to get her to relax with him present in the tepee. He gathered up Dawn Sky, who fit easily within his large hands. Softly, he began to sing her a lullaby. Perhaps his singing, which all in the tribe had said was wonderful to hear, would help Cante Tinza relax.

The deep, slow chant moved through Serena. She closed her eyes, remembering that voice from some lost part of her memory. It was his voice that had given her refuge in the turbulent state of her violent emotions. But he was a man. And capable of hurting her any time he chose. She was now a prisoner of the Sioux. Yet each time a new fear arose, it was neutralized by his chanting.

Unable to fight all her fears, Serena succumbed to the tone of his voice, allowing it to wash across her and cleanse away the tension making her rigid.

Wolf finished the chant, smiling down into the baby's round features. Dawn Sky broke into a delightful laugh and he chuckled.

The rumbling laughter that filled the tepee made Serena tense. Her eyes flew open and her gaze locked on his.

Wolf was wildly aware that Cante Tinza's green eyes were upon him. It was one of the few times in his life that he didn't know what to do, so he followed his heart, his unerring guide. Tucking Dawn Sky in the crook of his right arm, he carefully broke contact with the *wasicun*'s frightened gaze and returned to caring for his niece.

Throat constricted, Serena gulped. The man was aware of her, but he made no move to attack her or even approach her. Sweat bathed her and she lay there, soaking in her own fear. Taking several gulps of air, Serena lay tensely, waiting. When nothing happened for several minutes, she pried open her eyes, forcing herself to look at him.

"Now, little one," he told Dawn Sky, drawing the cradleboard to him and placing her into it. "If we can find Deer Woman, perhaps she will take you to the river with her to gather willow for the basket she plans to weave."

Wolf avoided looking at Cante Tinza as he rose slowly, not wanting to alarm her. One did not move quickly around a wild horse, and that was how he was going to treat her. Slipping out of the tepee, he carried his niece toward the central fires where the cooking for the village was undertaken. The morning was warm, and the sky was a blinding blue color. Birds were singing melodically, telling Wolf that no enemy stalked their camp.

Little Swallow was skinning a rabbit caught by her husband earlier when she saw Wolf approach her tepee.

"Tiblo?"

"I look for Deer Woman," he answered, halting nearby. Little Swallow looked rested this morning, and for that, he sent a prayer of thanks upward to Wakan Tanka, the Great Mystery.

"She is nearby."

"I want her to care for Dawn Sky. Cante Tinza is awake and I must try to get her to speak with me."

Little Swallow's skilled hand hovered over the partially removed skin from the rabbit. "I have not heard her scream yet."

"Yet," Wolf muttered nervously. "I am sure she will. If she does, will you come and help? Deer Woman is going to be of little use to me in this matter."

Smiling, she nodded, continuing to cut away the skin with sure, short strokes of the knife. "Of course I will. Leave Dawn Sky here. My oldest daughter will care for her until we see Deer Woman."

Wolf hesitated, knowing that Little Swallow's duties were many. He was torn between getting back to Serena and finding Deer Woman.

"Leave her, *tiblo*. She will be fine with us," Little Swallow chided.

"Very well. I can see why no warrior would want Deer Woman. She acts childish and will not take a woman's responsibility as she ought to."

"Stop muttering, Wolf, and go back to your red-haired one. Do not give your power away to such a young woman who has yet to mature into her body."

Wolf wiped his sweaty hands on his buckskin leggings as he walked back through the busy village. Everywhere he looked, the women were preparing skins, sewing or cooking. Most of the men, the hunters among them, had left hours ago to catch game. The children all played happily down by the river. Some of his nervousness abated as he allowed the peace that pervaded the village to be absorbed within his pounding heart.

Serena's gaze moved to the entrance when she heard a scratching noise. Her eyes widened considerably when she saw the same warrior come inside. Hands tightening against the robe, she watched as he faced her. There were twenty feet between them. Twenty feet between assault or peace.

Wolf held out his hand to her. "Name Black Wolf. I not hurt you. Understand?"

For once, he wished mightily that he'd worked harder on perfecting his English with the traders who frequented the tribe throughout the summers of his youth. Tensing, he saw the fear and hatred return to her eyes. The silence hung heavily on his shoulders, and he now knew what real helplessness was as he waited those pregnant moments to see what she would do. He tried to prepare himself for her to scream once again.

Serena struggled to sit up. As the robe fell away to reveal the white cotton gown she wore, she stared down at it and then up at him. She wrestled with the harshness and cruelty that were a part of his features compared to the softness of his low voice. What could she believe? His sincerity of tone or his threatening male countenance? And who had undressed her and put her in this gown?

Wolf saw indecision and fear in her emerald eyes. Little Swallow had been right: he must switch to the *wapiya* side of himself, the one that enabled him to sense and feel. Sensitivity never led him wrong, and he consciously shifted to that compass called his heart. Making each movement slow, as he would with a wild horse to be tamed, Wolf eased back on his heels and crouched, his hand still extended.

"Suna?" It was a pretty name, a melodic one, he thought.

Her eyes narrowed on his face. "How do you know my name?"

"My sister, Little Swallow. You spoke it to her last night."

Already her arms were shaking from supporting her weight. Serena felt light-headed and even a little hungry. She sat up straighter, still unsure of him. "Stay away from me!"

Wincing at the anger and plea in her husky voice, Wolf froze. "You are safe here. I—no one will harm you."

Sweet Mary, how she wanted to believe him! She saw the kindness in his wide, intelligent eyes but could not cling to that one piece of evidence. His mouth was generous, but pursed and thin. Kingston had thick, fleshy lips that always pouted when he was stalking her. Serena rasped, "I do not believe you!"

Grimly, Wolf glared at her, inwardly railing at her stubbornness. "I am Black Wolf. You live here. I want you well." He chastised himself for the clipped way his words came out.

His tone didn't go unnoticed by Serena. She compressed her lips into a stubborn line. "If you so much as lay a hand on me, I'll fight you until I'm dead. No man is *ever* going to touch me again! Do you hear me?" she shrieked.

Wolf leaped to his feet and retreated, his chest heaving with anger and hurt. Stupid woman! Could she not *see* he was being kind and careful with her? He heard someone enter the tepee, breaking his dazed state. It was Deer Woman with his niece.

"What is wrong?" she asked, looking quickly from Wolf to Serena.

"Everything!" Wolf roared at her. He stalked to the entrance. "Stay here for once and take care of things as you are supposed to do! I will return later."

Stunned by his anger, Deer Woman stood holding the baby for a few moments after Wolf's departure. She placed the cradleboard on his pallet and folded her hands in front of her, then walked over to the *wasicun*. She knew no English, but wanted somehow to speak with her.

Serena sat there, watching the young woman in a golden buckskin dress beaded on the bodice with brightly colored flowers. There was eagerness and excitement in her eyes as she approached her.

Smiling shyly, Deer Woman leaned down and dipped the wooden ladle into the bowl, offering her the water. "*Mni,*" Deer Woman said.

Serena stared at the bowl filled with clear water. She was thirsty.

Deer Woman repeated the Lakota word for water, sliding the bowl into Serena's hands, which rested in her robed lap. "*Mni.*"

Nodding, Serena gave her a grateful look, shakily lifting the bowl to her cracked lips. The liquid spilled out both corners of her mouth as she gulped down the contents.

Deer Woman smiled encouragingly, taking the bowl and filling it again. "*Mni,*" she repeated.

Serena nodded. "*Mni,*" she whispered, taking the bowl.

A dazzling smile of triumph blossomed on Deer Woman's mouth. "*Han, mni.*" Yes, water.

Her thirst sated, Serena sat there, looking around. She was in some kind of skin abode. It was large, circular and neatly kept. There was a central fire, from which smoke curled upward to a hole at the top. Fur robes of every

imaginable kind covered the dirt floor. The fact that there
were three pallets made her feel better. Was this woman
the wife of Black Wolf? She must be, for she cared tenderly for the baby in the cradleboard.

Eager to help Serena, Deer Woman went to a skewer
that held a cooked rabbit on it. She knelt down and offered the meat to Serena. *"Yuta,"* she urged. Eat. Making smacking sounds with her lips and pulling a piece of
flesh from the rabbit, Deer Woman popped it into her
mouth.

Yuta must mean eat, Serena surmised. She was fam-
ished and the rabbit looked inviting. Knowing she must
regain her strength, she took the offered flesh from the
woman. The meat was tender and juicy. Her jaw hurt,
and so did her temple each time she chewed, but Serena
ignored the pain.

Wolf entered the tepee. He glared at Deer Woman,
who was kneeling at Serena's side, feeding her.

"Look, Black Wolf, she eats!" Deer Woman announced proudly. Now he would be pleased with her.

Disgruntled, Wolf sat down, several dried roots in
hand. "You finally decided to return to your duties," he
rasped. He spread one root across a large flat stone.
Taking a larger stone that fit his hand, he exerted all his
strength and began to crush and grind the root into a
powder.

"I was down gathering fresh willow for a basket I intend to make," Deer Woman whispered, hurt by his censure.

"Yes, and you left my niece behind. I have things to
do, girl! I cannot tend Dawn Sky and this red-haired
cougar plus all my other duties!" Wolf glanced up into
Deer Woman's wounded features. "I do not intend to
have Little Swallow care for my niece just because you

ignore your womanly duties. Next time, you take Dawn Sky with you.''

"But it is hard to watch her and hunt for willow," Deer Woman whined. "You were all sleeping well when I left. I saw no reason to awaken your niece.''

Each grinding movement with the stone bled away some of his frustration and anger. Wolf glanced over at Cante Tinza. She'd stopped eating the moment he'd entered the tepee. Her eyes were shadowed, wary of his every moment. Curse the day he'd come upon her! And yet the urge to make contact with her as a woman, not as a frightened wild horse, was eating him alive. She hovered in every waking thought of his like fog lingering above a river. At night, he dreamed of her in his arms. In his arms, of all things! If anyone knew of his torrid dreams, they would poke fun at him. Only young braves were smitten thus. Not him. Not men of his age or of his importance to the tribe.

Serena saw tears gather in the woman's eyes after the harsh words Black Wolf had hurled at her. She didn't understand what they had said, only that he'd been sharp and wounding. It was easy to erect a wall of hatred toward him because of his treatment of his wife. He probably beat her, too. Just as Kingston had beaten her on numerous occasions. Yet Serena was mystified by how her heart reacted to the warrior. She remembered his songs of healing and how they had moved through her, assuaging her pain and fear. And she couldn't ignore the liquid kindness burning in his eyes and the low, dark tone of his voice as he'd tried to establish peace between them.

"No more," she told the woman. "Thank you."

Deer Woman nodded shyly, taking the rabbit off the skewer and placing it in a nearby pot for stew that she would fix later. The red-haired one was tired, revealed by the darkness beneath each of her glorious green eyes.

"*Asnikiya,*" she coaxed, patting the robe.

Tilting her head, Serena whispered, "I'm sorry, I don't know what you say."

"She said 'rest'!" Wolf snarled in English.

Tensing at the snapping tone in his voice, Serena glared at Black Wolf. Her Irish temper welled up within her. But the warrior could come over and knock her silly, or rape her if she foolishly made the scathing retort that she wanted to. Without a word, Serena slowly stretched out and lay down. Deer Woman patted her shoulder awkwardly, tears streaming down her cheeks. Serena wanted to comfort the woman, but didn't know how. Instead, she whispered, "Thank you."

Jealousy ate at Wolf. In that moment, he hated Deer Woman's ability to gain Cante Tinza's trust. Her words had come out in a husky breathiness that stirred his loins. What would it be like to tame all that fire and spirit and have her give the gift of herself to him? Pushing down brutally upon the stone, he crushed the root, the powder spilling off the sides and onto the skin that would collect it.

Nothing could erase the haunting, husky quality of Cante Tinza's voice within him. Wolf heard the emotion in it, wanting it for himself. Somehow, someway, he would gain her trust. He would tame her with the intent of making her his wife. This was the woman he wanted to carry his children. Despite her torture at the hands of the *wasicun,* her spirit moved him powerfully. It didn't matter if she was already married or had a family. He understood real love because of his sisters and their husbands. But could he really keep Serena selfishly for himself if she was truly in love with her *wasicun* husband?

Wolf's conscience chafed at him, and yet he was unwilling to look too closely at the questions—and the possible answers.

Stealing a glance at Cante Tinza he saw that she had closed her eyes. Her thick red lashes caressed her almost translucent flesh. She walked in beauty in his eyes. Her abundant red hair was a brilliant halo of fire framing her thin face. Wolf ached to brush her hair as she sat with her back to him, to run the strands through the elk-bone comb and watch them curl and slide cleanly through his fingers. And she would enjoy his worship of her, too. There were many ways for a man to love his woman. He would teach her that not all men hurt. Not all men brutally took without asking or giving something of beauty in return.

No, Wolf thought, the grinding becoming less angry now, *I will show her that a man can be her friend as well as her lover. She won't want to leave our tribe. I will make her stay. Somehow, I will convince her to stay and be my wife....*

Chapter Four

Serena moaned and moved restlessly, the nightmare of Blackjack raping her now invading her dreams. With a cry, she jerked upright. Perspiration clung to her skin. The tepee was empty, save for the baby in the cradleboard, who was softly whimpering. She had no idea what time it was, but she could still see soft sunlight touching the pine poles that came to a point far above her.

Heart still pounding, Serena discovered she felt a bit stronger, perhaps because of Deer Woman's kindness in giving her something to eat last night. She focused all of her attention on the baby, who was now beginning to sputter in earnest. The child's cry forced Serena to stir. Why did the wife of the warrior leave her baby behind? The fire was near the cradleboard, and Serena worried that the end of the long-haired buffalo robe might ignite.

Pushing off the heavy, thick robe, Serena slowly moved into a kneeling position. She brushed her hair away from her face, realizing it desperately needed washing. The baby's cries strengthened, so Serena crawled on her hands and knees the necessary ten feet to reach the cradle.

"Ohhh," she cooed softly as she turned the cradleboard toward her. The Indian child was snugly wrapped in several rabbit furs, her tiny round face and huge brown eyes visible. A lock of black hair had escaped and curled across her forehead. A slight smile tugged at Serena's mouth as she carefully removed the furs and set them aside. "Why are you crying?" she asked as she explored the baby's fawnskin diaper, which was filled with the soft down of cattails. Her fingers detected that the material within the diaper was very damp.

"Ah, I see. You're wet." Serena was amazed that the Indians used nature's material, and it worked just as well as a cotton diaper! Looking around, she saw a number of square and rectangular rawhide parfleches, all colorfully painted with individual designs in reds, blues and yellows. Sliding her hands beneath the baby, she eased her into her arms. Serena examined the fawnskin diaper and discovered it was held in place by two knots. Cooing to the child, who had stopped crying, she laid her in her lap. Serena smiled down at the infant, who stared up at her in fascination. In no time, she had taken off the diaper.

"I'm different, am I not?" she asked the infant quietly as she held her against her bosom. Her breasts were still sore and swollen, but Serena fought to ignore the pain because she intuitively understood that an infant needed the cradle of a mother's bosom to feel safe and loved. The tepee was warm because of the still glowing fire that burned inside in a deeply dug hole. Still, Serena worried about the baby becoming chilled, so she took the rabbit furs out of the cradleboard and covered her with them.

The baby cooed and lifted her tiny hands, entranced with Serena's long, tangled red hair. Little fingers touched the burnished hair, and Serena's smile deepened.

"You're a pretty colleen." Serena leaned down, pressed a kiss to her brow and inhaled deeply. Babies always smelled so clean, so fresh. Serena's heart blossomed with a fierce feeling of motherly concern over the vulnerable child. The months of hell Serena had endured with Blackjack subsided as the baby's bowlike lips broke into a smile, her fingers happily investigating strands of Serena's hair. For the first time in a long while, Serena felt an unparalleled peace flow through her. In amazement, she realized it was due to the baby in her arms, who was studying her with so much adoration and trust.

The elkskin hide across the entrance to the tepee was pulled open. Serena tensed, her eyes widening. It was the same warrior. He was dressed in a buckskin shirt and leggings. The breechclout was made of red wool and hung to midthigh. There were porcupine quill designs on the shirt in vivid red, yellow and blue. His thick, black braids were wrapped in glossy, dark brown otter fur, with bright red cloth above and below the sleek fur. He wore a white bone choker around his neck, which held a round, pale pink shell in the center of it. Below the choker was another necklace displaying a single, large tooth.

Wolf halted halfway into the tepee. He saw Cante Tinza sitting there, tense, holding Dawn Sky. The woman's eyes were huge with vigilance. Realizing he was holding the flap open and the warmth was escaping from the tepee, Wolf quickly shut it and moved inside. Where was Deer Woman? She had promised to take the baby with her. Had she left the infant behind again?

Wolf carefully held on to his anger because he realized the red-haired one was able to sense such a thing even if he didn't show it. He moved slowly to his pallet, a mere five feet from her. The driving need to reach Cante Tinza, to make her understand that he wasn't going to hurt her, overwhelmed Wolf. He set the freshly killed rabbit aside and devoted his attention to her.

Pointing to himself, he said, "Tashuunka, Wolf." Then he pointed at her and asked, "Suna?"

Mouth dry, Serena clutched the baby to her breast. The dark look in the warrior's eyes made her uncomfortable. Yet when he spoke his name, Wolf, her heart slowed its frantic beating. Again, he repeated his name and her name.

Gathering up all her courage, Serena whispered, "Wolf?"

A pleased look came to his face, and he nodded gravely. "*Han,* yes. Wolf. You, Suna?"

She shook her head. "Not Suna. Serena."

Wolf scowled and quickly looked down at the moccasins on his feet. The deerskin leather was wet from his foray into the woods and he needed to change into a dry pair. Her voice, trembling and husky, sizzled through him. English was not an easy language to speak. The *r* sound wasn't used by the Lakota, and he found it difficult to even form the sound on his lips.

Looking up, he slowly met her wary gaze. "Sunan?"

A part of Serena relaxed as she saw Wolf's face lose its hardness. She saw him trying to move his lips into the correct position to say her name. It was his eyes, a curiosity gleaming in them, that kept her on guard.

"Serena."

Snorting, Wolf shook his head. He lifted his hand in a gesture of patience. He pointed to her and said, "Heart," and he thumped his chest where his heart lay. "I not say other name. Cante Tinza, Brave Heart," and he touched his chest again.

The baby cooed happily, her attention and fingers lost in the array of Serena's red hair. Sensing Wolf's effort to communicate with her, Serena repeated, "Heart?"

"Yes, *Cante, chonteh.* Heart." He gave her a slight nod and added, "Brave. *Tinza, tinzah.*"

"*Tinza?* Brave?"

Wolf grunted, pleased. "*Han.* Yes!" He pointed to her. "You Brave Heart. Cante Tinza, not Suna."

"I'm Cante Tinza?"

"Yes!"

The pleasure radiated from Wolf's rugged features, and for an instant, Serena felt his joy over establishing communication with her. *Brave Heart.* It was a beautiful name, a courageous name. She watched his facial expressions closely. Deer Woman had had trouble pronouncing her name, too. Perhaps it wouldn't hurt to let them call her whatever they wanted. And then Serena realized it didn't matter, because she was a prisoner.

She looked down at the baby. "The baby's diaper was wet. That's why I took her out of the cradle."

The English words came too fast, and there were too many of them for Wolf to understand. Frustrated, he opened his hands. "Eh?"

Serena pointed to the baby.

With a grunt, Wolf said, "Dawn Sky."

"Dawn Sky."

"*Han.*"

Serena pointed to the baby's bare bottom and the discarded diaper in the cradleboard. "Wet," she said.

"Ho," Wolf muttered. Showing her he understood, he unwound from his crouch and moved to locate the parfleche that contained several folded fawnskins and dried cattails. He heard Cante Tinza gasp. Realizing he'd moved too quickly, that she still was highly mistrustful of

him, Wolf halted. Cante Tinza sat there, the baby
clutched to her breast, her eyes narrowed. It wounded his
pride that she continued to fear him. Hadn't he shown
her he was her friend? That he'd just honored her with a
sacred and powerful name? To be given a Lakota name
by a medicine man was considered the highest of hon-
ors. Wolf admitted she knew nothing of his people's
customs. But surely Cante Tinza realized he had treated
her in a friendly fashion.

Lifting his hand, he murmured, "Safe. Cante Tinza,
safe. No hurt."

No hurt. Serena stared up at Wolf, his bulk filling her
vision, the shadow of his form dancing against the skin
of the tepee behind him. Shadows frightened her even
more because Blackjack would often appear out of the
shadows of the night after silently entering her bedroom
and rape her. Forcing herself to relax, Serena placed the
baby in her lap as Wolf moved with deliberateness to the
rear of the tepee, behind the cradleboard. He brought
forth a rawhide container and placed it in front of her.

Crouching down, Wolf opened the container. "Look,"
he invited, and gestured for her to come and investigate
the parfleche. She eyed him and didn't move. Understanding all too clearly how much she continued to fear
him, Wolf stood up and backed away.

Keeping one eye on the warrior across the tepee Serena peered inside the container. Delighted to find the dry
diapers and cattails, she realized Wolf was trying to help
her take care of the baby. Licking her dry, chapped lips,
Serena nodded. "I understand."

Again, moving slowly, Wolf knelt nearby and removed the damp fawnskin from the cradleboard. Taking out a clean, dry skin, he laid it on the robe between
them and placed a handful of the dry cattails across the

surface. Looking up at Cante Tinza, Wolf held out his large hands, silently asking her to pass Dawn Sky over to him.

Serena nodded and gently lifted the baby toward Wolf's outstretched hands. The baby's fingers were twisted among several strands of her hair, and as Serena placed the infant in Wolfe's care, she was forced to lean forward. Her heart beat raggedly as she moved closer to Wolf and untangled her hair from Dawn Sky's little fingers.

"Hair like fire," Wolf said with satisfaction. Although Cante Tinza's hair was dirty, the copper and red strands still danced with the color of firelight. Cante Tinza was so close. Wolf realized the importance of the moment, and silently applauded her move to protect the baby's delicate fingers by gently easing her hair from the baby's grasp. He tried to smile, and dipped his head in thanks. "*Pilayama,* thank you."

Serena watched the grooves around Wolf's mouth deepen as he rewarded her with a slight, nervous smile. Another little piece of her fear dissolved beneath the warmth that moved from the curved corners of his strong mouth to his dark brown eyes. She was feeling weak once again, glad that Wolf changed the baby's diaper and placed her back into the cradleboard. Moving slowly over to her pallet, Serena curled into a sitting position, drawing the robe across her lower body. Wolf was his name. She watched him tenderly handle the baby, amazed that his large hands could be so careful, so caring. When he slowly turned toward her and their eyes met, Serena quickly lowered her gaze. His eyes burned with a deep fire in their depths, and she felt suddenly uncomfortable. Would he attack her now?

"Food?"

Serena lifted her chin. She saw Wolf go to another parfleche. He pulled out a piece of dried meat, and moved across the tepee to hand it to her.

"*Tatanka,* buffalo. Eat."

Her mouth watered. Serena gladly took the dried buffalo meat from him but was careful not to touch his sunbronzed fingers. "Th-thank you."

With a shrug, Wolf nodded and forced himself to turn away. Cante Tinza was looking very pale, which worried him. She needed to eat to bring back her strength. First, Wolf made sure that Cante Tinza had water to drink. He then placed *wasna,* pemmican, in the shape of a cake in front of her, and made a gesture to his mouth, meaning that she should eat that as well. *Wasna* was made of dried, lean meat, grounded into paste with animal fat, a great rarity in his people's diet. Normally, only hunting or war parties carried the prized food, but Wolf knew the woman was in desperate need of it to regain her strength.

Where was Deer Woman? Agitated by the absence of the lazy girl, Wolf went to the opening. Before he pulled the skin aside, he turned. "Sleep, Cante Tinza."

How did Wolf know she was beginning to feel sleepy? Chewing the last of the tasty dried meat, Serena nodded her head. "Yes, I'll sleep."

"*Washtay,* good. I be back later. Be safe."

His husky words, deep with concern, flowed across her. How badly she wanted to trust Wolf, but he was a man—and an Indian too. Serena knew absolutely nothing about the Sioux except what she'd been told by Blackjack, and Lucinda. While Lucinda had spoken of them compassionately, Blackjack had filled her head with terrible stories of how they scalped and tortured their white prisoners, which included raping the women. Wolf exited as quietly as he'd come, and she was alone once again.

Wolf sought out his sister, Little Swallow, who was busy tanning a deer hide that would be used to make moccasins.

"Have you seen Deer Woman?" he asked irritably as he approached her.

Little Swallow looked over her shoulder at her brother. She stood near a rectangular pine frame that held stretched clean deerskin tightly across it. The elk scraper, or *wahintke,* was used to scrape the hide free of hair and flesh. "Yes. I saw her ride on the back of Swift Elk's horse. He was going hunting for rabbit, I believe. Why?"

"Deer Woman cannot be trusted," Wolf growled, and he told her about Cante Tinza and the baby.

"So, she spoke to you?" Little Swallow asked, pleased. She continued the short, scraping motions on the hide.

"In her own manner, she did," Wolf acknowledged, standing beside the frame, his arms crossed against his chest. He felt the chill of the morning air and saw that Father Sky was dotted with many white cloud spirits. He knew that soon he and his people would have to move for fear of the horse soldiers coming once they discovered the dead miners by the riverbank.

He heard his sister chuckle and focused on her. "You laugh?"

"Not at you, *tiblo.* Every time you mention Cante Tinza, you are like a grouchy old lone wolf who has his paw caught in a trap." She waved the scraper at him. "I told you, she will trust a little at a time. Thank the Great Spirit that she loves children just as we do, or poor Dawn Sky would still be sitting in wetness!"

Wolf scowled and dug the toe of his wet moccasin into the ground. "Dawn Sky did not cry when Cante Tinza held her."

"Babies always know who they can trust." Little Swallow gave her brother a tender look. "*Tiblo,* do not look so unhappy. You have made progress with her! And if Deer Woman continues to ignore her duties to your niece, why not have Cante Tinza care for her instead?"

The idea was a good one. Perhaps. Wolf stopped digging his toe into the rich, red earth. "Cante Tinza is still weak and needs care herself." With a frustrated sound, he added, "She needs to sweat and have her hair washed. That would make her feel better."

Running her slender brown hand across the damp deer hide, Little Swallow was pleased with the even scraping. "Then," she said lightly, "why not get Deer Woman to take her into the sweat lodge and help her wash her hair afterward?"

Looking around the large encampment, Wolf snorted. "If she ever comes back!"

"If Cante Tinza awakes and Deer Woman isn't here, I'll come over and help her."

Wolf started to protest and then shrugged. "Cante Tinza doesn't trust me enough to help her."

With a soft smile, Little Swallow bent down to a bowl that contained the cooked brains of the deer. They were whitish, and pasty in consistency. She scooped up some of the matter and began to smooth it across the surface of the hide. "Then, *tiblo,* let me help."

Serena awoke slowly this time. Bright sunlight struck the buffalo hides of the tepee, and it created a hazy golden glow within the structure. Feeling better—less sore and stronger—Serena stretched and looked around. She was alone except for Dawn Sky, who slept in her cradle-board. Serena noticed that someone had placed the baby very close to where she lay. Had it been Wolf? With a smile, Serena rose up on her elbow and peeked into the cradleboard. Dawn Sky slept soundly. She reached in and touched the baby's soft cheek.

"You are awake."

Startled, Serena jerked back her hand. She looked in the direction of the entrance. Wolf had entered so quietly that she'd been completely unaware of his presence. Shaken, Serena slowly sat up. His face, usually a hard, unemotional mask, looked less threatening than before. Perhaps it was the velvet darkness in his eyes; she wasn't sure. He appeared pleased she was paying attention to the baby.

Serena watched Wolf as he came toward her. His mouth formed a slight smile and he crouched next to the baby, resting his hand on the top of the beaded cradle-board.

"I put Dawn Sky beside you," he said in slow, painful English.

"Th-that was all right," Serena whispered, unable to hold his dark, penetrating stare. There was such overwhelming power in Wolf that it sent her into an internal panic. Her gaze was riveted to his long, large-knuckled fingers that were draped across the cradleboard. For his size and the masculinity that exuded from him, he was extraordinarily gentle.

"Cante Tinza, you must clean."

Serena lifted her head. "What?"

Wolf made a scrubbing gesture, as if washing himself. "Clean?"

"I am rather dirty," Serena admitted, looking down at herself.

"Little Swallow take you to sweat. Clean hair." He touched his braids.

Serena nodded. She desperately wanted to bathe herself and wash her hair.

Satisfied, Wolf slowly stood. He was pleased to see that this time Cante Tinza wasn't looking at him as if he were going to attack her—well, at least, not like before. A song flowed through Wolf, and he hummed it as he strode across the tepee and left to get his sister. Did Cante Tinza realize that she was beautiful in his eyes? Wolf looked forward to the time when he could tell her that. The language barrier was so frustrating. He would have to teach her Lakota quickly, so that they could converse more easily.

Serena had changed Dawn Sky's diaper when Wolf returned with Little Swallow. The young Indian woman smiled and came toward Serena.

"How much better you look," she praised slowly in English. Little Swallow fussed over the baby. "And you took good care of her, too."

Serena tried to smile, because Little Swallow's spontaneity and obvious warmth made her feel safer. "I just changed her diaper. I mean . . . her . . . whatever it is."

Little Swallow smiled and placed the baby aside. She came over and held out her hand. "Come, I help clean you."

Another Indian woman entered just as they left. Serena looked at the woman as Little Swallow kept her hand firmly on her arm.

"Who is that?" Serena asked.

"Dove That Flies. She give milk to Dawn Sky."

"Oh."

Serena took small steps, unsure of her legs and balance. Little Swallow, who was shorter, placed her arm around Serena's waist and invited her to lean on her if necessary. Gawking, Serena saw at least fifty tepees built along the winding river. There were children playing, large cooking fires here and there and warriors on horseback. Little Swallow led her up a small incline and down into a protected area lined with quaking aspen.

Serena saw a hut made out of willow and covered with two large buffalo hides. The river flowed ten feet away, hidden by the bulrushes. Nearby, an older gray-haired woman was tending a large fire that had many rocks placed in the flames.

"This sweat lodge," Little Swallow explained. She stopped Serena next to the opening and allowed her to stand alone. Little Swallow took off her deerskin dress and stood naked. She placed the dress on a low-hanging limb.

"Come," she invited, motioning for Serena also to undress.

Serena had no idea of what was going to happen. To have a woman undress in the open was unheard of! Further, she was ashamed of the burns upon each of her breasts, afraid of what the Lakota women would think. Little Swallow smiled and helped her because she was so weak. There was no choice, and Serena choked down a lump in her throat and tried to trust Little Swallow. She braced herself for their reaction as she stood naked, her breasts fully visible.

The old, gray-haired woman clucked sympathetically and began speaking in rapid Lakota, gesturing to Serena's breasts, but Serena couldn't understand what was being said. The look on the woman's lined features showed compassion, and as she came over to Serena, gently placing her thin hand on Serena's shoulder to pat her, tears rushed unexpectedly to Serena's eyes. She stood there while both women discussed the burns on her breasts, which were red, swollen and seeping.

"Dreaming Bear says she has *icahpe hu,* purple coneflower root," Little Swallow said in her best English. "She says it help heal wounds and it leave less scars. She bring the *pejuta,* medicine, after she tend rocks in fire pit."

Blinking back her tears, Serena was overwhelmed with the sincerity and care on their faces. The shame she felt over her nakedness began to dissolve because these women acted as if nothing was wrong with being naked among other women. She didn't know if it was proper to reach out and touch their shoulders, but she did, in silent thanks for their care.

"Yes, I'd like that."

"*Washtay,* good," Little Swallow praised. She gestured for Serena to follow her into the very low, concave lodge, getting down on her hands and knees. Moving in a clockwise circle around a deeply dug fire pit, Serena followed the Indian woman. The lodge was very dark except for the opening. After her eyes adjusted, she saw a wooden ladle in a birchbark basket that was filled with water, a pipe and ceremonially wrapped sage. Fresh, pungent-smelling silver sage had been plucked and scattered all over the floor of the sweat lodge. Serena watched as the Lakota woman placed tiny bundles in colored cloth up above them, weaving them in and out of the bent willow framework.

"These tobacco ties," Little Swallow explained slowly. "I made these for you. Each tie is prayer to Wakan Tanka, the Great Spirit, to heal you and return strength. When spirits enter lodge and see ties for you, we will pray they answer my prayers for you." Sitting back down, she handed several sprigs of sage to Serena. "Place this over left ear. It tell spirits you serious about being here in lodge of Ina Maka, Mother Earth, and that you ask their help. If the heat too hot for you, make fresh sage into ball and place against nose and mouth and breathe through it. That way, you breathe the sacredness of this powerful herb, and it, too, is healing.''

Serena nodded and did as Little Swallow instructed. She watched as the Lakota woman took some of the fresh sage and vigorously rubbed her body with it. Serena followed her example and found the fragrant scent of the sage encircling her as she finished scrubbing herself with the plant. As she sat there cross-legged and naked, a sensation of peace blanketed her. Struck by the utter naturalness of being with nature in a way she'd never fathomed, Serena found herself eager to learn more from Little Swallow.

Dreaming Bear began bringing in glowing red rocks, one at a time, on the tines of an elk antler. Each of the first seven rocks to be placed into the deeply dug pit was blessed with the stem of a pipe held by Little Swallow. She told Serena to place a pinch of sage upon each rock to welcome it as her relative, for then the rock spirits would work their powerful healing on her for showing such respect. Soon there were twenty red-hot rocks in the pit.

The flap was drawn down, plunging the sweat lodge into complete blackness. Already, Serena was beginning to sweat. She heard Little Swallow dip the ladle into the container with water. She threw the water on the rocks. In seconds, hissing, hot steam shot upward and filled the lodge. Perspiration dripped from Serena, and she closed her eyes, enjoying the sensation of heat combined with steam.

The moments flowed together as Little Swallow began to sing one Lakota song after another. The music of her voice united with the warmth of the steam and Serena began to feel odd sensations. They weren't uncomfortable sensations, no, they were wonderful, giving her a sense of tranquility that seemed to move like a living, breathing thing within the darkness of the lodge.

The women remained in the sweat lodge for four rounds, and at the end of each round the flap was lifted to allow the steam to escape. Then more glowing rocks were placed into the fire pit, more water was added, and the door closed once again. By the end of the fourth round, Serena felt a new kind of strength, something she couldn't define. She only knew that when she crawled out of the door and stood with the other two women's help, she felt reborn.

They took Serena to the river and sluiced cold water across her to cleanse her of the sweat drawn out by the lodge ceremony. Next, they made her kneel on the bank and scrubbed her hair with *hupestola*, soapweed. Dreaming Bear used the herb, wild bergamot, a very sweet-scented flower, to rinse her hair, leaving it smelling clean and fragrant. Serena was very weak by that time, so after the women dried her off, they sat her on a flat stone, wrapped in a wool blanket.

Dreaming Bear brought forth the purple coneflower root that had been painstakingly ground to a fine consistency and mixed with bear grease. As gently as possible, she applied the healing herb to the burns on Serena's breasts, the whole time murmuring soothing sounds. Then, with old and trembling hands, the elder bound Serena's breasts with soft buckskin to protect the seeping wounds so that the herb could work its healing magic.

Serena wished she knew more Lakota to thank Dreaming Bear for her care. The elder treated her as if she were a frightened child, constantly clucking and soothing her with pats and touches to her shoulder. Next, they dressed her—this time in a lovely gold-colored buckskin dress with beading across the shoulders and down the arms. As Serena stood, each woman bracketing her, she felt her knees go wobbly. All the exertion, the excitement and strain combined to make Serena feel suddenly faint.

Little Swallow made her sit down on a fallen log so that she could place a pair of beaded deerskin leggings on her calves and moccasins on her feet. She turned to Dreaming Bear. "I will ask Wolf to come and help. She is too weak to walk, and we cannot carry her."

Serena watched Little Swallow leave. She touched her damp, fragrant-smelling hair, which was badly tangled and hung in thick ropes about her shoulders. She looked up at the woman who had stood at her side, tears in her eyes. "Thank you, Dreaming Bear."

With a toothless smile, Dreaming Bear patted her gently on the shoulder.

Serena saw Wolf appear at the top of the bank minutes later with his sister. He wore a worried expression, but when he saw her, his eyes darkened with some undefinable emotion.

"Wolf, she is very weak. Will you carry her back?" Little Swallow asked in Lakota.

He tried to contain his surprise at how lovely Cante Tinza looked. The gold buckskin emphasized her pale features, but the curled, damp strands of the hair that framed her face made her look beautiful to his heart. "Yes."

By now, Wolf knew he must approach Cante Tinza slowly, so he held out his hand toward her. "Come," he coaxed.

Serena gave Little Swallow an uneasy look and tried to stand up. "No! I can walk. Let me walk!" Her protest was cut off as Wolf easily slid his arms beneath her back and legs and lifted her. Serena gave a little cry of alarm and stiffened as she was brought against him.

"Safe," Little Swallow said, patting her arm as she walked beside her brother. "You safe, Cante Tinza."

Wolf tried to swallow his hurt over her reactions. He could feel Cante Tinza trembling in his arms, her hands tight against her body. He was alarmed at how light she was, and as he walked, he caught his sister's attention.

"Do you have any stew?"

"Yes. For Cante Tinza?"

"As usual, you read my thoughts," Wolf grunted.

With a pleased look, Little Swallow said, "I will send one of my daughters over with a small kettle of deer stew. Let her eat all she wants."

Mortified that she'd had to be carried, Serena was never so happy as when she was deposited outside Wolf's tepee. She tried to ignore his long fingers wrapped around her arm to ensure she did not fall as she climbed through the opening. The warmth of the tepee and the fragrance of the dried herbs conspired to ease her fears. Wolf released her once she sat on her pallet. He went over to a parfleche and drew out an elk-bone comb.

"Here," he said, making motions for her to comb her hair.

Stunned by his sensitivity to her needs, Serena reached out for the comb. She took a handful of the damp strands and slowly drew the teeth of the comb through them.

Minutes later, a little ten-year-old Indian girl came in with a small kettle of stew, which she placed over the fire. Then she silently left. Wolf busied himself by stirring the fragrant food in the kettle, and occasionally he glanced over at Cante Tinza.

The silence deepened in the tepee as he pretended interest in the kettle of food. The sounds of snorting horses, talking men and laughing children gently permeated the buffalo-hide walls. Wolf saw pain flit across Cante Tinza's face when she tried to lift her arms above her head to comb. She would wince, bite down on her lip and try again.

He placed the wooden spoon aside and moved over to her. She was on guard instantly, but this time there wasn't as much fear in her eyes as he crouched in front of her.

"Here," he said, holding out his hand and asking for the comb. She hesitated, then gave it to him. Wolf realized that Cante Tinza's breasts were still very sore, preventing her from lifting her arms high enough to comb the tangled hair on top of her head. He would do it for her.

He slowly moved his hand toward her hair, aching to touch the burnished strands. "Safe," he told her as his fingers barely touched the crown of her head.

Serena winced and cowered.

Wolf froze. She was acting like a beaten dog. His heart bled for her, and again he murmured, "Safe." He ran the comb through her damp, strong strands, trying to tame them into place. With each stroke of the comb, Cante Tinza relaxed more and more. Then, Wolf remembered that his songs, his chants, had stopped her from becoming restless and frightened when she walked in the shadowy darkness of unconsciousness.

Serena heard low, soft sounds begin in Wolf's chest as he continued combing. She closed her eyes, relenting in degrees. Each time his fingers barely grazed her scalp, her skin tingled wildly in response. Wolf's chant went on, subdued and deep, and Serena responded. No longer did she clench her hands in her lap, or cringe. Instead, with each stroke of the comb, she straightened a little more.

She had never been touched by a man until Blackjack had raped her. Serena would never forget his groping, bruising touch. Now she was in awe of Wolf's size, and yet despite his hands being so large, he was incredibly careful combing her hair. Wild, confusing emotions began bubbling up through Serena, and she didn't know what to feel or do. She had never seen before a man comb a woman's hair. Was it ever done? Struck by how different Indian men were from white men, Serena could do nothing but sit there and hungrily absorb Wolf's occasional touch to her scalp, and listened to the wonderful song that somehow fed her starving soul.

Wolf felt the vibration of the song flowing through him like a thunder being sending his sound across Father Sky. He watched his song work a miraculous kind of magic on Cante Tinza. No longer was her face pale. Instead, a rosy blush stained her gaunt cheeks, and her compressed lips softened and parted in the wake of his ministrations. He had great satisfaction in feeling those strong, fiery strands of hair flow in and around his fingers. She had strong hair, like a horse's mane, and that was good.

Finally her hair, which hung in copper-colored sheets below her breasts, was combed, and looked like a fiery, shining cape. Wolf allowed his hands to drop to his thighs as he shifted into a kneeling position. As her lashes lifted, his breath lodged in his throat. Cante Tinza's green eyes were filled with gold flecks of sunlight, not the darkness of fear. He silently thanked White Buffalo Calf Woman, who had brought the seven sacred ceremonies to his people, for her intervention. Cante Tinza's lips were parted, and Wolf wanted to reach out and touch them, to explore their shape and their texture with his fingertips.

Wolf controlled his desire, for he realized that somehow the song had created a fragile bridge of trust between them as he'd combed her hair. With a slow gesture, Wolf pointed to her hair and then to his braids. She would be unable to braid her hair herself, and he could do that for her, too. But would she allow him? He held his breath.

"Han?" he asked.

Serena blinked, caught within the webs of the chant he had been singing. It felt as if the baritone music was still moving through her. Her scalp tingled, and Serena could smell the sweet fragrance of the wild bergamot in the folds of her hair. She lifted her gaze and met Wolf's inquiring eyes. When he pointed to his braids, she understood. Her arms were weak, much more so than she liked to admit, and Serena knew she could never braid her hair right now. Perhaps, in a few days, but not now.

"Yes...please?" A part of her looked forward to Wolf's butterfly-light touch once again. She saw pleasure shining in Wolf's eyes. His chiseled mouth drew into a smile, and she felt as if the sun itself were shining down upon her. This time, when he gathered up her hair to braid it, Serena did not wince. Nor did she cringe. She sat there consuming Wolf's touch, which somehow was healing her. How could that be?

Just as Wolf completed the second braid, about to tie it off with a bit of deerskin, a scratch came to the door.

"Enter," he ordered.

Serena looked beyond where Wolf kneeled beside her. She saw Deer Woman come through the entrance. Her young face was bright with happiness until she saw them together.

"You!" Wolf growled. He quickly knotted the piece of deerskin and rose in one fluid motion. "Where have you been? Half a day has passed."

Pouting, Deer Woman lifted her chin defiantly. "I was with Swift Elk! Why do you snarl at me, Black Wolf? I was getting us dinner for tonight!" She tried to hide her jealousy. She knew that only a husband combed and braided his wife's hair. Wolf was braiding the *wasicun*'s hair. Oh, how she had dreamed of Black Wolf someday coming and braiding *her* hair. Pain twisted through her heart, and she couldn't accept the fact that he wanted the stranger.

"You left Dawn Sky alone—again," Wolf snarled. His nostrils quivered with fury as he moved around the altar and fire to face Deer Woman. Her young lips were set with petulance. He pointed to the baby who had just been fed by her wet nurse. "And Cante Tinza had to take the baby from the cradleboard because she was crying and wet. You call yourself a help? I think you ran off with Swift Elk because you are lazy, Deer Woman. I will not continue to tolerate your lack of attention to my niece."

Deer Woman's lower lip trembled. She glanced angrily over at the red-haired *wasicun*. "She is the reason I left! I got us food!" She held up the rabbit. "Swift Elk gave me one of the rabbits he killed."

With a cutting gesture, Wolf silenced her. "If you ran off with him to make me jealous, it is of no avail, girl. You have made me angry, and I do not forgive you for leaving my niece alone and unattended. We already have enough meat. If you'd looked in the other parfleche, you would have seen the dried buffalo meat."

Hanging her head, Deer Woman bit down hard on her lip. "I—I did not mean to displease you so, Black Wolf. I only wanted to help."

Wolf didn't know what to do. He couldn't palm off his niece on his sister. He glanced over at Cante Tinza, whose eyes once again had become shadowed. Realizing that he'd raised his voice and caused her to fear him once again, Wolf forced himself to speak in a more reasonable tone. "Do you want to stay here?"

"Oh, yes! Yes, I do, Black Wolf. More than anything." Deer Woman pleaded with him. "Let me stay. I give you my word, I will stay around the tepee."

Wolf didn't believe her, but what was he to do? He dug into Deer Woman's golden eyes, luminous with such undisguised love for him that he felt nothing but compassion for the girl. "I will give you one last chance, and then I will send you back to your mother if you displease me."

Eagerly, she walked over and picked up Dawn Sky, nestling her in her arms. "Thank you, Black Wolf. I promise, I will be of more help."

Wolf didn't like the jealous look Deer Woman threw in Cante Tinza's direction. He wasn't even sure she realized that the girl was jealous of her. That could be dangerous, as Tall Crane had warned him. Unhappy, and still grieving over his sister's death at the hands of the miners, he left the tepee. He had a healing ceremony to perform later that night for another family, and he couldn't afford to remain in a black mood. No, the Great Spirit asked all healers to be of peaceful mind and of good heart when they performed such a ceremony.

Still, Wolf was needled by the deadly look Deer Woman had given Cante Tinza. Surely the girl wouldn't do anything harmful. Yes, she was frivolous and young, but not mean or cruel in her heart.

Chapter Five

The next morning, Serena realized the entire Lakota camp was being moved. Deer Woman had quickly packed all the supplies into parfleche containers and rolled up the buffalo robes. Serena left the tepee and gazed around the camp. Activity filled the air, cutting through the fog that rose off the river in silent fingers and wove through the dark green, thick bulrushes that lined the banks.

Serena tried to stay out of the way as Deer Woman hurried back and forth between the tepee and the pack-horses that would carry most of their goods. Horses were fitted with travois, which would carry not only the heavy buffalo robes, but the hides that created the tepees. Where was Wolf? She missed his presence. He had not returned last night before she fell asleep. Had he come home at all?

Deer Woman placed the cradleboard containing Dawn Sky into Serena's arms, asking her to watch the baby. Serena wanted to remain warm in the late October chill, so she took the infant closer to one of the large cooking fires still burning. Above her, the sky was pale blue and cloudless. Pine trees surrounded her in every direction.

Serena sat on a log with the cradleboard in her lap, and inhaled the fresh scent of pine. Everywhere she looked, the Lakota were busy. She began to appreciate how the people all worked together for the common interest of the community. Even the children, no matter what their ages, seemed to have duties assigned to them, and they willingly carried them out.

There was such peace here, Serena realized. How different from her life of near starvation in Wexford, Ireland, and then the deepening nightmare of her months in America. The smell of wood smoke, the steam from horse's nostrils, the yip of dogs and the laughter of children all conspired to make Serena feel as if she were part of some large, undefinable family.

From the center of the village, Serena saw Wolf on a small black horse that pranced eagerly in the chill of the dawn. Her arm tightened automatically about the cradleboard as she realized he'd spotted her and was coming in her direction.

Today, he wore several brown and white eagle feathers in his hair. The buckskin shirt and leggings outlined his proud form. In Serena's eyes, he was a magnificent warrior. Even the black mare realized that her master was special as she arched her neck, and proudly lifted her fine, delicate legs. Serena gulped as Wolf's dark eyes met and held hers. Instantly, her heart picked up in ragged beat, but this time it wasn't out of fear—it was out of awe.

She recalled the morning the miners had attacked the Lakota women, and how, at the last second, she'd seen Wolf ride up to the rise just above her. That was her last conscious memory, she suddenly realized. So much of that day's events was blocked—until just now. On one side of the horse, to the rear of the cottonwood saddle

draped with a red wool blanket, was Wolf's shield. There
was a running black wolf painted on it, with red flannel
over the top edges of the shield, and a dozen eagle feathers sewn below. The shield looked as if it were alive as the
horse danced beneath his guiding hand and legs.

Her gaze lingered on Wolf's expressionless face. In his
own fashion, he was ruggedly handsome, with high
cheekbones and a broad, lined brow, his mouth full and
chiseled, his nose hawklike and thin. The authority surrounding him as he rode with such ease made Serena feel
light-headed.

As Wolf drew near, Serena saw his dark eyes grow
warm with silent welcome. She felt shaky as he pulled the
black mare to a stop a few feet from her.

"Hau kola," he greeted.

Serena shrugged and opened her hand to indicate she
didn't understand.

Wolf said, "Hello, friend, *hau kola.*"

She liked the way the words rolled from his lips. *"Hau
kola,"* she whispered shyly, trying to speak Lakota herself.

"Washtay, good!" Wolf praised. He dismounted with
ease. How could he tell Cante Tinza how beautiful she
looked this morning? Her red hair was a bit frayed at the
crown, and Wolf realized it needed combing and braiding. But he'd had to leave early this morning to help with
the jobs that came with being second in command.

As always, Wolf monitored his body language with
her, because more than anything, he wanted to gain
Cante Tinza's trust. Moving slowly, he came within a foot
of where she sat. "Dawn Sky?"

Serena glanced down at the sleeping baby. "Yes. Deer
Woman asked me to care for her while she packed."

With a grunt, Wolf shifted his attention to his tepee. He could see Deer Woman working hard, and he nodded his approval. Perhaps the girl was going to become more responsible. He hoped so.

"Your horse is beautiful," Serena said, hoping that Wolf would understand her.

"Wiyaka, Feather, is her name. She buffalo runner." Wolf saw the admiration in Cante Tinza's eyes for the mare.

"Buffalo runner? What's that?"

Crouching down, Wolf dropped the rawhide rein. The mare, trained to be ground-tied, didn't move. With his hands, he tried to imitate a horse running after a buffalo.

"Oh, a hunter!" Serena was delighted. Finally, they were able to talk somewhat with each other, even if it was part language and mostly hand gestures.

"Han!" Wolf smiled suddenly as he saw Cante Tinza's cheeks once again grow rosy. She bowed her head to avoid his gaze.

"Come," Wolf told her, holding out his hand.

Serena stared at his large hand and realized how long and graceful his fingers were—the fingers of an artist, she thought. What was he going to do?

Wolf read her expression. "Come. You ride Wiyaka. You and Dawn Sky."

"Oh...but...Wolf..." There, she'd said his name. Panicky, Serena blurted, "I've never ridden a horse!"

"Ah," Wolf murmured. He took the cradleboard from Serena, set it on the yellowed grass and placed his hands around Cante Tinza's small waist. He saw her eyes go wide with surprise, and he felt her hands grip his thick wrists as he lifted her into the saddle.

Luckily, the buckskin dress had slits in the sides of it, she thought. Even luckier, she had been given leggings that stretched up to her knees so that none of her skin was revealed as she settled her legs across the saddle. Nonetheless, her face flushed, and she gripped the front of the saddle so tightly her knuckles turned white.

Chuckling, Wolf retrieved the cradleboard and handed it to Cante Tinza, who was forced to release her death grip on the saddle. In one easy motion, Wolf mounted Wiyaka. He heard her gasp as he settled against her back, one of his arms going around her and the cradleboard.

Serena stiffened instantly, making her less steady as the horse began a slow, plodding walk. She was more worried about dropping the baby than anything, even though Wolf's sun-dark arm and hand was wrapped firmly around them. The feeling of entrapment was very real to Serena, and she closed her eyes to fight back a cry. Wolf wasn't hurting her, she told herself.

Deer Woman's mouth dropped open in amazement when she saw Wolf approaching with his passengers aboard the black mare. She scowled as he halted in front of her.

"Don't you have anything to do," she flared hotly, "besides giving the *wasicun* a ride around our camp?"

Wolf frowned. "You are not my wife, so do not chastise me, girl."

Pouting, Deer Woman threw the heavy buffalo robe to the ground. "You act as if *she's* your wife! Last night you combed and braided her hair!"

"And what I do is not your business, Deer Woman."

"You treat her as if she will break!" she cried, angrily stomping her feet. "And yet I work like a camp dog for you and get nothing but your harsh words and angry looks."

Wolf held on to his temper. There was no doubt that Deer Woman was jealous. He'd hoped otherwise, ignoring the other subtle signs. "If you were injured like Cante Tinza, I would treat you the same. But you are not. You are young and healthy. You have not been raped and starved as she has been. You saw her wounds. She cannot comb or braid her hair for herself yet." Wolf watched his words shake Deer Woman from her angry stance. "And if *you* had been there yesterday in the tepee as I wanted, you could have taken Cante Tinza to the sweat lodge, washed her hair and combed and braided it. As it was, my sister had to do your duties. So, do not admonish me, Deer Woman. Cante Tinza is to be treated with respect because she saved many women's and children's lives. I owe her much for saving my sister, and if she cannot comb and braid her hair, then I will do it for her if you are not around as you should be."

Breathing hard, her breasts rising and falling sharply beneath her buckskin dress, Deer Woman glared at Wolf. "I can do nothing right for you! I brought a rabbit home—"

"No one asked you to go hunting with Swift Elk," he reminded her less harshly. Wolf felt the tension in Cante Tinza as their angry words were traded. He wondered why she became so frightened by raised voices. There was much he wanted to know about his red-haired woman, in time.

"At least Swift Elk pays attention to me! He's glad I'm around."

"I am too, when you *are* around," Wolf reminded her grimly. "I am going to take Cante Tinza and the baby to my sister. Then I will come back here and help you."

Mollified, Deer Woman muttered, "Very well. It is the least you can do."

Wolf allowed her disrespect to go unchallenged for now. The girl was upset enough, and he didn't want to endure her pouty anger tonight around the campfire. For three days they would be traveling south through the Paha Sapa, the Black Hills, following the star constellation of Wincincala Sakowin, the Seven Little Girls. Normally, Chief Badger Mouth didn't range that far south with his band, but because of the miners being killed, he didn't want his people to be blamed by the horse soldiers. It was better, he felt, to go far past their usual wintering camp, and avoid any confrontation or blame for the event.

As Wolf nudged the mare away from his tepee, he felt Cante Tinza once again begin to relax. This time, she leaned lightly against him, using his body to steady herself on the moving horse. Smiling inwardly, his heart sang because he realized that his sister was right: Cante Tinza *was* beginning to trust him. Wolf longed for a time when he could speak privately and at length with her about her past. He had so many questions.

Wolf made sure that Deer Woman took Dawn Sky with her when she went to help the other women skin several deer that a few warriors had killed along the willow-laden banks of the river where the band of Indians now made their new winter camp. They worked quickly because Father Sky was a leaden-gray color, and snow was sure to come by midday.

The three-day ride had been hard on Cante Tinza. However, Wolf attributed her exhaustion to trying to do too much to help his sister, with whom she rode, and to not resting as much as she should have. Little Swallow was inundated with work, and Wolf had watched from the distance as Cante Tinza had tried her best to lend support. She took instruction well, and soon was cooking, feeding the Old Ones and almost exclusively caring for Dawn Sky.

Wolf moved quietly about in the tepee he had just raised the day before. He still needed to unpack many items for his altar, as well as the cooking utensils. Deer Woman was glad to flee her cooking duties, so Wolf decided to rest today. He would remain with Cante Tinza and enjoy her presence. The red-haired one still slept, wrapped in the dark brown buffalo robe that revealed only the shining crown of her hair. Wolf felt contentment as never before. Just her presence made him happy.

He cut up pieces of freshly killed deer and put them into a small cooking pot that was suspended over the fire pit. Adding water and dried wild onion to the mixture, he stirred it. The fragrance soon filled the tepee. Cante Tinza awoke during his cooking duties. Wolf crouched before the fire and enjoyed watching her awaken.

Cante Tinza's eyes were heavy lidded and slightly puffy with sleep as she roused herself and then braced herself on one elbow. Her messy hair was the result of three days without combing or braiding. Her cloudy emerald gaze settled on Wolf.

"Good morning," Serena murmured, her voice thick.

"It is good to see your face," Wolf replied.

Serena sat up and rubbed her eyes. As sleepy as she was, Wolf's voice blanketed her with such vibrancy that she gave him a shy smile. First, she had to attend to her toilet needs, so she located her moccasins and went outside. The dawn air was icy, and the first snowflakes began to fall as Serena hurried back to the warmth of the tepee.

No longer did she think Wolf was going to jump her as Blackjack had done. The past three days had been a series of exciting lessons for her. Little Swallow had made it clear that Wolf was a medicine man, a healer, to the tribe.

"Take this," he told Serena as she entered the tepee.

She took the wooden cup. "Thank you." She held it close to her nose and inhaled the pungent fragrance. "What is it?"

"*Ceyaka,* mint. We drink often. Good for you." He was thrilled to see the grateful look on Cante Tinza's face. Again her cheeks grew a rosy-pink color, and Wolf was beginning to realize that meant she was pleased.

Sitting down on her robe, her legs beneath her, Serena sipped the fragrant tea. "It tastes sweet."

"Honey," Wolf told her. Then, in a mixture of Lakota and English, Wolf continued, "Last summer I came upon a fallen tree that a grizzly was digging into. He hunted the bee's honey. After he left, I gathered what I could find in my birch container." His mouth curved. "Honey is wanted, but hard to find."

Sitting there, only six feet separating them, Serena sipped the tea. Having learned much Lakota, she understood Wolf perfectly. Today he wore his usual buckskin shirt, leggings and breechclout, she noticed. Except for the choker around his neck, he wore no other accoutrements as he had during the journey to Dried Willows. His hair was shining black, clean and neatly braided. She had found out that the otter fur the Lakota wore around their braids protected their hair.

As Serena watched Wolf prepare the stew, she felt bold enough for the first time to ask him a question. This morning, he didn't appear to be so overwhelming to her, or perhaps, Serena thought, she was finally adjusting to his presence.

"Wolf?"

He lifted his head and studied her. Cante Tinza had both her long, thin hands wrapped around the dark cup, the rim of it inches from her lips, her eyes huge and velvet green. "Yes?"

"I—I've been meaning to ask you something?"

"Yes?"

The burning light she saw in his eyes no longer frightened her. Wolf was a man of intense focus, she realized. When someone spoke to him he devoted all of his attention to that person. Nervously, Serena licked her lower lip. "Am—am I a prisoner? A slave? I've heard so much about Sioux warriors stealing white women and—"

"What? Prisoner?"

Tensing, Serena held his gaze. "Yes, am I a prisoner of yours?"

He laughed. It was a booming, rolling laugh, filled with pleasure. "No, Cante Tinza free."

She saw the puzzlement in his face over her question. Wolf's laughter, which she'd heard often when he played nightly with the baby, wasn't aimed at her. He'd found her question funny, that was all. Setting down the cup, she laced her fingers together and once again met his amused gaze.

"Free?"

"Yes." He gestured around the tepee. "Like us. You are free."

"You mean, I could leave if I wanted to?"

Wolf lost his smile. He stirred the soup vigorously. The silence deepened. His heart cried out against her question. Did Cante Tinza want to leave? He had been dreading this moment. Finally, he stopped paying attention to the stew. He sat cross-legged in front of her, tensely resting his hands on his knees. He knew he must be truthful with her.

"Cante Tinza is free to go where she pleases. Do you have husband?"

It was her turn to laugh, and the sound spilled melodically through the tepee. She saw Wolf's face once again take on that puzzled look. "Me? Married? Heavens, no."

"But—" he gestured "—you are of marrying age."

Sobering, Serena cleared her throat and looked away. "I'm not married. I don't think anyone will ever marry me, if the truth be known."

Perplexed, Wolf considered her words. They carried so much pain with them; he could see the hurt reflected in her green eyes. "You come from far away?"

"Yes. Ireland."

"This land, is it near?"

"No. Far away. Across an ocean."

"Eh?"

Serena smiled softly. "I come from across a large lake," and she pointed toward the east. "Far, far away from this country, America."

With a grunt, Wolf understood. "Your tribe is red-haired, yes?"

Nodding, Serena realized how badly Wolf wanted to know about her. How much should she tell him? Although she was ashamed, Serena knew Wolf didn't deserve anything less than the truth. He had saved her life when he could have left her to die, as Blackjack had done. She opened her hands and looked down at them.

"Wolf, I come from a very poor family. My parents are dead. I was barely surviving in Wexford, Ireland, my home. A man named Calvin McIntire paid my ship passage to come to America. He promised I would make good wages as a washerwoman." She looked up for a moment and blinked back the tears. Glancing at Wolf, she realized he was entirely focused on her.

More nervous now, Serena felt her hands flutter over the mint tea in the cup. Then she whispered, "McIntire lied to me. When I got off the ship, he said my job was here, in the Dakota Territory. He said that a man named Blackjack Kingston, a very rich gold miner, needed a washerwoman. I came west on a wagon train. When I arrived, McIntire took me over to Kingston's house."

It hurt to think about it, and Serena hung her head. Tears blurred her vision, and she tried desperately to hold them back. Sniffing, she went on, her voice broken. "McIntire made a deal with Kingston. I became his slave. He didn't need a washerwoman. He wanted a—a soiled dove. I wasn't one, but it didn't matter to either man." Touching her brow with trembling fingers, Serena said hoarsely, "Blackjack raped me. For four months he kept me a prisoner in his house. He had a wife and son but they didn't seem to care about the situation. No one did. I—I fought him, trying not to let him take me, but he was so strong.... And when I fought him, he'd beat me until I was senseless."

Lifting her head, Serena made a little motion toward herself. "I had to escape. I couldn't take it any longer. Even death was preferable to him. The night I tried to escape, Blackjack caught me. He beat me. I—I guess he was tired of me, so to punish me he took a hot poker and burned my breasts. He laughed at me and said that if I managed to survive being dumped into the Black Hills, no man would ever touch me again."

Serena choked on a sob. She willed herself to go on, to tell Wolf the truth because he deserved to know what kind of woman she was. "I woke up the next morning beside the river. I was in much pain from the burns, but I was alive. I remember seeing a group of miners, so I hid in the bulrushes. And then they disappeared around the corner of the river." Wiping her eyes quickly, Serena added, "Soon I heard the Lakota women screaming, and I ran to help them. When I saw the miners were hurting them...raping them as I'd been raped, I became crazy with anger. I remember running down the hill screaming at them and waving an oak branch around my head."

It was impossible to lift her head and look into Wolf's face. Serena knew the shame that the rape stamped upon her. She was a fallen woman—no longer a virgin. No man would be interested in her as wifely material now. And the scars on her breasts would remind her until the day she died that a man had hated her enough to brand her like an animal.

Serena buried her face in her hands, waiting for Wolf to ask her to leave because she was a scorned woman. She didn't know her status here, anyway, and she was sure that now Wolf knew the truth he would not allow her to stay. Hadn't Blackjack dumped her out in the wild with the hope that wolves would find her and kill her off? Serena knew she was worthless, and waited her sentence.

Wolf sat there, stunned. He hadn't understood half of Cante Tinza's story, but he quickly pieced together her explanation. Blackjack Kingston was his mortal enemy, but she did not know that. The shame he'd seen on Cante Tinza's face had torn at him, and when he understood that she had been brutally raped and beaten by a *wasicun* he hated more intensely with each breath he drew, Wolf could not longer stand her pain.

He knelt down inches away from Cante Tinza. Gently, his hands closed over her hands. She was trembling, and Wolf knew that even though she made no sound, she was crying. How many times had she cried alone after Kingston had hurt her? How many? He eased her hands away from her face. Wolf shared her anguish when she lifted her red lashes and revealed the haunted terror in the depths of her eyes. Tears wound silently down her pale cheeks, caught and held on the corners of her parted lips.

Framing her face with his hands, Wolf began to methodically wipe away the tears on her cheeks with his thumbs. "Tears are good," he told her, his voice husky with emotion. "Tears show that we are alive. It is good to weep for what has been taken from you." How badly Wolf wanted to lean down and touch her lips with his. How badly he wanted to simply enfold Cante Tinza into his arms and hold her. Hold her and rock her like the hurt child that she was.

Wolf's hands were large and warm against her flesh. His unexpected gentleness released months of suppressed grief and terror from her enslavement by Kingston. As the sobs started to well up and be released, Serena tried to pull out of Wolf's grip.

"No," he whispered, "do not run from me, Cante Tinza. Run to me...." And he opened his arms to her. She came without fighting him, and Wolf bit back a groan deep within himself. He raised his head, allowing her to nuzzle against his shoulder and chest. As he placed his arms around her shaking form, Wolf closed his eyes. He felt her pain as if it were his own, but then, he was a healer and he always felt the patient's pain.

This time it was different, his wolf spirit guide whispered, as he held Cante Tinza. Yes, he felt his patient's pain, but this time his heart was open to her, too. Wolf understood compassion and the healing power of touch, so he caressed her as he would a sick child. Stroking her hair, her shaking shoulders and long, deeply indented spine, he began to ease the burden she'd carried so long by herself.

A spirit-departing song welled up within him. Wolf began to sing softly, his deep voice bringing the words to life. Almost instantly, he felt Cante Tinza cry even harder, her weeping sounds filling the tepee. He sang for what she had lost—for what had been taken from her by a man who was selfish in his eyes. He prayed in his own language to White Buffalo Calf Woman, to Wakan Tanka and to Tunkasila to come and help Cante Tinza heal her broken heart and splintered soul.

As he knelt with Cante Tinza in his arms and felt her fingers digging into his buckskin shirt as she wept, Wolf finally understood why she had been so fearful of him. He was a man, and a man had hurt her. He had kept her confined to the tepee since her arrival, so she thought he was keeping her a slave just as Kingston had done. Worse, Wolf realized that Cante Tinza had been waiting for him to rape her, just as the *wasicun* had done.

And yet, throughout the past quarter of the moon, Cante Tinza had disregarded her own fears to reach out in generosity and help others, whether it was Dawn Sky, Deer Woman or his sisters Little Swallow and Evening Star. With a shake of his head, Wolf ended the song and rested his brow against her hair. He found himself wanting to heal her completely, but the process would be long, and often painful for her. Was that what she wanted? Did she even want to stay with his people? Or did she want to return to a *wasicun* town to live among her own?

He gently eased her away from him, and caught and held her tear-filled eyes. The corners of his mouth curved slightly as he framed her face with his hands. "I named you well, Brave Heart. For you are all of that and more, my woman. I do not think you know your own courage, your own fighting spirit." He wiped away the last of her tears and saw the shame in her eyes. "You have nothing to be ashamed of. You fought like a warrior. You were not meek, and the Lakota people will honor you. They will not judge you."

Serena hiccuped through her sobs and wanted nothing but continued closeness to Wolf. His eyes burned with such fierceness and care for her that she trembled. "B-but, I'm a soiled woman," she cried. "I'm no good to anyone!"

"Hush," Wolf commanded, "the Lakota do not see you as soiled. You did not give yourself to a man. You were taken against your will. Even our women are sometimes taken by our great enemy, the Crow. Some have been forced to marry Crow warriors, and as prisoners, they fight back, too. If a Lakota woman escapes and comes back to us, we have a great ceremony to welcome her among us once again. She is honored and given many gifts. If she was single before capture, then she is looked upon as a maid once again, regardless if a Crow raped her or made her his woman."

Blinking, Serena pulled out of Wolf's gentle hands. If she didn't, she was going to throw herself into his arms to be held once more. Never had she felt so protected— or so fiercely cared for. Somewhere, in the back of her spinning senses, Serena had heard him call her his woman. What did that mean? Utterly torn and confused, she dried her face with her shaking hands.

"I-if I go back to that town I don't know what will happen. I don't have any money, and no one would give me shelter or food." She looked up at Wolf's suffering features. "I don't have anywhere to go. I'm lost...."

"Ah, Cante Tinza," he breathed huskily, briefly touching the crown of her head, "you are never lost. As long as you know where you stand—where your feet rest upon Mother Earth—you are not lost." He touched his chest. "Your heart is your home. We would welcome you into our tribe, for you have not only saved our people's lives, but you have more than proved yourself worthy to us in so many other ways."

"Y-you would?" Hope flared strongly in Serena. She searched Wolf's dark, liquid eyes, wanting to believe him as never before. How could she have feared him so much when he had given her nothing but understanding and respect? Serena realized with a start that if Wolf had been indeed like his white counterpart, he would have taken full advantage of her while he held her—and he had not.

Wolf smiled slightly and gestured around the tepee. "It is an honor if you would stay with us."

"B-but, you're married to Deer Woman, and you have a baby. I—I'm an interloper."

Wolf reached over and began to untie the deerskin thong wrapped around one of her braids. "Cante Tinza, I am not married to Deer Woman. She has agreed to help because my sister was killed, and I am the baby's uncle. I must see that Dawn Sky is raised and loved."

As Wolf began to unbraid her hair, Serena gave a little gasp of surprise. She was wildly aware that he was going to not only unbraid her hair but brush it, too. Oh, how she'd enjoyed the experience the first time, once she had rid herself of her initial fear and distrust of Wolf. She watched him now, mesmerized as his dark brown fingers divided the copper strands of her hair.

"You aren't married?" she asked in a whisper.

Wolf heard the tremor in Cante Tinza's voice. Was it fear? He wasn't sure. He released the rest of her hair and gently began to run an elk comb through her strong, thick strands. "I am thirty summers old, and once, long ago, I fell in love with a maid." He frowned slightly, enjoying the closeness—the beauty of the moment as he combed her hair. "Pretty Shield was out picking chokecherries alone, and a Crow war party found her." Wolf's mouth twitched and he stared hard at the red hair in his hand. "They raped her, killed her and scalped her."

"Oh, no!" Serena cried. She felt Wolf's pain, and saw the loss in his burning eyes.

"That is the past and all things must move forward, as Wakan Tanka teaches us." The memory no longer haunted him, for he had released his anger and hatred toward the Crow over the many years since the incident. Wolf was touched by Cante Tinza's response to his sad story. "It is over now," he reassured her. "It is the past. For many summers, I grieved for Pretty Shield. But then my work, learning the ways of medicine, gradually took on importance, and now the people of our tribe own my heart."

Serena could hear the maturity and wisdom of years in his voice. Scalp tingling, she held still as he expertly began to braid her hair. "I thought you were married and Dawn Sky was your child."

"All children belong to the tribe," Wolf said, tying off the first braid. He enjoyed sliding his fingers through the silky sheets of her hair. This was something he could do forever, and envisioned waking up with Cante Tinza every morning and each taking turns combing and braiding each other's hair. Such was the way between a husband and wife: respect and love. Wolf realized Cante Tinza was watching him with a soft expression. He ached to lean down and explore her full mouth, but he controlled the unbidden urge.

"The Lakota is one large family," he added. "It is not uncommon to take in a child if the parents die. We do not let our old ones go hungry. After a buffalo hunt, we give the elders the hearts, tongues and livers to honor them and their wisdom.''

"In Wexford," Serena whispered, "people die in the gutters for lack of food, no matter what their age."

Wolf flexed his mouth into a thin line and said, "*Wasicuns* respect nothing. They see themselves as dominant. They do not realize that we are all related. We are tied to our Mother, the Earth, and we are her stewards, not her conquerors."

Serena sat there as Wolf finished braiding her hair. He brought over a parfleche and opened it.

"You will stay among us?" he asked, fearful that she would say no.

"Yes—I'd like to," she ventured softly, watching as he drew out two otter skins.

Joy coursed through Wolf, but he tried to hide his reaction because he didn't want to influence Cante Tinza's decisions. "You may stay with whomever you choose." Wolf wrapped the first otter skin around her braid and tied it off with red cotton cloth. On the end of the first braid, he placed a small, fluffy brown-and-white eagle feather as a symbol of her newfound freedom.

Serena courageously lifted her lashes and looked directly into Wolf's eyes. "I think Dawn Sky needs more attention than Deer Woman can give her. I'd like to stay here—if you'll let me."

Wolf's heart took a galloping beat, and his hands trembled ever so slightly as he fitted the second otter skin on the other braid. "We would be honored with your presence. And you are right—Deer Woman has many other duties and I worry that my niece is not being properly attended. You are a free woman, Cante Tinza. The Lakota people honor generosity, bravery, responsibility and hard work. You possess all these things. No one owns you. If you want to leave at any time, you are free to do so. If you want to stay forever, that is your decision."

The words, spoken so low and with such feeling, drove tears into Serena's eyes. Free. She was free. For the first time after four months of brutal captivity.

106

He could...

Chapter Six

Serena had barely dried her eyes and composed herself when Wolf, who had gone over to his robe, asked, "Would you care for my niece? I have need of a woman here, to live in my tepee."

"I've never been a mother, but I could try."

"Dove That Flies, who just had a son two moons ago, provides her milk whenever Dawn Sky is hungry. Would you see that my niece is taken to her for that purpose?"

Serena nodded. "I love children, Wolf. I know you are busy, and I want to help." How could she turn down any request he had? Wolf had saved her life.

He grunted. She had spoken like a true Lakota maiden, he thought. The eagerness shining in Cante Tinza's eyes opened his heart, and he felt her joy in being able to care for his niece. As he sat there mulling over the situation with Deer Woman, the unbidden thought of Cante Tinza having *his* children struck him. Right now, she needed to put meat back on her bones. The winter and spring would serve to strengthen her. What then? Swallowing hard, Wolf knew what he wanted—Cante Tinza as his wife. What would she do if she knew that? Run? Scream in terror because he was a man, and he could also hurt her?

Whatever he did, Wolf knew that as never before, he must allow his spirit guides to lead him through this thorny situation with Cante Tinza. Soon the village would know that she was going to stay with him. That meant any warrior could rightfully begin to court her. And who among them would not?

"I will ask Deer Woman to show you how to cook and to bead and...well, perform the tasks that Lakota women are taught."

Wolf was about to say more, but Deer Woman entered the tepee with his niece. Her golden skin was flushed because of the chill. She smiled at him brightly in greeting and placed Dawn Sky's cradleboard on the appropriate pallet. He watched Deer Woman's smile disappear when she looked at Cante Tinza. Disturbed, sensing more than seeing, Wolf could feel the young woman's jealousy.

"Deer Woman, come over here," Wolf invited. "We must talk."

Deer Woman eagerly came and knelt near him. "I await your words, Black Wolf. What may I do to please you?"

Wincing inwardly, Wolf held her golden gaze. "Cante Tinza has decided to stay with us, and not go back to the *wasicun* town to live."

"Oh...."

"She has further agreed to take care of my niece for me and live in my tepee."

Deer Woman's mouth fell open, and she jerked a look over at Cante Tinza and then back to Black Wolf. "But— you have me!" she protested as she touched the breast of her quilled buckskin dress. "Have I not agreed to live with you and be your niece's helper?"

Wolf tried to soften his words because she appeared distraught, and he saw tears in her eyes. "You are but a child yourself," he said quietly, "and you would rather run off and play than do the work required of a woman."

"But—"

Wolf held up his hand and his voice grew firmer. "There is no argument on this. I have made my decision. And you are not shamed because you are being replaced. I feel you will have more time to allow Swift Elk to court you properly."

Deer Woman leaped to her feet, curling her hands into small fists at her sides. "How can you choose Cante Tinza over me?" She struck her breast. "I am Lakota! She is *wasicun!* How can you expect her to care properly for your niece? She knows nothing of our ways, our beliefs! And I *will* be shamed if I am sent back to my parents' tepee!" Tears flowed down her cheeks as she cried out, "And I do not love Swift Elk. I love you!" There, it was finally out. She stood there in front of the medicine man, taut and trembling. "My heart," she whispered brokenly, "has never belonged to anyone but you, Black Wolf. All my life, I have watched you and loved you from a distance. I know you think I am young, but in my heart the summers do not matter. It is the feelings that lie there that are more important. I—I want the chance to prove myself to you, to show you that I am deserving of being looked upon as a good Lakota wife for you."

Wolf moved uncomfortably. He had seen Cante Tinza's face change markedly when Deer Woman leaped to her feet and began to cry. He wished she did not have to see this. Mouth moving into a grim line, he spoke in a low tone. "You are a child in my eyes, Deer Woman. I cannot give my heart to you, for it belongs to the tribe."

"Ho!" she spit, whirling around and pointing at Cante Tinza, "I think you hide from yourself, Black Wolf. I see the look in your eyes when she stirs. I see your mouth soften. I see longing in your eyes. Perhaps you do not lie to me about this, but you lie to yourself. You *want* her! And somehow," she sobbed, "you have convinced Cante Tinza to not only stay, but to live in your tepee! You are a medicine man...you have put a spell on her—"

Wolf slowly got to his feet, towering over Deer Woman, whose face was contorted with rage and jealousy now—not hurt. "Girl, do not accuse me of such things. I would never place a spell on anyone. If anything, I remove spells from others!"

Deer Woman sniffed loudly and took a step away from his imposing presence. "Yet, you do not deny that you *want* this *wasicun!*"

"Cante Tinza is a free woman who will walk among us," Wolf gritted out between clenched teeth. His niece began to cry, and he glared at Deer Woman because she'd caused him to nearly lose his temper. The girl had a nagging trait of knowing the truth. Wolf saw Cante Tinza slowly get up to attend to his niece in the cradleboard. The baby, reassured, stopped crying instantly. He swung his attention back to Deer Woman, who stood breathing hard and glaring at him.

"I had hoped that I could ask you to stay long enough in this tepee to teach Cante Tinza the womanly things she should know, but I see now that is impossible."

Startled, Deer Woman reached out and gripped Wolf's arm. "No! I will stay. I will do whatever you want."

Sadly, Wolf pulled his arm out of her grasp. "No, you cling to this opportunity to stay the winter just to be with me, not to be here for Cante Tinza or my niece."

Deer Woman just stood there while her lips trembled and tears slid down her cheeks. She had not realized that Wolf had intended to allow her to stay upward of six moons with him to teach Cante Tinza. "Please," she begged hoarsely, "let me stay. I can teach the *wasicun* well. I *want* to be here with you."

Wolf foresaw the danger in Deer Woman's staying. She was a child instead of a woman, and one with dangerous emotions. He didn't want to have such dissension in his tepee. His work as a medicine man demanded serenity and peace, to put him in the proper mood to conduct ceremonies, and it couldn't be done with Deer Woman's jealousy, or belief that he loved her, when he didn't.

"No, I think it's best you pack your belongings and go now," he told her heavily. "I thank you for what you've done. I will bring three of my best horses to your father in thanks for your services here. At least, when you marry you will have a good dowry of three horses to bring to your husband. People will admire these horses I give you, and you will admire them, too."

"I want Wiyaka, then!" Deer Woman cried. "You have fifteen horses. You are rich, Black Wolf. Make one of those you give me your very best buffalo runner, Wiyaka."

Anger sparked through Wolf as he watched the cunning in Deer Woman's eyes come alive. Wiyaka, Feather, was his black mare, his personal favorite. "You may walk among my herd and choose any three horses other than Wiyaka."

"I suppose you are going to give the *wasicun* your black horse?"

Stung, Wolf held on to his temper. Deer Woman had incredible insight into him, and it disturbed him greatly. Had she read his mind? He had thought of giving his buffalo runner to Cante Tinza after he taught her how to ride. "What I do, and to whom I give, is not your business," he warned her darkly.

Deer Woman glared at Cante Tinza, who held the baby in her arms, and then swung back to Wolf. Without a word, she went over to her pallet, quickly wrapped her belongings in a gray wool blanket and left without another word.

Wolf sighed and glanced over at Cante Tinza. He knew she had understood very little of the argument, yet she was disturbed. There were so many fine lines to walk with her. How much could he tell her about Deer Woman? Realizing he had just made an enemy out of the girl, Wolf sat down and frowned.

But Dawn Sky's happy cooing and laughter gradually broke down the tension that had accumulated in his shoulders and neck from confronting Deer Woman. He looked up. Cante Tinza held the baby so that her tiny brown feet touched the robe. Wolf could see joy in Cante Tinza's green eyes, and that joy evaporated the rest of his anger as if it were fog beneath hot sunlight.

The laughter of his niece and the soft smile of Cante Tinza's lips spun threads of hope in Wolf. He ached to go over to the two. That could not be. At least, not yet, he reminded himself grimly. Although many barriers had been broken down between her and him, he knew Cante Tinza still feared and distrusted men—no matter if they were *wasicun* or Lakota. And she had a right to own that fear.

"Why was Deer Woman crying?" Serena asked softly.

Wolf's mouth tightened. "She wanted to stay and care for the baby."

Serena studied his expression carefully. "She was upset."

"Yes, she was." Wolf didn't want to divulge the ugly conversation to Cante Tinza. She was just beginning to recover, and it wouldn't help to know that Deer Woman was jealous of her. "Do not worry yourself," he soothed. "I go to talk with my sister, Little Swallow. She will teach you Lakota ways."

Serena smiled and nodded, caught up in the joy and laughter of Dawn Sky. She brought the baby back into her lap and cuddled her. "I want to learn, Wolf. Just tell me what I have to do."

His mouth moved into a slight smile. "You are doing it right now. I have never seen my niece laugh like that since her mother died." He motioned to the child as he got to his feet and moved toward the entrance. "Dawn Sky accepts you as her real mother. That is good."

The tepee became quiet after Wolf left. Serena looked around at the large, roomy structure. This was her new life. Had it been the right decision? Any other choice would mean starvation as it had in Wexford. White men couldn't be trusted, and she certainly didn't want to go back to the miner's camp owned by Blackjack Kingston.

Gazing down at Dawn Sky, who moved her arms and legs in happy abandon as she lay on her back, Serena smoothed the baby's black hair away from her small brow. The quarrel between Deer Woman and Wolf had disturbed her. There had been such hatred in Deer Woman's eyes when she left. Was it because of her? So much was changing in her life that Serena felt terribly insecure and unsure of her decisions. In Wexford she had had to live one day at a time, without seeing a future. She would have to do the same here. She could not afford to hope; she wouldn't know what to hope for, anyway. The Lakota had taken her in. If she could prove to them that she wasn't a liability, but rather, an asset, perhaps she could make a new life for herself. Perhaps.

"Soon," Wolf told Cante Tinza, "the moon will come when geese return in scattered formations. After the equinox, when Mother Earth turns toward the warmth once again, we will break camp and begin our trek toward Pte He Gi, the Gray Buffalo Horn region." He used his hands to indicate that they would make their summer camp high in the hills. "A stone rises out of the earth and has the claw marks of a grizzly bear all around it. It is very tall, and very sacred. We will hold our summer solstice Sun Dance beneath its shadow."

Busy beading, a craft that she had learned from Little Swallow, Serena looked up at Wolf who sat on the opposite pallet. "I can hardly wait to see it. I will be glad when winter is over, too."

The Lakota camp had taken on a new energy of late, and Serena had been busy making her second pair of moccasins for Wolf. The first pair had been a disaster, but with Little Swallow's help and guidance, the second hadn't turned out too badly. Wolf wore them, she noticed, with great pride. It made her feel good that he liked them. Dawn Sky lay beside her, playing with a deer bone, happily gurgling and cooing.

"This is sacred land we live upon," Wolf said. "And nowhere is it felt more powerfully than where we go to make our summer camp. We will move the camp many times before we reach the Gray Buffalo Horn. In the moon when berries are ripe, we will finally arrive."

"I never realized how much you move."

"We must, for to remain in one area too long is to take away Mother Earth's food and animals. The Great Spirit taught us to take only what is needed, and leave the rest. It is a good way to live."

Serena smiled at his flawless logic. How different the Lakota were from white society. And yet Serena preferred the Lakota way of life. No one went hungry. No one had to sleep in gutters. The camp was a large, extended family. Sometimes there were problems, but they were settled fairly and without bloodshed.

"Are you happy with us, Cante Tinza?" The moons had flown by for Wolf, and she had worked unerringly to learn Lakota ways. To his delight, she had made a fast friendship with his sister, Little Swallow. But there had been those who were not so pleased with Cante Tinza's presence. Chief Badger Mouth told Wolf that if the horse soldiers found out a *wasicun* lived among them, a woman, they would attack their camp and drag her off to live with *wasicuns* once again. Deer Woman's nasty gossip about Cante Tinza had hurt her deeply when she found out about it after learning their language. She had cried, and that had hurt Wolf.

"Very happy, Wolf," Serena answered, glancing up from her beading. "Why?"

He shrugged. "You work very hard." He gestured to her hands. "Even harder than my sister, who is a model Lakota woman. Your hands are always chapped and bleeding."

With a laugh, Serena said, "That's because I still haven't gotten down the art of porcupine quilling!" Her smile dissolved as she discovered the worry in Wolf's eyes. "You've made me feel welcome. How can I not be happy?"

Grumbling, he said, "Deer Woman's gossip has hurt you."

"Oh, that. I'm not so sure it came from her, Wolf. I know there are several people in the tribe who don't like me here. It could have been one of them who said those mean things about me."

Mouth quirking, Wolf sighed. Gossip had gotten started about Cante Tinza's scarred breasts—that because of the terrible burns on them, she could never nurse a baby. Rumor had circulated that if she had a baby, it would starve for lack of milk. Wolf couldn't prove that it was Deer Woman who had started the latest round of gossip. To his surprise, there were several other maids who disliked Cante Tinza's presence in his tepee. They, too, had their eyes on him as a husband.

"I know the gossip has hurt you," he said in a low voice, studying her placid features as she beaded beneath the light of the fire.

With a nod, Serena said, "Maybe it's true." Yet, thanks to the herbs provided by Dreaming Bear, the scars on her breasts weren't as bad as they might have been.

"What?" Wolf demanded. "That you cannot give a baby your milk? That is nonsense!" He gestured toward her. "Only the outer skin is damaged."

The conversation was embarrassing to Serena, but she had found over the months that the Lakota people accepted the human body and human functions as natural—not something to be ignored, covered up or hidden. She wrestled with the moral taboos that had been taught to her. One just didn't discuss a woman's breasts this openly. Heat fled to her cheeks and she dropped her lashes.

Wolf was far from unaware of her changing moods. "I shame you by speaking on the matter," he muttered unhappily as he saw the color rise in her face. Cante Tinza's cheeks were now fuller, and gave her face more beauty, he thought.

"No...I...it's just that among my people, we don't talk about such private parts, that's all." With a little laugh, Serena glanced up at him. She melted beneath Wolf's ebony gaze. There was a fierce fire of life burning in the depths of his eyes, and she had come to treasure these quiet moments with him. Perhaps it was Dawn Sky who had brought them this close to each other, for the baby was greatly loved and cared for by both of them.

When Cante Tinza touched her flaming red cheek, Wolf felt for her. "You are a beautiful woman. Any warrior would be proud to have you for a wife. *Ho*. They would be crazy, *heyoka*, to turn you away just because of scars you bear on your breasts. A warrior would see them as battle wounds, and that is honorable. They are nothing to be ashamed of, so you should hold your head high, Cante Tinza, and not allow this gossip to hurt you so."

Serena's lips parted over his impassioned speech. Wolf had never called her beautiful before. No, if anything, he was the model of decorum around her. Since her wounds had healed sufficiently, he no longer combed or braided her hair. How much she missed that intimacy with him. Wolf slept on his pallet opposite her. He respected her privacy, and never touched her. An ache was centered deep within Serena as she held his fierce, searching stare. She had never forgotten that day when she'd fallen into his arms and he'd held her. His touch had been exquisitely gentle and healing.

"Well," Serena stumbled, "I've never seen myself except in the reflection of a pool of water, and no one ever said I was pretty." She gestured to the coverlet of freckles across her cheeks and nose. "I have freckles, and they are considered ugly looking. And my face is long and narrow, like a horse's face."

Wolf couldn't stand to hear her speak of herself in such a way. Getting up, he walked around the altar and fire. "You," he said, kneeling before her and barely grazing her fiery cheek with his fingertips, "are beautiful in the ways of a woman. These freckles remind me of the many stars in Father Sky. I see them as a reflection of Wanaglta Canju, the Milky Way. To me, they are a symbol of how special you are, Cante Tinza." He smiled and gently outlined the shape of her face. "And yes, your face is long, but you have high cheekbones just like the Lakota. Your eyes remind me of the quiet green pools found near the banks of the river. And your mouth is the color of ripe wild strawberries that the women gather each summer." He forced himself to sit back on his heels, his hands coming to rest on his buckskin-clad thighs. "And a horse's face? No. Your nose is too fine and thin."

His unexpected nearness, his touch, which she had come to hunger for and never received, was thrilling. Serena stared up at his features. Wolf's voice was low with feeling, and she absorbed his sincerity into her heart. "I love the way you see me, Wolf. It's so beautiful...."

Wolf tried to stop his hand from rising. He had fought himself throughout the moons, constantly battling with his need and hunger for Cante Tinza. She was still watchful and wary of men, which he knew because he would often see her shy away from the other warriors. She had shed that wariness with him, but he had to constantly remind himself that she had been raped, and that it would take her a long time to release that terrible memory, if ever. But the liquid look in Cante Tinza's eyes now made him do the unthinkable, and Wolf found himself reaching out and cradling her cheek and jaw against his large, open palm.

"You walk in beauty, my woman. Your heart belongs to Mother Earth, and your soul to the Great Spirit. Do you not think that I see how the children love you? How they beg you to play their games with you? And the elders talk respectfully of you, of your attention and care to them." Her skin was soft and pliant beneath his palm, and Wolf wanted to continue to explore her, to show her his love and reverence. When her ripe lips parted and tears made her green eyes luminous, he smiled a little. "Listen to the smiles given to you, Cante Tinza, the looks of adoration and respect from those whom you have unselfishly and generously helped. Do not listen to the wicked gossip spoken by a few who are jealous of you. They are the lazy ones, the ones who wish to receive such smiles and respect from others but who do not earn it."

Wolf forced himself to remove his hand. If he didn't, he would do something unforgivable, such as lean down and explore her red, full lips. A maid did not allow a warrior to kiss her unless she was thinking of marriage. Getting up, he moved away from Cante Tinza and took his place on his pallet.

Serena blinked once, and reached up to touch her tingling skin where he'd laid his hand against her flesh. A warm, melting sensation continued to blanket her in the aftermath of Wolf's unexpected touch, as did the trembling words that had come from his heart. She knew he wouldn't look at her, instead busying himself by crushing dried roots gathered the previous fall for medicinal purposes. The firelight shadowed his large form, revealing the deep lines around his mouth and eyes.

She was beautiful to Wolf. The discovery was as potent as it was frightening. But Serena wasn't frightened of Wolf as much as she was of herself. What were these feelings moving like chaos within her? What was the strange ache centered in her lower body? Even her breasts tingled with an oddly disturbing sensation. She bowed her head and forced herself to pay attention to the beading. A part of her had been silently crying out for Wolf's touch, and now that he had grazed her skin, she felt shaky and breathless in the wake of the experience. Would she feel this way all the time? Blackjack's touch had been painful and bruising. Serena had experienced only hurt from him. Wolf's touch was the opposite, and she had no one to share her discovery with.

"Come," Wolf told Cante Tinza. He gestured for her to follow him. The April sunlight was strong and warm, sending away the winter chill. They walked just outside of the circle of tepees toward the large herd of horses. Wolf held a rawhide jaw cord in one hand, and a cottonwood saddle in another. The snow was less than ankle deep, and was quickly melting.

"Where are we going?" Serena asked, running to catch up with his long stride. She wore a heavy elkskin dress that Little Swallow had made for her. The elkskin leggings and moccasins kept her far warmer than deerskin. As she hurried to Wolf's side, she squinted against the glare of the snow and her breath came out in white clouds of steam.

"You are going to learn to ride," he announced. When he realized she was struggling to keep up with him, he shortened his stride.

"Really?" Serena laughed and clapped her hands. With the melting of the snow and the longer hours of sunlight, she'd felt more alive than she had ever felt before.

Wolf met her smile, admiring her green eyes dancing with life. He knew he was going to have trouble keeping his hands off her today. Cante Tinza's long, heavy braids were wrapped in otter. She wore the fluffy eagle feather and porcupine medicine wheel that he had made for her two moons ago. He had told her that only a person who had a Lakota name could wear the eagle feather and medicine wheel. From that day forward, Wolf had seen her plait her hair and tie the gift into her burnished strands. Pride swept through him, because she walked so tall and straight now, her shoulders thrown back with confidence, her chin high. No longer was Cante Tinza the cowering dog who had come to them so many moons before.

Wolf chose the oldest of his horses for her to learn to ride upon—a gray mustang mare so old that her knees were arthritic. The midday sun was warm, and the air clean and fresh as he showed her how to saddle the mare and place the jaw cord into its partially toothless mouth. A number of children looking for something to do had followed them out to the horse herd, which was guarded by two Lakota riders. All warriors took turns protecting the herd from potential Crow raiders.

"Now," Wolf counseled her, "you do it," and he removed the saddle and the jaw cord from the gray mare.

The children gathered around Serena to give her advice. She glanced up at Wolf and then at the saddle in her arms. "The poor horse will hate me when I'm done."

"She's too old to care," Wolf said.

Serena had learned long ago to pay attention whenever Wolf tried to teach her something. She timidly approached the gray mare, who stood there with her head hanging down, and petted the thickly furred animal. With help and suggestions from the children who crowded around her, Serena saddled and bridled the mare. She turned, smiling triumphantly.

"There!"

Wolf laughed. "I think your helpers did most of the work for you."

The children came up for hugs and embraces from Serena. She did not disappoint them.

"Now, you must learn to mount," Wolf instructed her.

Serena watched Wolf approach the horse while the children crowded close to her, hanging on to her elkskin dress and moving beneath each of her arms. Wolf placed his foot in the cottonwood stirrup and moved easily into the saddle. She sighed. "You're so graceful, Wolf. I'd be lucky to have half of that."

Dismounting, Wolf grinned and handed her the jaw cord. "A woman who walks in beauty is *always* graceful. Try it. You will see."

Serena nervously patted the gray mare, and burying her doubts, tried to mount. It took several attempts, along with Wolf's cajoling to realize that the key to success was balance. Finally, she climbed into the saddle. All the children broke into yells and cries of victory. Laughing, Serena bowed her head in thanks to them. But it was the warmth in Wolf's eyes, his admiration, that made her feel so good.

Wolf quickly caught, bridled, and mounted Wiyaka, his black mare. He rode up to Serena. "Now, we ride." He showed her how to use the calves of her legs to squeeze the sides of the horse to make it move forward.

They rode at a walk along the willow- and bulrush-lined riverbank. At first, Serena clutched at the front of the saddle, but after a while, she established a rocking motion with the mare and finally released her grip. Wolf praised her. The children ran after them for some distance, and then went back to the village to play.

All around Serena was beauty she would never tire of seeing. The sky was wide and blue, the sunlight warm against the elkskin dress, and returning birds trilled their hearts out among the bare willow branches. Occasionally, Wolf's leg would brush against her own, and she would look over and smile at him. He rode with such naturalness, Serena realized, that he was beautiful to watch, too. His thighs were long, curved and hard from being born to a horse, his back ramrod straight, and his arms loose and relaxed. It was obvious that Wiyaka loved her master as much as he loved her; Wolf would sometimes lean forward and slide his fingers across her ebony neck to pet her, and the mare would arch her neck and dance sideways in response.

Serena wondered what it would be like to have Wolf touch her the same way.

Wolf thought she looked beautiful as she rode the mare. With time, as she relaxed and trusted the horse, she would become a good rider. "Tomorrow," he told her as he gestured to the north of them, "we begin to pack and move toward our summer grounds."

"I can hardly wait!"

"You grow bored, Cante Tinza?"

"Oh, no! It's just that I've heard everyone talk of how lovely the Gray Buffalo Horn area is. I'm excited!"

After a few minutes, he asked, "Do you miss your people?"

Serena saw the worry in Wolf's eyes. "Sometimes," she admitted softly. "But it's Ireland I miss, not America. My parents are dead, and so are most of my relatives. I have nothing to go home to." She looked around and smiled softly. "The trees are so green here, Wolf.

They remind me of my home. Ireland is so green. We don't get snow like this where I live, but it does get cold and rainy."

"So you are happy among us?"

"How could I not be?"

"*Washtay,* good. Come, let us turn back. Your legs will protest enough tomorrow morning when you get up. You will use the gray mare as your personal riding horse from now on."

Delighted, Serena said, "Thank you, Wolf. She's so old, bless her heart. I worry I'll hurt her."

With a chuckle, Wolf said, "The gray will be steady for you. She will teach you well, Cante Tinza. In time, you will own a horse like Wiyaka."

It was her turn to laugh. "I'm afraid not! She's very spirited and I'll never be that good a rider."

Wolf gave her a burning, searching look. "No, you are exactly like this fine black mare, Cante Tinza. There is a fire in your soul. I see it burn in your eyes. Like this mare you have a heart that feels deeply and hard. You will someday ride a horse much like yourself. You will see...."

Chapter Seven

"What are you making?" Serena asked Wolf. She had just finished changing Dawn Sky's diaper and had placed her in the cradleboard for the night. The moon of the green leaves had come, and the village had just made camp deep within the Paha Sapa, surrounded by the towering pine trees.

Wolf glanced across the shadows of the tepee. The fire was small tonight because it was warm. Soon, the cooking fire would be placed outside. When night came, the darkness would be complete within the tepee. "I am crushing the seeds of wild rose."

Serena had always been interested in Wolf's herbal knowledge, but had shied away from showing her curiosity. He must have seen the look in her eyes, because he seemed to sense her needs before she ever spoke of them, which sometimes startled her.

"Come." He gestured. "Come see what I am doing." He was using a flat rock that fit into the palm of his hand to roll the bright orange rose hips against a larger stone, crushing them into a powder. He was thrilled that Cante Tinza was finally expressing an interest in the medicines, and he waited to continue until she came to his side. Over the moons, she had lost all her wariness toward him, and now she could kneel only inches away from him without tensing.

"What do you use this for?" she asked, pointing to the fine, orange powder.

He smiled. "This is not a medicine. I am going to crush enough of the seeds so that Little Swallow could show you how to make a jelly from the powder."

Serena straightened, her hands resting on her thighs. She met his smiling eyes. "You're playing the *heyoka* again, Wolf," and she laughed.

Cante Tinza's laughter created a longing so sharp and deep through Wolf that he avoided her sparkling green eyes for a moment. How beautiful she looked in her new deerskin dress. During the late spring and throughout the summer, the women wore deerskin, which was much lighter than elk. The dress had been lovingly fashioned by Dove That Flies for Cante Tinza, who often cared for the woman's three other children while she fed Dawn Sky from her breast.

Wolf continued to crush the rose hips methodically. Cante Tinza seemed to be able to read his mind, and she brought over a small birchbark container that had been sealed with pine pitch. Carefully scooping a handful of the powder into the container, he looked up at her very serious face.

"You show interest in what I do." Wolf watched her facial expression closely.

"Well—I—"

"There is nothing wrong with being curious about what I do."

With a shy shrug, Serena laughed. "I've always loved plants and flowers. Almost every night, you crush some plant, and I've often wondered what it was for."

Wolf nodded. "Perhaps you have a skill for such a thing, as I do."

"Oh, no! I couldn't . . . I'm sure."

He ignored her exclamation. "Come with me tomorrow morning? I go to gather *hehaka tapejuta*, wild bergamot. I need this for elk medicine."

Thrilled, Serena stared down at Wolf's rugged, shadowed profile. Normally, at dawn, both went about their own duties, which were considerable. The demands on Wolf's time were heavy. He doctored the entire tribe, which included performing many kinds of healing ceremonies, and collecting and making his own medicines.

"What is elk medicine? Once I heard Deer Woman speak about it in the moon lodge. She giggled and covered her face when she spoke of it."

Wolf grunted. "She probably wants some to put into Swift Elk's food to force him into marrying her."

"What?"

"Some medicine men and women possess elk medicine. It is a love medicine, Cante Tinza. I take the elk's heart and part of its hoof, and mix it with this herb. If you place the elk medicine in someone's food or drink, then they will begin to love whoever placed it there. It is a very powerful medicine. I once knew a young warrior madly in love with a maid who didn't want him at all, who brought many horses to me for just a pinch of the powder."

Her eyes widened. "Does it work?"

Wolf smiled over at her surprised features. The moons had filled out Cante Tinza. Her face was no longer painfully narrow and drawn. She looked beautiful to him. "Ask Tall Crane."

"Him? He used it?"

Chuckling, Wolf said, "Many years ago my friend Tall Crane came to me. He'd fallen so much in love with this maid that he begged me to help him. The maid had eyes for another, but I felt her heart wavered between the two warriors, so I promised to help Tall Crane." Wolf held up his hand and placed his thumb and index fingers close to each other. "One pinch into the maid's food and her heart swung to Tall Crane within a week. He played his flute for her outside her parent's tepee, and she went for walks with him. Tall Crane's mother had gifted him with a trading blanket, and he used that as a courting blanket.

"Of course, Tall Crane had competition. Each of the suitors would stand in line outside her parent's tepee with their courting blankets. Each warrior had his turn placing the blanket around himself and the maid to talk."

"What did they talk about?" Serena asked. Like a child, she loved it when Wolf would stop and spin a story.

"Many things. Understand that this went on at dusk every evening. Each warrior would tell the maid of his exploits that day. If he had been on a hunt, he would tell her how he did. If he counted coup against the Crow he would relate that story. And if the warrior took too long, the other suitors would throw pebbles at his blanket to remind him his time was up. If he refused to move along and give the other warriors a chance to speak with the maid, they often forcibly ejected him."

Serena smiled. "So the elk medicine you gave Tall Crane worked?"

"It did. Within a month, the maid chose him for her husband." Wolf placed more of the ground powder into the birchbark container. "They were very happy together." He frowned.

"But Tall Crane lives alone in his tepee now."

"Yes."

"Oh, dear. What happened?"

Wolf sat up and scowled. "A man named Blackjack Kingston gathered his many miners and attacked our village two summers ago. He timed it so that all the hunters were gone for the day to hunt for food. He also knew, through someone who has never come forward to admit their deed, that the warriors who normally remain close to the village to protect it from such attacks, had left to count coup against the Crow, who were trying to take the Paha Sapa away from us. I was with that war party, for the medicine man always goes along to care for those who are wounded."

Serena felt the agony radiating from Wolf, and his eyes were filled with anger and pain. "You know Blackjack?" she asked, her throat closing with fear.

"I do," Wolf rasped. "The *wasicun* attacked our village late in the afternoon. His intent was to murder as many of our people as he could. He was a coward, because the only ones left in the village were the children, women and elders. There were fifty miners. Our women fought courageously, and killed ten miners. Among our people, Tall Crane's wife and baby were murdered."

"Oh, no!" Serena cried, pressing her hands against her mouth.

"The hunters came back at dusk and heard our women wailing and crying. Fifteen of our people were murdered, and as many others had various wounds. One of the hunters rode after the war party. He caught up with us two days later to tell us the news. We hurried back to camp. By the time I arrived, five more people had died." Wolf shut his eyes. "Most of the tepees were burned to the ground, and the miners had stolen everything they could, including some of our young maids."

Fists knotting against his thighs, Wolf growled, "From that day forward, I vowed to kill Blackjack Kingston if the Great Spirit ever put him in my path. I wait for that day."

Tears smarted in Serena's eyes. "What happened to the women the miners stole?"

"We went after Kingston's men. I led the war party with Tall Crane. I prayed for a thunderstorm to slow Kingston's progress toward his camp. That night it rained and hailed, and the thunder beings hurled bolts of lightning all around the Paha Sapa. We sneaked through that storm and located Kingston and his men. Their wagons were buried in mud, and at dawn we fell upon them. Our maids were in chains and ropes, but we brought them home.

"Kingston managed to escape, but he knew that Tall Crane and I were after him. We killed ten more miners without suffering any wounded among our warriors. All of our maids had been raped, and it was a bittersweet homecoming. But the women were honored at a special ceremony, for they, too, fought their captors."

Serena was silent for a long time. "I didn't know this. Poor Tall Crane. He's such a good man. I often wondered why he looks so sad. I sometimes find him outside his tepee, at the end of a day's work, just sitting looking off in the distance, his eyes filled with tears."

"Elk medicine works both ways," Wolf told her gravely. "The person using it also falls more deeply in love with the maid he gives it to."

"Will he always grieve for his wife and child?"

With a shrug, Wolf said, "The Lakota take the bond of marriage to their heart. Tall Crane loved deeply. I know several maids are interested in him as a husband, but he shows no interest in them."

"How terribly sad," Serena whispered. She watched as Wolf's face became a mask of anger as he continued to grind down the rose hips. "Why didn't you tell me you knew Blackjack?"

With a snort, Wolf glanced over at her. "I wanted you to heal first. My heart went to you when I understood he had raped you. It made me angry once again. In a way, he murdered a part of you that will never be given back to you. The *wasicun* has no heart. He cares for no one but himself."

With a shiver, Serena wrapped her arms around herself, the terrible memories of her days as a prisoner flooding back to her. "I'd almost forgotten about him," she admitted softly, "because I'm so happy here."

Wolf saw the fear in her eyes once more and admonished himself for bringing up the *wasicun*'s name to her. He reached over and gently eased her arms from around herself. "You are safe here with us. With me."

Serena tried to smile but failed. Wolf's touch, as always, was gentle. She clasped her hands tightly in her lap. "Sometimes," she admitted, "I have terrible nightmares about him coming to get me again."

"He will have to kill me first," Wolf growled. "I will never allow him to take you, Cante Tinza. Never. If he tried, I would come after you. You have my word upon that."

Serena felt an incredible power radiate from Wolf as he ground out those words. She drowned in his black, velvet eyes, lost in the deep tenor of his promise. "I believe you."

"We are never truly safe, Cante Tinza. The Crow wait to attack us, and the miners sneak onto our sacred land, which is bound by treaty to be ours alone, to steal the gold from the creeks and rivers. The Lakota have many enemies, and this is why we move so often, to avoid an attack. That is why you must always go with a group of women to gather roots or berries. There is safety in numbers, my woman, and I always want you to be on guard." Wolf looked away, realizing he'd called her his woman once again. How had the words slipped out of his mouth? Only a warrior who wanted to marry a maid would use such a reference. He wondered if Cante Tinza understood that. Little Swallow and the other married women were sharing much of the Lakota culture and customs with her, but she could only learn so much at a time.

Serena stared at Wolf, who had resumed his grinding and crushing duties. *His woman.* That was the third time he'd used the phrase with her. What did it mean? Shaken by their talk, yet longing to have Wolf touch her once again, Serena forced herself to get up and leave his side. As she moved to her pallet to unbraid and comb her hair, which she did each evening, Serena couldn't explain the ache in her lower body, or the yearning in her heart each time Wolf was near.

"Tomorrow morning, you take Dawn Sky to Dove That Flies and ask her to care for her. Tell her that we will be back by early afternoon."

Serena nodded and opened the parfleche she had recently made and painted. Wolf had gifted her with many items over the previous months—among them, an elk bone comb. As she picked it up, she wondered if that, too, was considered elk medicine. Did that explain why, in quiet moments, unbidden thoughts of Wolf came to her? Why she dreamed of him touching her in a loving way? Had he placed the powder in her food? That was nonsense, Serena decided, for Wolf had been the epitome of a gentleman around her. He treated her with great respect—as an equal—and never touched her.

Serena sighed as she unbraided and combed her hair. Would Wolf do such a thing without her knowledge? A part of her wished that he had, but that scared her, too. Her rape was still too fresh in her memory. Another, larger part of her whispered that Wolf was too honorable to resort to such trickery. She understood as never before how much trust the Lakota had in him. Wolf never lied, and never stretched or embellished the truth in any way. He was a man who walked with great humility, even though he was the second most powerful person in the village.

A fierce emotion that had no name flowed through Serena as she considered all these things. Dawn Sky was greatly loved by Wolf, and several times each day, he would pick up the baby and play with her to give Serena a break from watching her. Serena was amazed at how the men, when they weren't busy with their own duties, would pitch in to help the women.

Every moon, Serena spent five to seven days in the women's moon lodge as they gave their blood back to Mother Earth. She looked forward to those times spent with the many other women who shared the same moon time. Those five days gave her the rest she needed from the dawn-to-dusk work demands upon her. Serena had learned to bead, quill and make leather goods during those times. The women taught her the ways of women— their songs, their stories and what was expected of a Lakota maid. Yes, the moon lodge was a wonderful hiatus from the backbreaking work, and yet Serena missed Wolf acutely during her time there. A woman who was on her moon was considered too powerful to be around men. And she, especially, because she lived in the tepee of the medicine man, and could pull the power from all of his medicines and render them weak or impotent.

During those days, Wolf cared for Dawn Sky and took over her womanly duties without complaint. He always had her favorite meal, deer stew, waiting for her upon her return to the village. And always he had some small gift for her—usually sweet-smelling flowers lying on her cleaned and folded robe. Serena realized that life had taken a turn she'd never expected, and she was happier now than she'd ever been.

After combing her hair, Serena allowed it to fall free around her shoulders. Would this happiness last? She wasn't sure, because she always felt dread stalking her. Placing the comb back in the parfleche, she lay down with her back to Wolf, and closed her eyes. It was too hot to sleep beneath the robe, so she now slept on top of it.

As sleep claimed Serena, her last thought was looking forward to hunting herbs with Wolf. How long she had wanted to go with him, but she'd lacked the courage to speak up. She didn't know if it was proper to ask such an important favor from him. A soft smile shadowed her mouth and a joy flowed through her like the quiet river they camped beside.

"There it is," Wolf said. He pulled Wiyaka to a halt. They stopped at the edge of a large, oval meadow surrounded by pine trees. Cante Tinza was riding the old gray mare.

"The bergamot?"

"Yes." Wolf dismounted and dropped the rawhide jaw cord. Wiyaka would stand where the cord dropped. The day was young, and Father Sun was still not above the pines of the Paha Sapa as Wolf came around to the gray mare. Cante Tinza was not a good rider yet, but she tried her best. Often, she would have trouble dismounting because her dress caught in the cottonwood saddle.

Wolf smiled and held out his hands to her before she dismounted. "Do you want help today?"

With a laugh, Serena nodded. "I can see the story of my falling off and ripping my dress has gotten back to you." She watched pleasure come to Wolf's dark eyes as he opened his large hands and spanned her waist. He easily lifted her up and out of the saddle and placed her lightly on the green grass of the meadow.

"Thank you," she said breathlessly, aware of his hands still lingering around her waist. She felt his strong fingers against her, and an unexpected heat flowed through her lower body. Serena lifted her chin and gazed up into Wolf's strong, harsh features.

"Yes, Deer Woman came running over to me to tell me that you'd fallen off the horse and ripped your new deerskin dress."

Serena smiled wryly. "Everyone was laughing, Wolf. I had been with the women gathering dandelions for a meal. Luckily, I had given Dawn Sky's cradleboard to Little Swallow before I tried to dismount." She reached down and touched the hem of her newly repaired dress. "The fringe was too long, and caught between two pieces of wood. I had thrown my leg across the horse to dismount when I realized—too late—that my dress was staying with the saddle! So I screamed, lost my balance and pitched off into a heap. The old mare didn't move a muscle. She just turned her head around and looked at me, wondering what I was doing flat on my back. I started to giggle because I was so embarrassed, but all the women, bless them, laughed *with* me, not *at* me. Dove That Flies got my foot out of the stirrup and helped me up."

Wolf smiled and forced himself to release Cante Tinza. "Like a Lakota, you have a good sense of humor. It takes humbleness to laugh at oneself. I am glad you and the baby were not hurt."

"No," Serena assured him with a chuckle, "only my pride was hurt."

Once his laughter had subsided, Wolf gestured for Cante Tinza to follow him. Today, she wore her work dress—deerskin without any fringe on the sleeves or hem. It was obvious that she had taken a sharp knife and cut off the offending fringe on the hem before she wore the dress again. Fringe could get caught in brush and grass, so the women rarely wore their better dresses when working. Wolf had made her a belt many moons ago, and she carried what all Lakota wives carried in them: a knife, an awl case and a strike-a-light pouch containing flint and steel.

Because the day was going to be warm, Wolf had chosen to wear only his red breechclout and moccasins. He carried a quiver of arrows on his back, and a knife around his waist. The bow would remain on Wiyaka. Wolf had taken these precautions just in case they ran into Crow warriors or miners.

Picking up from the rear of the saddle one of the dried buffalo bladders that was used to store valuable medicines, Wolf walked toward the patch of wild bergamot. He purposely slowed his stride so that Cante Tinza could keep up with him. This morning her cheeks were a bright red, and he saw the delight in her eyes. Wolf realized that she was enjoying this outing as much as he was.

Standing over the growing flowers, Wolf gave her the bladder to hold. "You will now learn what a medicine person does." He gestured toward six sturdy plants growing in the meadow. "We never take without asking first. Remember the Lakota belief—*Mitakuye oyasin,* we are all related.''

Serena nodded, standing opposite Wolf and the flowers. "Yes, we're all bound to one another."

"Invisibly, but yes, nothing is separate from the whole, the hoop of the Great Spirit." Wolf drew out a small leather bag from his belt that contained sacred tobacco known as *kinnikinnick.* Squatting in front of the plants he said, "First, I close my eyes, and in my head I send greetings to these plant spirits who reside here. I tell them who I am, and what my needs are. I ask if I may take some of them so that others may live. I then open my eyes, give them a pinch of the *kinnikinnick* and await their answer. Most plant spirits will willingly give up their lives for us, so that we may live. Some do not. The spirits of plant people are just like us—all different.''

"You hear them?" Serena asked in awe.

"Yes. You can, too. Come here, beside me."

Serena knelt down beside Wolf and he handed her a pinch of the sacred *kinnikinnick.*

"Now, close your eyes. Tell the plants your name, and ask them if they would give their lives for you. Tell them that they will be used in a good and sacred way." Wolf watched as she spread the sacred tobacco over the plants and then closed her eyes. How lovely she looked, kneeling there, her lips slightly parted as she concentrated on the mental questions. After a minute, her lashes lifted and she looked at him.

"Well? Did you feel their answer?"

With a little laugh, Serena reached out and gently touched several of the tall hairy plants. "Wolf, this might sound silly, but I *felt* this joy wrapping around me. It was so strong! I must have been making it up!"

His smile deepened and he watched as her long, work-worn fingers caressed the bergamot. He wished that she might touch him with such love, such reverence, some-day. "You did not make this up. The spirits are happy to give their lives for our needs. You see, it is a great honor to give your life for another. The spirit is blessed for such a deed by becoming reborn, perhaps next time as a bird or butterfly."

"But, I didn't *hear* them speak."

"No, they do not know our language, but they know the language of the heart." He gestured around the meadow that was thick with green grass and many colorful wildflowers. "There is no such thing as anything being evil that was made by the Great Spirit. Only good. It doesn't matter if it is plant or animal—they know only love and respect for one another."

Serena frowned. "Except for white men."

"The Great Spirit doesn't make them evil, either. It is a choice they make on their own. You did well, Cante Tinza. I feel you will make a good medicine woman if you want to begin training. I knew in my heart you were close with the plant people. Now, I am proved right."

"But how do you know?"

He touched his bare chest. "I know this in my heart. A person who has skills with plant people will *feel* their response, just as you did. Not everyone can walk up to a plant spirit and communicate with it as you just did."

Serena felt a giddy excitement. "I really can learn about herbs?"

The radiant joy in her face took Wolf off guard. The shining light in her green eyes reminded him of Father Sun's rays sliding through the pines. Every morning, Cante Tinza placed the eagle feather and medicine wheel decoration into her fiery red hair. It made him feel good, because it was a gift he'd made for her, and she wore it proudly every day. He longed to reach out and graze her pink cheeks with his fingers. Before he could control himself, he did just that. As he gently stroked her cheek, Wolf saw her eyes widen in surprise over his daring action, but then they became lustrous. And as he drew his fingers away, he realized that she had enjoyed his touch. It was a thrilling discovery for Wolf. Could he dare hope that she liked him just a bit?

Wolf found himself trembling inwardly as he drowned in the splendor of Cante Tinza's verdant eyes. There was such life in them, such love. Love? He wondered if he was going *heyoka,* crazy. Was there truly love in the depths of her eyes or was he fooling himself into wishing such a look was there? Grimly, he forced himself to pay attention to teaching her about herbs.

"Yes, I will take you on as my student if you desire," Wolf finally said, his voice strained.

"Oh, Wolf!" Serena threw her arms around his neck. She gave him a quick hug and felt him stiffen instantly. Realizing that she might have committed a mistake by doing it, she quickly released him. The shock on his face was obvious. "I—I'm sorry," she said breathlessly, still giddy from his invitation. "I shouldn't have hugged you."

Shaken, Wolf just stared over at her. For the first time, Cante Tinza had been spontaneous. She was like a happy child, he realized with humbleness. This was the same woman who had been hiding beneath terrible pain. Wolf sent a prayer of thanks to White Buffalo Calf Woman, to whom he prayed nightly for Cante Tinza's healing.

"No, it was good," he praised her.

"I never see people hugging one another," Serena offered, opening her hands, "but I just couldn't help myself. I'm so excited!"

A wry smile pulled at Wolf's mouth. "They hug. You just do not see it."

"What do you mean?"

His smile deepened as he held her gaze. "This act of holding the other is something a husband shares with his wife. It is a good thing, but it is never done in public."

"Oh...dear...." Serena touched her fingers to her lips. She saw the amusement in Wolf's face. Heat crept into her cheeks, and she knew she was blushing furiously over the error. "I—I'm sorry, Wolf. Among our people—in my family—we hugged all the time. It was showing our love, I guess," she explained lamely.

"Is it not the same as the Lakota?" he suggested wisely, watching the strawberry color flood her cheeks, making her look even more desirable to him.

"Well—I guess, I really don't know...."

"Do not apologize for your actions toward me," he told her. "What we share is ours alone."

"Then you weren't offended by what I did?"

"If a meadowlark comes and sits on the poles of our tepee and sings her beautiful song, how could I be angry with her? She blesses us with her music and her voice. How can I be upset with you for sharing your joy with me in your own way?"

Touching her hot face, Serena gave a little laugh. "I've wanted to ask you about the herbs. I just never dreamed you would want to teach me, that's all. I've wanted to for so long, Wolf, but I was afraid to ask you."

Capturing her hands against her face, Wolf drew them into his. "Never again be afraid to ask anything of me, Cante Tinza. Honesty and truth are the way among our people." His fingers tightened around her long, pale hands. "You were a crushed flower beneath Kingston's boot. We rescued you, and we replanted you in hopes that you would grow strong and healthy once again. You have. I see you as a many-petaled sunflower, Cante Tinza. Each time you take back your power and make it your own, a new petal of you unfolds. You have strength, intelligence and a good heart trapped within your injured spirit. I *want* you to blossom. Do not ever be afraid to speak to me of what lies in your heart."

In that golden moment, Serena *felt* like a fragile new bud on the verge of unfolding her petals to the sunlight. Only Wolf was her sun. Wildly aware of his strong, brown hands holding hers, she wished she had the courage to tell him of her dreams of him, of the longing that gnawed away deep within her. His mouth, strong and chiseled, was drawn into a sad curve and his large, intense eyes held hers as gently as he held her hands.

"I'll try to speak up more," she promised in a hoarse whisper.

"*Washtay*, good," Wolf praised. He forced himself to release Cante Tinza's hands. If he didn't, he was going to lean down and taste her ripe lips. And that was something he couldn't do without her permission. "By the moon when leaves turn brown, you will know much about herbs and how to use them. Then you will be known as a medicine woman among our people. I have always needed help, and I welcome you working beside me."

So many wonderful sensations flowed through Serena as Wolf released her tingling hands. What she wanted to do, what lay in her heart, was to embrace him once more. Only this time, she wanted him to return that embrace. They were dreams, Serena thought, turning her attention to what Wolf was going to teach her. But were they? She had seen a fierce, burning light in his eyes whenever he touched her. Serena wished she had more experience in the ways of men. But she had none, except for Kingston, who had been only cruel and hurting.

Chapter Eight

The sun was blisteringly hot. Serena could feel the intense heat on her back while she picked chokecherries along with five other Lakota women. Dawn Sky cooed happily in her cradleboard, which was propped on a low-hanging oak limb not far away. A breeze gently pushed it back and forth.

Serena's deerskin dress was hot, and she longed for a bath in the cold waters of the creek below. The water was nearly hidden by the nearly five-feet-tall bulrushes along the banks. The chokecherries were ripe for picking, and her fingers were stained a dark purple. Wolf had taught her earlier that the seeds of the chokecherry were highly poisonous, and the leaves and twigs were just as deadly. The berries, when black, however, were not poisonous. They would be pitted and laid out to dry, and then used for winter food or for ceremonies.

The women were bent over large shrubs that looked like a wall of thickets covering the hill. The area was surrounded by fragrant pine. Serena loved living in the Gray Buffalo Horn area. The Sun Dance, the Lakota four-day celebration, had come and gone. During the celebration she had seen Mato Tipila Paha, Bear's Lodge Mountain. The tower of brown and black rock rose well over a thousand feet out of the earth. Its mighty sides looked clawed, as if some giant bear from long ago had used the mountain as a scratching post.

Soon, Wolf told her, they would leave this sacred and beautiful region and begin their yearly travel toward Pte Pute Ya, the Buffalo's Nose area. There was a powerful and revered mountain there known as Mato Paha, Bear Butte. It was there that Wolf would put many young warriors up on the slopes for their vision quest. He told her the profile of the mountain looked like a pregnant woman reclining on her back, with her face lifted skyward. It would be a very busy time, he warned her, and he would often be away from the village for days at a time. She would be responsible for doctoring the tribe's ills in his absence.

Serena smiled to herself. She had easily absorbed the knowledge that Wolf had taught her over many moons. Now he allowed her to dress wounds, pack them with herbs and, upon occasion, sew up a large wound under his guidance and direction.

Now her birchbark container was filled with chokecherries, so she left the thicket area and carefully picked her way back to the meadow where the horses were grazing on the succulent green grass.

The gray mare lifted her head and nickered gently as Serena approached. Serena's parfleche saddlebags were now full, and it was time for her to return to the village to begin pitting the chokecherries. All the horses suddenly raised their heads, pricking their ears forward as they gazed down toward the stream. Serena was instantly alert, for this area was very close to Crow territory and the threat of attack was always real.

Her alarm turned to surprise. She saw Wolf riding along at a lazy lope on Wiyaka. Her knees felt shaky as she stood by her mare and watched him ride toward her. He wore only a breechclout and moccasins. His body was deeply bronzed by the hot sun, and each set of muscles moved in perfect unison with the flowing stride of his mare. He was holding something in his arms, and she frowned and walked toward him.

Ordinarily, she never saw Wolf during the day unless she accompanied him to gather herbs. She smiled as he drew to a halt and quickly dismounted.

"What do you have in your arms?"

Wolf grinned and walked toward Cante Tinza. Her red hair was arranged in two thick braids, and the deerskin dress accented her slenderness. "A gift for you," he said. "Open your hands."

Serena did so, and her eyes widened in surprise. "A puppy!" she cried as she eagerly took the fluffy black animal into her arms. She saw Wolf's smile change and deepen. How handsome he looked to her, so proud and strong as he stood beside her.

"No, not a dog. A wolf."

Serena gasped in surprise and studied the puppy, who now looked up at her with big, inquiring yellow eyes. "But—he looks like a dog!"

"*She* is not a dog. Tall Crane was with the hunters earlier this morning when they came upon this mother grizzly bear who was attacking a white wolf. The wolf had to defend her babies against the grizzly, who was angry over the wolf's nearness to her two cubs." Wolf shrugged. "The wolf lost the battle, and so did all her pups except this one, who hid beneath an old, rotted log. Tall Crane brought the pup back to me because he said he had a dream of finding a black wolf. He said he came back to the village in this dream and gave it to you." He smiled as she gently petted the pup. "That was a powerful dream Tall Crane had, a foretelling dream. When he told me about it, I knew that I must find you to give you the female wolf pup."

"Oh," Serena sighed, "she's so pretty! Look at her yellow eyes!"

"All wolves have yellow eyes. That is how you can tell them from dogs. Dogs do not possess such a color."

Worriedly, Serena examined the three-month-old pup. "Well, is she all right? No injuries?"

"She is fine. A bit frightened, but if you give her some meat to eat and a little water, she will become bonded with you for life."

"I can keep her?" Serena asked. "I thought wolves were wild."

"I am wolf. Am I not domesticated?" he teased with a laugh.

She became lost in the dark, smoldering look in Wolf's eyes. "I suppose you're right."

"You must think of a name for her. Perhaps you will dream it tonight. Now you have wolf medicine just as I do. It is a great honor."

"What does wolf medicine do?" Serena knew that each Lakota had at least one invisible spirit guide who was in animal form. She thought of them as guardian angels. Wolf was guided and taught by a wolf spirit. Tall Crane had shown her the great blue heron that plied the waterways, and told her that that bird was his spirit guide, which was why he was named for it.

Wolf watched Cante Tinza pet and soothe the shaking puppy. "Wolves are teachers," he told her seriously. "They care for one another, too. If one is sick, they lick it and bring food to it. If one is old, they allow it to eat from the kill, whether it helped in the hunt or not.

Among the Lakota, a person who has wolf medicine is a teacher."

"You certainly are."

Wolf watched softness come into Cante Tinza's face as the pup began to lick her fingers with her tiny pink tongue. "You must be the same as me if you have wolf medicine."

Thrilled, Serena hugged the puppy. "Do you think she will stay if we feed and care for her?"

"For the next moon, you will keep her tied and take her everywhere with you. All night, you will allow her to sleep with you. She will see you as her mother, and a bond that cannot be broken will form. The only way this bond will break is if one of you dies."

Sobering, Serena nodded. The pup had an ebony color, with fuzzy, soft hair. There was a bit of white around her eyes, as if she wore a mask, but it wasn't pronounced. "How long do they live, Wolf?"

"Fifteen summers, perhaps longer. It may be shorter if they tangle with a grizzly. I have seen a wolf pack kill a grizzly, but one wolf against such a powerful animal will lose. Now I must return to the village. We will speak more of wolves tonight."

Serena reached out and caught Wolf's large, callused hand. She squeezed it. "Thank you," she whispered. "You are so wonderful to me. I don't know how to thank you...."

Wolf groaned inwardly. Every passing day it became harder not to touch Cante Tinza. She was blossoming before his very eyes, gaining new confidence in herself, and becoming more spontaneous. He squeezed her fingers gently in response. "You thank me with your presence, Cante Tinza. You are a gift to me. Never forget that. I will see you at dusk."

Unwillingly, Serena released his fingers. "Yes, tonight...."

"Look at her," Deer Woman muttered angrily as she sat outside her parents' tepee at dusk. Swift Elk stood next to her with his courting blanket, but she would not allow him to cover her and him with it. "Now, she has a wolf pup!"

"Tall Crane gave it to her," Swift Elk said as he stood beside her.

Deer Woman's heart hurt. She had never recovered fully from Black Wolf's sending her away. She refused to have anything to do with the red-haired *wasicun*. If she had to pick berries, she would go with a second group of Lakota women. If they were bathing at the river or stream, Deer Woman refused to be in the water with Cante Tinza. At all costs, she avoided being with the woman who had Black Wolf's attention and heart.

"She has cast a spell on him," she muttered angrily. "I'll wager she has put elk medicine in his food time and again, and that is why he follows her around like that wolf pup of hers! Both tag along at her heels with their tongues hanging out!"

Chuckling, Swift Elk said, "Let us talk of more important things. Will you go with me for a walk this evening?"

Pouting, Deer Woman glanced up at the youth. Swift Elk was a hunter by nature, not a warrior. She wanted a warrior like Black Wolf, a man of stature, not a youth who had yet to prove himself in battle. Swift Elk wore no eagle feathers in his hair, which was an honor given to those who had counted coup against the enemy.

"No, I want to watch the *wasicun* and her wolf."

"That wolf is very protective of her," Swift Elk warned. "Once, I approached their tepee, and she came leaping out the entrance and crouched, her teeth bared, snarling."

"That wolf reflects the *wasicun,* only she is more subtle than the animal. But she does not fool me. She sneaks around like that wolf of hers."

"The elders praise Cante Tinza," Swift Elk reminded her. "Did she not save Strong Fox, Chief Badger Mouth's wife?"

"Pah! Strong Fox ate too much, that is all. She vomited up all her food. The *wasicun* ran over with a medicine given to her by Black Wolf. *He* saved her."

"Black Wolf was with the band of warriors that was gone for a week at that time. No, Cante Tinza knew what to do, and she saved the chief's wife."

"Yes," Deer Woman cried, leaping to her feet, "from vomiting. That is all! Even you make her out to be something sacred, and she is not! She is just a woman like me!"

Swift Elk quickly lowered his head. "I do not mean to make you angry, Deer Woman."

Glaring at the youth, she whispered fiercely under her breath, "Everywhere there is talk of her having power. Power! Pah! Black Wolf has taught her everything she knows. She mimics, that's all."

"Still," Swift Elk persisted more gently, "no one else has ever gentled a wolf, nor had a wolf follow them around as this one follows Cante Tinza. That is powerful medicine, you must admit, Deer Woman. That wolf could have left her at any time, but she does not. She goes everywhere with her. Just two weeks ago, when the Crow were stalking us, wasn't it her wolf that alerted us to their presence? It wasn't our dogs, but Cante Tinza's wolf who howled the warning.''

With an exasperated sound, Deer Woman stalked off. Her heart was beating with such fury that she knew she must leave the village for a while. It was dusk, and Father Sun had just set. It was the tenth moon of the year, and all the trees had lost their leaves in preparation for the coming winter. The Lakota had just returned to their winter location by following the Dried Willows constellation in the sky. The village now sat near a small river thick with willows and bulrushes. Deer Woman walked to the water's edge.

The bulrushes were dried and brown, cracking and moving in the chilly breeze. She could feel the first snow of the season in the air and realized that the sky above had turned cloudy. In her heart, she worried for Black Wolf, who had left a week ago to ride with the warriors to chase off the Crow, who were foraging deeply into their territory once again. Word had spread that the miners had paid the Crow to harass the Lakota into leaving the gold-filled Paha Sapa. She would die if anything happened to Black Wolf. Sitting down on a gray rock near the river, she closed her eyes and pressed her hand to her heart. How could this *wasicun* have captured her people's heart? Everyone, with few exceptions, loved the woman.

Why couldn't they speak of her, Deer Woman, in such glowing terms? Opening her eyes, she glared out across the quiet ribbon of water flowing in front of her. She didn't possess fiery red hair or pale skin. All the women liked to touch Cante Tinza's hair because of its color and unusual texture. They also touched the brown spots across her cheek and nose, and decided that she was like the spotted tree, the Appaloosa, of the Nez Percé people.

It hurt Deer Woman to know that each morning before the *wasicun* left to go with the women for the day, Black Wolf would smear her cheeks, nose and brow with a herb-and-bear-grease mixture to prevent her white skin from being sunburned! Of course, Deer Woman refused to acknowledge that every good Lakota husband did the same for his wife each morning. That, and they combed and braided each other's hair. Jealously, she wondered· if Black Wolf and Cante Tinza shared that, too.

Tongues wagged constantly in the village about Cante Tinza and Black Wolf. Would they marry? It seemed only a matter of time, the old women had agreed when they tanned buffalo hides earlier in the year. Among the warriors, Tall Crane longed to court Cante Tinza, but he held off. Why? Two other warriors, both good men who had lost their wives to the miners' attack two years ago, also wanted to court Cante Tinza. They had talked among themselves, but neither was quite sure of Black Wolf's intentions toward the *wasicun*. No one knew if they shared the same robe at night or not. And, of course, no one would ask, because that was considered rude.

Deer Woman fumed over the question. Knowing how honorable Black Wolf was, he would never share his robe with Cante Tinza unless he officially announced to the village that he wanted her as his wife! The whole village talked of that possibility. Now that Strong Fox had been cured by Cante Tinza, she wanted her son, Short Bull, the next chief, to begin openly courting the *wasicun*.

Knotting her small fists in the lap of her elkskin dress, Deer Woman sat there trying to plan how the *wasicun* could be taken away from Black Wolf so that she could have him for herself. Several ideas formed in her mind.

She would go to Short Bull, who was a young, impetuous warrior, and full of himself. She would whisper in his ear that Cante Tinza liked him. It was a lie, of course, but Short Bull wouldn't know. Then she would go tell the other two warriors the same thing. A smile formed on her lips. Deer Woman could hardly wait to see Black Wolf's face when the three warriors scratched at the door of his tepee with their courting blankets over their arms, asking for the *wasicun* to come out and speak with them! Oh, the excitement that would create! Deer Woman knew that the war party would be coming back very shortly, and when they did, she would spring her plan into action.

Kagi lifted her head where she lay near the fire in the tepee. Her ears were pricked forward, and her attention was focused on something going on outside. Serena glanced at the wolf as she changed Dawn Sky's diaper. Whining, Kagi got to her feet, wagging her brushlike tail.

"What is it?" Serena demanded.

The wolf looked over at her and then trotted to the entrance flap to be let out. Children's voices drifted through the camp and Serena gasped. Had the war party returned? She picked up the baby and went to the entrance. Instantly, Kagi leaped out and disappeared.

"They're coming! They're coming!" the old village crier, Lame Dog, proclaimed. "The war party is home!" His high, piercing voice rolled through the village with the announcement.

Wolf was coming home! Or was he? Anxiety shot through Serena as she placed Dawn Sky back into her cradleboard. For a quarter of a moon, Serena had worried about Wolf's safety. War parties were dangerous, according to Little Swallow, and many times men were killed. All of the wives waited in silent terror until the returning war party was spotted by the village crier.

The first snow of the year had fallen the night before, and Serena had to keep the fire in the pit burning more brightly to rid the tepee of the chill.

Despite the joy proclaiming the warriors' return, Serena didn't feel right. She'd had terrible nightmares the past three nights and was uneasy. Had something happened to Wolf? Worry blotted out any happiness from the prospect of seeing him as she quickly slipped outside into the icy dawn air. Everyone, it seemed, was coming out of the tepees to greet the warriors. Women and children stood in clumps, all facing west. Serena moved away from the tepee and saw fifteen warriors riding over the hill into the valley where they camped.

As the warriors drew near, Serena's blood turned cold. She recognized a number of Lakota warriors riding with their heads down on their horses' necks—a sign that they were wounded. Biting her lower lip, she searched frantically for Wiyaka, Wolf's black horse. Her heart took off in painfully rapid beat as she finally spotted Wolf near the rear of the group. Kagi was at his side, leaping happily and racing around the mare. Something was wrong. Wolf was not sitting on his mare properly. Was he wounded?

All Serena could do was stand and wait just as the rest of the Lakota women, children and elders had to do. It was anguish to wait another half hour before the group finally entered the village. Youths rode out to greet them, yipping and giving victorious yells of welcome. The boys trailed behind the warriors, waving their weapons and calling to them. The horses of the war party were tired, dragging their feet through the snow and hanging their heads. Their long, thick winter coats were twisted and matted from sweat, and then frozen that way.

Serena waited impatiently at the tepee because there was no sense in joining the ever growing group of children and wives. There were wounded, and her services would be needed shortly. Clasping her hands to her breast, she caught her first good glimpse of Wolf as he split away from the group and headed his weary mare in her direction.

"No!" Serena cried, pressing her hand to her mouth. Wolf had a buffalo robe over his shoulders to protect him from the snow and cold, but she saw the rust color of blood stained upon his buckskin shirt near his right shoulder and collarbone. His face was grim and tight, and as he drew close, she saw his mouth set against pain.

"Wolf!"

He drew Wiyaka to a halt at the tepee and gave Cante Tinza a tired smile. "You are bright sunlight to my dark days without you, Cante Tinza," he said to her wearily, holding out his hand to her. She flew to his side, her arms stretched toward him, panic in her face. As her hands touched his thigh and arm, he tried to smile, but it was impossible.

"You're hurt," she whispered brokenly, looking at the blood stain on his shirt as he allowed the robe to fall off his shoulders.

He gripped her cold fingers. "I will live," he soothed. "Come, help me. I have lost much blood, and I do not know if I can stand."

Serena clamped down on her worry. She watched Wolf move with great pain as he tried to slide off the mare. Serena placed her arm around his waist and felt his arm fall around her shoulder. Wolf was weak, and he leaned heavily on her.

"Come," she whispered, "let's get inside. I can care for you there."

"No," Wolf said, fighting the weakness that threatened to bring him to his knees. "There are others who need your care more than I, Cante Tinza. Take the medicines and go to them. If I can lie down, I will be fine until your return. I need sleep more than anything."

Once inside the tepee, Serena made Wolf comfortable. She pulled off the bloodstained shirt and choked back a cry. An arrow had lodged in his right shoulder, and although Wolf had pulled it out, the gaping wound needed tending.

"Oh, Wolf," she cried. "What happened?"

He gripped her hand. "Cante Tinza, go help the other warriors. There are three. As a healer, you must tend to the worst first. Go, woman. I will not die on you."

Shakily, Serena got to her feet. She covered Wolf with a robe. "I—I'll be back as soon as I can."

Closing his eyes, Wolf nodded. "I am home now. I am with you. That is all I need to get well."

His words haunted Serena. But somehow, she put her anxiety for Wolf behind her. She moved from one tepee to another to care for the warriors who had been hurt by the Crow.

It was nearly noon by the time Serena ran back to Wolf's tepee. Inside, the tepee was warm. Dawn Sky had just been fed and was now sleeping peacefully in her cradleboard. Anxiously, Serena's gaze moved to Wolf, who slept deeply beneath the robe. She knew what had to be done to help his wound heal without infection. It was a puncture wound and it had to be kept open so that it could drain. Moving as quietly as she could, because she knew the warriors had ridden for two days and nights without any rest, she pulled out several buffalo bladders that contained medicine used primarily for arrow wounds. Then she heated water in a small iron kettle.

Wolf roused himself as he felt the robe being pulled away from his chest. Through his short, black lashes he saw the anxiety and tension in Cante Tinza's face as she knelt at his side. She gently touched the area of his wound to test its temperature. Heat would mean it was infected. He weakly raised his left hand and slid his fingers across one of her thick braids.

"I dreamed of your hair—of you," he told her in a low voice, ragged with pain. "I was hit by a Crow arrow and tumbled off Wiyaka during the battle. I remember hitting the snow-covered ground and losing consciousness. And then you were there, bending over me, telling me to get up." His smile was crooked with pain. "You shook your finger at me and ordered me to rise and mount Wiyaka. You were with me from then on, my woman. You gave me the strength to fight to come home."

Tears stung Serena's eyes as he stroked her braid, which lay against his chest as she leaned over him. "You could have died," she rattled, as she examined the wound with her fingertips.

"And leave you behind?" Wolf teased her. "No, Cante Tinza, I promised, remember? I would never leave you alone."

"Y-yes, you did." She sniffed and wiped her tears away with the back of her hand. "The wound looks good, Wolf."

He allowed his arm to drop back to his side. "What I am in need of is your love and care. That will get me well."

Her love. Shaken, Serena looked into his half-closed eyes. She knew that Wolf was in pain. Further, he'd lost a great deal of blood. His flesh was pale compared to the usual copper color of his skin, and his words were slurred with exhaustion. "Love and care can help," she admitted brokenly as she took a moist, warm cloth and cleaned around the edges of the ugly-looking wound, "but you'll need rest, food and your dressings changed daily to get well."

"I have all I need in you." Wolf lingered at the edge of consciousness. Was he dreaming once again? Or was he really home, with Cante Tinza caring for him? He wasn't sure. The past two days had been fraught with danger. "We counted coup on the Crow. We scattered their herd of horses and brought many back with us. Five Crow are dead, and we lost no one. It was a good battle. I counted coup against the chief, Gray Horse. I touched him with my lance."

Serena listened to Wolf's mumblings, her heart bursting with fear. He could have been killed. As she packed the wound with purple coneflower powder, which would keep it free of infection and speed healing, she could think of nothing else but nearly losing him. Shortly after that, Wolf fainted. It was just as well because she had to press other herbs deep into the wound to pack it, and then wrap clean buckskin around his shoulder to keep it uncontaminated.

Kagi came over, whining. She lay down, her muzzle resting against the robe that covered Wolf's legs.

"He's going to live," Serena told the wolf in a low, off-key voice. "He will get well."

Kagi whined once more and then closed her eyes and slept. Serena kept busy. She prepared the nutritious and strengthening deer stew. A scratch at the door made her jerk in reaction. Chiding herself for being so jumpy, Serena went over and opened the deerskin flap.

"I heard that Black Wolf was injured," Deer Woman cried. "Is he all right? May I see him?"

Gathering her scattered emotions, Serena said, "He's going to be fine, Deer Woman. Wolf is sleeping now. Why don't you come back tomorrow sometime? He desperately needs his rest right now. He lost a lot of blood."

Wiping her eyes, she nodded and peered into the tepee. "I—I just wanted to know if he was going to live. I—I will return tomorrow."

Serena replaced the flap so that the heat would no longer escape. She stood there in the graying light and stared down at Wolf, who slept deeply. Her heart burst open with longing, and she knew without a doubt that she loved Wolf.

Wolf awakened much later. He felt someone gently drawing an elk comb across his scalp and through his hair. With great effort, he forced his lids to open. Cante Tinza was kneeling at his side, the comb and his hair in her hands.

"I thought I was dreaming," he rasped, his mouth gummy. "I remember the very first time you allowed me to touch you—to comb your hair. You were like a wary wild animal." The corners of his mouth drew in, and he tried to smile but didn't succeed. "It gave me great pleasure to do that for you, to show you that not all men would reach out to hurt you, Cante Tinza."

Serena smiled gently and began to braid his hair. "I remember that," she admitted softly as she admired how his thick, black hair glinted blue highlights beneath the firelight. "I'd never had my hair combed by a man before and I remember sitting there thinking how odd it felt. I felt like a pampered horse being curried."

"You are not a horse, and I did not see myself currying you. A woman should be shown respect, and combing and braiding your hair was a silent way to tell you that I respected you."

Serena became lost in his dark, pain-filled eyes. "You've always been good to me, Wolf. I feel spoiled, if you want the truth. Now, let me spoil you. How do you feel? I tried not to wake you as I combed your hair."

"I feel more rested. You act as a wife, Cante Tinza. A wife does not want her husband to look unclean, so she combs and plaits his hair every morning." He stared into her shadowed features. There was peace and tranquility in her, as she braided his hair. More than ever, Wolf wanted Cante Tinza as his wife. In his drowsy state, he'd said things he'd never think of sharing with her. Wolf watched her pale cheeks stain with the color of ripe, wild strawberries.

"I love to braid your hair. It's so thick and clean. Now I see why you liked to do mine." Serena couldn't risk looking into Wolf's half-closed eyes. He'd said "wife," and how often had she wondered about being *his* wife. Too many times. Clearing her throat, she said, "It's dark now. Would you like some deer stew?"

"Yes," he admitted, "I need to regain my strength, and eating is the only way to do it."

"I've made dock tea for you, too." Serena finished tying off the last braid, satisfied with her work. Wolf needed to sweat in a sweat lodge to cleanse himself, but that would have to wait. Instead, Serena had warmed water in the kettle and had washed his upper body as he slept.

"The dock tea will make my blood strong," Wolf agreed. He caught her slender, work-worn hand in his and squeezed it. "Thank you, Cante Tinza."

She fell beneath the burning look in his eyes, wildly aware of his hand upon hers. "Didn't you nurse me back to health at one time?" she teased unsurely. The look in Wolf's eyes made her go weak with longing—a strange yearning that was growing within her day by day.

"You care for me as a wife would her husband."

Serena pulled her hand from his. She knelt at his side, clasping her hands tightly in her lap. "Wolf, I'm frightened."

"Of what?"

She made a small sound of frustration and looked up at the shadows high on the tepee. "Of myself."

Wolf caught and held her gaze. "Remember? There are no secrets between us? We can share what we hold in our hearts for each other."

Touching her brow, Serena gave a little laugh of embarrassment. "I—I have all these crazy feelings going on inside me, and I don't know what they are. What they mean!"

The rest of the sleep was torn from Wolf, and he focused entirely on Cante Tinza's flushed features and the fear he saw in her dark green eyes. "Talk to me, my woman," he urged quietly. How badly he wanted to pull Cante Tinza into his arms and hold her.

My woman. A thread of heat spiraled up through her, and Serena took a deep, nervous breath. "Wolf—I, this is silly." Touching her heart, she whispered, "Every time you look at me, my heart starts beating in my breast like a drum. If you touch me, I feel this weakness spread through me, as if I will fall. Your voice…well, your voice is like a warm blanket to me. It makes me feel safe and good and—" She searched for the words. Forcing herself to look down at him, she whispered, "Your voice gives me hope. When I'm with you, I'm so very happy.

Even when I go with the women in search of food, I think of you! At night, I dream of you...."

His eyes narrowed to slits, the silence deepening between them. The crack and snap of the fire broke the tension. "Dreams of me? Will you tell me about them?"

Serena touched her hot cheeks and avoided his sharpened look. "Good dreams, Wolf, not bad ones, believe me." Serena knew how much importance Wolf placed on dreams. Biting her lower lip she said, "I dream of you with me, that we are happy. Sometimes I am riding on Wiyaka with you. Other times you're playing your flute for me while I'm sitting beside the river with Dawn Sky in my arms." She shrugged, completely embarrassed by the admissions. "Oh, Wolf, they are silly dreams, that's all. They mean nothing."

Wolf remained silent for a long time, digesting her admission. "Have you ever felt this way about any other men?"

With a small laugh, Serena said, "What other men? Wolf, I knew no men in Wexford because I was living in the alleys of the city, foraging for food. I lived with my mother until she died. I don't even remember having a father. I had no brothers." She frowned. "The only man I knew was Kingston, and he hurt me."

"Does your heart feel glad when I am with you?"

"Always."

"I see."

"Wolf, what do all of these feelings mean? I'm so confused. Sometimes, I feel so ashamed of them, and at other times I feel as if I'm dancing on clouds in Father Sky. Can you help me? Can you answer my questions?"

Chapter Nine

Serena could see how exhausted Wolf was becoming by continuing to talk with her. "I'm a fool for prattling on when you should be eating and then resting." She helped Wolf sit up and placed several buckskin pillows stuffed with cattail down behind his back so that he could lean against one of the poles of the tepee. "We can talk later. Let me get some food into you."

As Wolf leaned wearily against the lodgepole, surrounded by the warmth of his thick, shaggy buffalo robe, his pain eased somewhat. Perhaps it was watching Cante Tinza cook over the fire, her thick braids gleaming like the tongues of flame, that made him feel better.

"I never thought I would see you again," he said, his voice a rasp.

Serena glanced at him as she ladled the thick deer stew into a wooden bowl. "I knew something was wrong, Wolf. I had terrible dreams the past three nights about you." Serena brought over the bowl and placed it in his robe-covered lap. She realized how weak he was as he tried to pick up and hold the spoon.

"I'll feed you," she whispered, taking the utensil from his fingers.

"I'm as helpless as Dawn Sky," he joked. "You may mother us both."

She smiled gently and spooned the stew from the bowl. Blowing on it for several seconds, she placed it between Wolf's lips. Just the act of feeding him made her go shaky once again. Serena forced her hand not to tremble as she fed him. How the man affected her! Wolf tipped back his head after she finished feeding him and shut his eyes.

"You're tired," Serena said as she set the bowl aside.

"I want to talk with you," Wolf protested, barely opening his eyes.

"Later," she said firmly. "Come, slide down between the robes. A good night's sleep will make you feel much better tomorrow."

Wolf didn't have the strength to argue with Cante Tinza. Not that he would argue. He knew she had made the correct decision and acquiesced without a word. The last thing Wolf remembered before he sank into a healing sleep was Cante Tinza covering him with the robe.

Serena jerked awake. It was pitch-black inside the tepee. What had awakened her? Instantly, sleep was torn from her as she heard Wolf moan. Kagi was sleeping at his feet. Serena placed a few sticks of wood on the fire and quickly made her way to Wolf's side. She was relieved to find that his skin was cool. He was restless, though, and kept muttering and turning his head slowly from one side to the other. Serena guessed that Wolf was having a dream, or worse, a nightmare. She, of all people, understood the terror of a nightmare.

Her heart told her to lie down beside him and place her arm around him. Serena knelt there several seconds digesting that unbidden thought. Hadn't Wolf always told her to follow her heart? He'd often said that the *wasicun* had cut off the cord between their head and heart. All they did was think, not feel. And to not feel was to isolate oneself from all the beauty of life's feelings, and all of Mother Earth's relatives.

What would it hurt? Serena told herself that she didn't want Wolf moving and jerking around and opening his wound. She slid down beside him, laid her head on the pillow next to his head and inched closer until her body was pressed against the contour of his. Her heart pounded with imagined fear, because she vividly remembered Kingston sliding down beside her in her bed.

The sensation was nothing like what she remembered a year before with Kingston. As Serena settled near Wolf, only heat and longing throbbed through her. Wolf stopped muttering almost instantly, and ceased his restless movement. The tepee was chilly as Serena lay there in her sleeping dress. Soon the flames would rise and again warm the tepee.

Sometime during the night, Serena finally slept amid the rainbow feelings that sleeping next to Wolf evoked. Her dreams were vivid, colorful and provocative. In them, she told Wolf that she loved him, unequivocally. He smiled at the admission and opened his arms so that she might step into them.

Wolf awoke slowly, filled with a sense of well-being and peace. He was warm, his wound wasn't aching half as much, and— His attention swung to the person at his side. The tepee glowed with the weak light of dawn. He turned his head just enough to realize that Cante Tinza slept beside him. Her arm was thrown across his torso and her fingers grazed his left arm.

Sleep was torn from Wolf as he humbly realized that
Cante Tinza was at his side. Her head rested against his
and her moist breath softly whispered across his shoulder. He could feel the roundness of her breast against his
arm and the length of her body following the line of his
own. A blinding, aching heat grew in his loins as he absorbed her innocent action. He must have been restless
during the night and she had come to him, transcending
her own fear of him as a man, to lie beside and soothe
him. Wolf's love for her was fierce and nearly uncon-
trollable as he realized her gesture toward him.

As he lay staring up at the many lodgepoles that came
together in a point far above him, Cante Tinza's words
from last night flowed back to him. She had been living
in his tepee for well over a year now. At some point, she
had learned to trust him—to relax her guard. Later, she
had begun to see him as a human, not just as a man.
Much later, she had fallen in love with him. Wolf realized that wonderful discovery with a gratefulness that
brought tears to his eyes. Cante Tinza loved him, but did
not know it. With a sigh, he closed his eyes and savored
her closeness.

A plan began to form in his mind. Come spring, as
they made their way back to the Gray Buffalo Horn area,
he would begin to court Cante Tinza the way every
maiden was courted by a warrior who wanted her as his
wife. Just because she lived with him did not mean she
didn't deserve to be accorded the same consideration.
Relief flowed like a quiet river through Wolf as he devel-
oped the plan. Yes, come the moon of the green leaves,
he would begin to court her in earnest.

Serena watched Dawn Sky play near her moccasin-
covered feet. They sat beneath the spreading arms of a

pine tree. Each late afternoon, she would take the infant, who now walked with unbridled energy, to the shade of the trees on this small hill that overlooked the village below. As Dawn Sky puttered around, testing her newfound skills of picking up stones and twigs and examining the wildflowers, Serena would watch her and do quill work.

The sunlight was very warm, and the meadow was alive with Lakota, busily performing their individual tasks. The leather in Serena's lap was a buckskin vest she was making for Wolf. She divided her attention between the vest and Dawn Sky, who still played happily at her feet. Smiling, Serena recalled the very first time that Dawn Sky had called her *ina* or mother. Wolf was *ahtay* or father. Serena was certain that Dove That Flies had taught the little child to say those words to them. Lately, Wolf had hinted that there should be a *hunka,* or relative-making ceremony, to make Dawn Sky officially their daughter by blood ceremony.

From her vantage point on the knoll, Serena viewed the entire village, which was nestled in a wide, circular meadow surrounded by the dark pine trees. Serena sat there with her hands idle over the vest and closed her eyes. Wolf had taught her to see, hear, smell and taste the beauty of Mother Earth. It was a year and a half since she'd come to the Lakota people, and she'd never dreamed of such contentment.

Just as she was about to busy herself quilling, she heard a different sound. A beautiful sound. A flute! Serena turned, wanting to locate where the flute music came from and who was playing it.

When she stood up, her eyes widened. Wolf, dressed in a breechclout, leggings and moccasins, sat on a large rock just below the summit of the hill. He smiled at her with his eyes as he continued to play the soft, raspy music.

Stunned, Serena could only stand there, clutching the vest in her hands, and listening. She had never realized Wolf knew how to play the flute. The instrument was decorated with trade beads and seven great blue heron feathers that hung beneath the instrument. Dawn Sky had stopped playing and was listening with equal intentness.

With a shy smile, Serena walked over and picked up the baby girl. Carrying the child on her hip, Serena sat down near Wolf and took advantage of the shade of the pine boughs overhead. Dawn Sky snuggled to her breast, sighed and closed her eyes as Serena embraced her. The music flowing from Wolf's flute was soft, poignant and stirring. She saw the familiar burning fierceness in his eyes and her heart responded with effortlessness to the call of his music. She, too, closed her eyes as she held the infant, and not only listened, but *felt* the magic of the music as it flowed through her heart.

Wolf played the flute for nearly a half hour. Some of the songs were sad, others were uplifting. When the music ended Serena opened her eyes. Wolf placed the flute gently across his hard, curved thighs.

"That was so beautiful." Serena sighed. "Thank you."

"A maid," Wolf told her in a deep voice, "should always be courted with music." He touched his chest. "The music comes from my heart to be given to your heart, Cante Tinza." Did she know how beautiful she looked with Dawn Sky in her arms?

Lips parting, Serena gazed at Wolf as she digested his words. "Courted?" she said finally, the word a bare whisper.

Wolf nodded somberly. "I have come to court you, Cante Tinza." Fear clashed with his need of her. Would she be frightened? Would she say no? Wolf sat very quietly, praying, as he did every day, to the Great Spirit, to turn the eyes of her heart upon him as husbandly material. He saw the surprise, the desire and the fear loom together in her huge green eyes that could hide nothing from him.

"Oh, dear...."

He cocked his head toward her, and she quickly looked down at the green grass, biting her lower lip between her teeth. "You are not pleased?"

Serena raised her chin. Wolf's face, despite its harsh quality, was gentle as he searched her eyes. "I—uh, no. No...."

Wolf slowly unwound from the rock and walked over to her. On one knee, he knelt before her and the baby she held. Stroking her fiery red cheek with his fingers, he asked, "Then what? I see many feelings in your eyes, Cante Tinza. Will you share them with me?"

Tears flooded Serena's eyes as she became lost in the tenderness of Wolf's gaze. His touch, fleeting and feathery, sent off a storm of tiny explosions throughout her. Heat pooled deep within her body, and that same raw, restless yearning awakened within her once again. Gathering her strewn thoughts, Serena whispered, "Y-you want me to marry you. Is that it?"

Wolf shrugged. "Marry?"

"Yes. You want me to share your robe—to be your wife."

He smiled a very proud smile. "Yes, I want to court you until you agree to share my robe every night." He ruffled Dawn Sky's thick, black hair. "And I want to create children to grow within your belly."

Molten heat spread quickly throughout Serena, and she gasped. Wolf continued to caress her cheek lightly "I—I thought these were all dreams," she admitted with a nervous laugh.

Wolf withdrew his hand and rested his elbow on his thigh as he held her startled gaze. "Dreams?"

Looking away, Serena whispered, "I dreamed so many times of this moment, Wolf. I dreamed of you covering me with your courting blanket. But then I got scared. ran."

Frowning, Wolf took the infant into his arms as he sat down opposite Cante Tinza. Dawn Sky fingered his necklace. "Why?"

Serena stood up, her hands tight around the vest she held against her belly. "Because of what Kingston did to me." She gave him a pleading look. "I *know* you'd never be like that to me, Wolf. You're too gentle, too sensitive." Frustration ate at her. "I—I try and tell my crazy head that. My heart believes you wouldn't be like that but my head doesn't trust even you. I feel so ashamed of that because you've never given me one reason to distrust you."

He nodded and gently ran his hands across Dawn Sky's small form. Cante Tinza had made the outfit the baby wore, even the tiny, neatly beaded moccasins. "Allow me to court you, Cante Tinza. With time, perhaps your head will know what your heart already knows—that I love you, that you already own my heart—my very spirit that walks Mother Earth."

Shaken, Serena nodded. Tears remained in her eyes as she gazed down at Wolf's upturned features. "I'm sorry to be like this. I don't want to be, but—"

"Hush, Cante Tinza. You cannot help how you feel. It is not your fault. Kingston hurt you. He stole from

you. I will never steal from you, my woman. I will come
honestly to you, I will speak the truth that lies in my heart
as to how I feel toward you." His voice was unsteady with
feelings. "Love can never be captured and tamed. Love
should be left wild, like an eagle flying. If you come to
me, it will be because you desire me as much as I desire
you. But, always, it will be your decision, not mine."

The bulrushes were growing tall and high, Serena noticed as she walked beside the river she had come to love.
They had just made camp in the Gray Buffalo Horn area
yesterday, and directly above her was the towering rock
with the bear claw scars deeply scored into all sides of it.
Serena had asked Little Swallow to care for Dawn Sky for
an hour so that she could take a walk alone in order to
think.

The past two weeks, Wolf had come every day and
played his flute for her. Beside him was a red wool
courting blanket. When he finished playing, he would
ease to his feet, come over to her and gently place the
blanket first around himself and then her. His hands
would rest lightly against her, but he would not draw her
those last few inches to rest against him. Instead, he
would tell her stories—stories she loved to hear about
Lakota myths. Beautiful stories about White Buffalo
Calf Woman, who had visited the Lakota only recently
to give them the seven sacred ceremonies, including the
pipe.

Serena reached out and touched the strong, thick bulrushes. Soon, they would be picked, woven into mats and
allowed to dry. Her heart was in utter turmoil, and she
hadn't slept well the past half moon. Was she going
crazy? How could all of her but her head want Wolf? Her
mind screamed that Wolf would hurt her just as Kings-

ton had. Biting down on her lower lip, Serena stopped and absently ran her hands up and down the bulrushes.

"You are torn."

Serena gasped and whirled around. Wolf stood on the bank, the flute in one hand, the courting blanket in the other. Touching her pounding heart, she whispered, "You scared me."

He gave her an apologetic look and came down the bank. Placing the blanket and flute on the grassy ground, he moved to her side. "I could not stand the pain I saw in your face any longer, Cante Tinza." Wolf captured her hands and held them in his own.

Wolf's touch was stabilizing as she looked up into his understanding features. "I am torn. It's so stupid, Wolf. I don't know what to do...."

"Listen to your heart, because it will never lead you wrong," he advised, stroking her fingers and feeling the roughness of her skin created by the many activities she performed daily. He smiled gently. "Each of us must, at some time in our life, have the courage to believe what comes from our heart—no matter what others say, or what our head tells us. The greatest courage is to live, Cante Tinza."

She felt his warmth silently embrace her. It was a wonderful feeling of love and protection. "You gave me a name that I haven't been living up to," she admitted in a raspy voice. "You called me Brave Heart because I attacked the miners. But I'm finding that the name you gave me means so much more than that. It's a daily challenge to live up to my heart's demands, not my head's demands."

"So, you see the sacredness of your name," he murmured with a pleased smile. "That is very good, Cante

Tinza. A name is more than just a name. It is a way of life. A way of becoming."

"I haven't been very brave of late, have I?"

He reached out and touched her red hair. "Each of us battles dark fears within ourselves," he told her, "so do not be hard on yourself. The name given to you asks you to live up to that possibility. You were brave once, and you can be brave again."

Serena's breath whispered from her lips as she felt Wolf's hand close across her hair and gently guide her forward. Closing her eyes, she came into his arms of her own accord, following her heart not her head. His arms, strong and powerful, held her close, but not tightly, against him. Serena rested her head against Wolf's chest, and for the first time she heard the thunderous beat of his heart beneath her ear. Her hands rested against his sun-hardened flesh, and she felt the latent tension in his muscles. Serena was wildly aware of a startling heat uncoiling rapidly within her.

Easing away from Wolf and lifting her head, Serena looked directly into his eyes. "Kiss me?"

The words, whispered so softly, caught Wolf off guard. As Cante Tinza lifted her chin, her green eyes wide and lustrous, he, too, followed his heart and framed her face with his large hands. As he leaned down to touch her lips for the first time, he prayed for control over his screaming need to make her his woman. This was a test, Wolf realized somewhere in his spinning senses—a test to prove to Cante Tinza that he would not take her violently as Kingston had done.

"My woman," he said thickly, as his mouth lightly slid across hers. "You are the rainbow in my life." Wolf felt her tremble and he grazed her lips more surely, asking her to explore him at her leisure. He was not going to force her into anything, so he waited. He waited in agony, the knots within him painful and begging for relief. Wolf would have gone through the worst torture imaginable before he would ever have taken from Cante Tinza. No, she must understand that between a man and a woman there was respect and sharing.

Serena trembled again as Wolf's mouth captured her lips. She felt the strength of his mouth grow gentle against her. She could feel the warmth of the sunlight on them, and taste the salt of perspiration. This was the mouth that sang to her, that played the flute, that stretched into a dazzling smile, and that released deep and strong laughter. The cherished movement of his mouth sent a yearning through Serena. Each light, coaxing touch of his mouth made her want more. She leaned forward on her tiptoes, holding her hands against his chest, to seal his mouth with her own. She heard a low growl from deep within Wolf's chest as she pressed her lips inexpertly against his. The vibration coursed through her hands, up her arms and into her body as if he had stroked her with his large hands. But he hadn't touched her body; his hands continued to span and frame her face.

With a small cry, Serena wanted more of Wolf, and knew instinctively she must ask for it. He did not disappoint her as his lips coaxed and shaped her mouth strongly to his. The moment his tongue slid across her lower lip, a heat shattered and seared through her lower body. Serena was beginning to shake in earnest, and her knees grew weak from the tender exploration Wolf was initiating. Barely aware that his hands had moved from her face to her shoulders to steady her, Serena felt her breath come in ragged gasps as she eased from his mouth.

Staring up into his dark, burning eyes, Serena became lost in a storm of longing that threatened to make her faint with need. Wolf's hands became firmer against her shoulders. She pressed her face against his naked chest and closed her eyes as his arms swept around her and held her tightly.

"This is love," Wolf rasped close to her ear. "We love each other, Cante Tinza. I want you for my wife. I want you to be the mother of all my children. Walk back with me beneath the blanket through the village. Let the people know that you have chosen me as your husband. I vow to always love you, cherish you and respect you. The children you hold in your belly will be children fashioned from our love for each other. Will you walk at my side, my woman?"

Without a sound, Serena nodded. In that moment, she had felt her heart burst open like a flower. She loved Wolf. She lifted her head, drowning in his gaze. She watched as his eyes filled with tears of joy. Reaching up, she touched his tears with her fingertips.

"Yes, I'll be your wife, beloved."

Wolf wanted to howl his joy like the animal he had been named for, but instead, crushed Serena against him. He held her and rocked her. "You will never be sorry for this decision," he told her in a choked voice. "I see the happiness in your eyes. I want always to see that gold light there, Cante Tinza. I want to make you smile. I want you to be happy, as you deserve."

"All I need, all I'll ever want is you, Wolf," she quavered. And Serena meant those words with her life. She saw him smile brokenly as he caressed her cheek, and tears blurred her vision.

"Tonight," he rasped, "I will be gentle with you, my woman. You will never feel pain from me, only pleasure, only my love. That is my vow to you."

Serena believed him. "I'm afraid, Wolf, but I'm not going to let it stop me from living. I can't."

Wolf leaned down and picked up the bright red wool blanket. Without a word, he placed it around himself and then draped it across Cante Tinza. When her arm went around his waist and she stepped next to him, his heart soared like the eagle. Picking up the flute, he smiled down at her.

"Let us walk through the village so that everyone knows that you will, from this moment on, be my woman."

Deer Woman was sitting outside her parents' tepee with a bored look on her face, even though Swift Elk stood speaking animatedly with her. The sun had just gone down, and the sky was a vibrant pink and gold color. The black nighthawks were now flying and screeching around them, dipping for insects buzzing in the air just above the river region. Nearly everyone in the village was outside at this time of night—either eating their meals around the community fires, talking in low voices or playing.

"Look!" Swift Elk said, pointing toward the end of the village.

Deer Woman looked. Her mouth fell open. Her heart beat painfully. "No!" she cried, jumping up from the log she sat upon.

With a laugh, Swift Elk said, "Finally! The Wolf captures Cante Tinza! Ho! This is good."

Angrily, Deer Woman watched Wolf proudly walk with Cante Tinza beneath his courting blanket. Hurt mixed with fury as she watched them draw closer. How

could Wolf do this to her? He didn't love that *wasicun!*
He only fell in love with the idea because she was pale
skinned and had fiery-colored hair! With a cry, Deer
Woman turned and ran behind the tepee. She kept running until she got to the pine forest that ringed the large
meadow. Once inside the forest she fell into a heap, and
sobbing, pressed her hands against her face and mouth.
She sobbed loud and hard, rocking back and forth in
pain.

How could Wolf have done this to her? How? She was
a comely Lakota maiden, and her father was rich with
horses. She loved Wolf! The cursed *wasicun* had cast her
spell over him—that was all there was to it! As darkness
began to fall, Deer Woman stopped crying. Her grief was
replaced with hatred. What could she do to tear the *wasicun* out of Wolf's arms? Somehow, Deer Woman vowed
to herself, she would make sure that Cante Tinza would
leave their village—forever. She prayed long and hard to
the Great Spirit to show her a way to do this.

Darkness was complete around Deer Woman. She
knew she must get back to the village. Worse, she knew
that Wolf would now take the *wasicun* to his robe and
make her his wife that very night. Bitterly, Deer Woman
got to her feet. She angrily wiped the tears from her face
and began the long walk back to the village, where several cook fires still burned in the distance. Deer Woman's pain nearly tore her apart, and she began to weep
again as she stumbled blindly down into the meadow toward her parents' tepee.

Tonight, Little Swallow had taken Dawn Sky home
with her. It was her gift to Serena and Wolf. Nervousness stalked Serena as she completed the normal nightly
tasks before they went to bed. Only this time, she would

be sharing Wolf's robe. The fire was small in the pit, mostly glowing coals, but the shadowy light chased away the darkness in their tepee. Wolf had shaken out the robes and laid them neatly on the dried bulrush mats. He had gone to the sweat lodge earlier and then to the river to cleanse his body and spirit for this sacred night. His hair was washed, hanging in dark black sheets about his powerful shoulders. A number of the married women had prepared a similar sweat lodge for Serena.

Hands trembling, Serena glanced nervously over at Wolf. He wore nothing but his breechclout. His skin was darkly shadowed and taut against the heavy muscle of his body. He sat there cross-legged watching her, his arms relaxed across his knees. She felt anything but relaxed. In the darkness of the sweat lodge the older women had counseled her on the ways of a new wife. They had accompanied her to the river, rinsed her off in the icy waters and dried her on the bank. Then they had unbraided her hair, combed it out and rubbed her skin with the fragrant wild bergamot.

They had told her how fortunate she was to be Black Wolf's wife, that he was looked upon with great respect and love in the tribe. They combed her hair until it shone like burnished copper, whispering and giggling like young girls the whole time. Serena finally laughed with them, some of her nervousness dissolving beneath their care and teasing.

She could no longer find anything to do. She knew that she was supposed to pull off the dress and walk naked to Wolf's robe, but she just couldn't do it. At least, not yet.

"Come here," Wolf invited softly, holding out his hand to her. He saw the fear in Cante Tinza's huge green eyes. As her damp, cool fingers met his, he drew her down so that she knelt in front of him. He released her hand and threaded his fingers through her heavy red hair. "The women have made you even more beautiful, if that is possible," he told her. Just the simple feeling of the heavy, silken strands of her hair flowing around and through his fingers sent unbidden longing through Wolf. He eased to his knees and began to gently massage her scalp.

"Do you know how many times I have dreamed of doing this?" he asked her, holding her unsure gaze. Her lips were parted, begging to be touched once again. "A husband loves his wife in many ways, Cante Tinza. He massages her scalp, combs her hair and braids it.... If the sunlight is harsh, he places grease upon her cheeks and brow to ensure she does not become burned by it. Each night, I want to ease the tension I now feel in your shoulders. You work very hard. You never stop to rest." He smiled into her eyes and realized the fear was dissolving with each caressing stroke of his hands against her tense shoulders.

"Your hair—" and Wolf sighed as he withdrew his hands from her now relaxed shoulders and cupped the weighty strands into his palms "—is living fire. I often felt that the fire you wore in your hair was like the fire you carry in your heart. I am not wrong, for I sense this about you. When you touched my lips near the river earlier, I felt your fire for the first time, and I knew...."

With a shaky breath, Serena surrendered to Wolf's dark voice—to the beauty of his words that she knew came from his heart—and to the gentle touch of his hands upon her. She had seen him tame wild horses with that same touch. Was she any less wild? No. She had been as frightened as a wild horse, but for different reasons. She felt him take the hem of her deerskin dress and begin to roll it upward. Closing her eyes, she allowed him to pull it off her.

Unable to look up at him because she knelt fully naked before him, Serena saw him carefully fold her dress and put it aside. Hesitant and unsure, she gasped as Wolf's hands lightly came to rest on her shoulders.

"Look at me," he urged. "You have nothing to be ashamed of, my woman. In my eyes, you are beautiful to look upon. You make me feel powerful and good because you sit before me with such innocence and trust."

It took every last vestige of Serena's dissolving courage to lift her chin those scant inches to meet Wolf's tender, dark eyes. Swallowing convulsively, she felt him begin to lightly stroke her shoulders, trailing his fingers down her arms to her hands and then back up to her shoulders. It was as if he were trailing fire up and down her arms, and she released a ragged breath, succumbing to his touch.

"Let me please you," Wolf begged hoarsely. "Let me show you the love a man can give his woman. This time, allow me to give you pleasure. At other times, when it feels right to you, I will teach you how to please me in return."

Serena nodded and closed her eyes, her heart beating like a wild rabbit in her chest. Wolf moved behind her, resting his thighs on either side of her as he began to gently soothe and massage her tight shoulders and stiffened spine. Each time he touched her, tiny rivulets of fire leaped through her. He was so close that she could feel the heat of his body—the energy that always surrounded him. As Wolf leaned down and pressed a series of small kisses against the length of her neck and across her shoulder, she shuddered. But it wasn't from fear, it was from longing. His tongue wove wet, subtle patterns across her sensitized skin, and Serena moaned as she fell back against his body. The instant they touched, she felt as if they were melting into each other, for their flesh was hot and tingling.

She was no longer thinking, simply feeling and responding to each of his butterfly caresses. Never had she been worshiped in such a way, never had she felt her body respond in such a fashion, as Wolf's hands created a hot, simmering magic wherever he stroked her. As his hands gently slid beneath her arms to cup her breasts, Serena froze.

"Do not run," Wolf whispered against her ear, "but ease back against me, my woman. I will not hurt you, I only want to give you further pleasure. . . ."

The shame of the scars made Serena stiffen. She felt Wolf release her. He stood up and came around to face her. "I—I'm sorry," Serena whispered, her hands pressed against her breasts. "They're ugly, Wolf. Ugly."

Whispering her name, he captured her hands and drew them away from her breasts. "Not ugly, my woman. The scars you carry are from a battle you fought. There is never ugliness in scars earned in battle." He gave her a soft smile and gently cupped her breasts once again in his hands. Wolf saw desire clash with fear in Cante Tinza's half-closed eyes. He began to use his thumbs to gently brush her nipples, and they hardened instantly beneath his onslaught. A gasp tore from her, but it was a gasp of shocked surprise and pleasure.

"Your breasts are beautiful to me, Cante Tinza," he told her in a roughened tone. "They remind me of the fullness of Mother Moon when she shines white in Father Sky." He leaned down, licking one nipple with his tongue. Instantly, she gripped his shoulders with her hands, a small cry issuing from her lips. Smiling to himself, Wolf knew he had pleased her. "The milk that spills from your breasts will feed our children, my woman. I do not see your breasts as ugly, nor will our babies. I feel your need of me when I suckle at your breast. I see your beauty and I taste the liquid gifted to me from your breast. How can any of these things be ugly?"

Serena gave another little cry as Wolf's lips closed around her nipple and suckled gently. Her fingers dug frantically into his dark, brawny shoulders. His head was pressed against her as his lips teased and drew each nipple into the moist, heated depths of his mouth. She lost her reason when she felt Wolf move his hand downward in slow, tantalizing patterns, across her torso, splaying his fingers out across her rounded belly. The earth tilted and Serena felt herself being carried in Wolf's arms to his robe. The soft, thick fur of the buffalo robe tickled her back as he laid her down. She saw the burning intensity in his eyes as he knelt above her.

Reaching up, she threaded her hands through his thick, loose hair. He gave her a very male smile and leaned over to once again capture one of her nipples. Serena lost all coherency as she surrendered to Wolf's gentle assault upon her stubborn mind. As his hand roved across her belly, brushing down across her tense thighs, she became lost in the multitude of wonderful sensations. Heat collected between her thighs, intensifying the throbbing ache below his fingers. Of their own accord, her thighs parted, and Wolf's hand moved downward caressingly.

Just as he lightly stroked her damp womanhood, he captured her parted lips and the cry caught in her throat. A moan tore from Serena as his fingers worked a new kind of magic, seeking and slowly exploring her moist depths. She was engulfed by a series of intense explosions wreaked by his caresses. Her breath was ragged as she clung to his mouth, and her hands gripped his shoulders in urgent need. Arching against him, Serena felt as if lightning were dancing up through her, each bolt striking and making her shudder with a pleasure she had never known existed. Wolf's dark voice was close, urging her to enjoy and to surrender to her womanly ways beneath his hands and mouth.

Dazed, Serena felt Wolf move across her. Suddenly, memories from the past slammed into her, and she gave a little cry, throwing her hands outward. Her palms met the hard flesh of Wolf's chest as she frantically tried to push him away. Mewing out cries of fear, Serena felt him move away from her.

"Easy, my woman," Wolf cajoled thickly. He realized Cante Tinza was reacting to the past—to Kingston's brutal rape of her. In one unbroken movement, he rolled onto his back and brought her across him so that she straddled his body. He saw the surprise in her eyes as he steadied her with his hands on her waist.

"This is the only way," he rasped, his body an aching knot of need. "Take as much of me as you want, when you want, my woman. If there is pain or pressure, do not go further." He smiled gently up at her. "Let your heart guide you on this. You need to do nothing if that is what you want. There is no hurry."

Trembling from need, and at the same time from the savage memories that had torn away the beauty of their moment, Serena gave a jerky nod. As she rested against his hard maleness, the signals were mixed, but her heart cried out that she wanted to love Wolf fully. Little by little, Wolf dissolved the memory as he caressed her, coaxing her to sink into the pleasure he had given her before. Only this time, he cupped her hips with his hands and slowly began to slide her against him. The shocking pleasure began once again, and Serena closed her eyes and rested her hands tensely against his hard, flat stomach. The intense, heated feeling began all over again; only this time, it wasn't his fingers wreaking such magic from her body, it was him.

It was as if she were riding a horse, Serena realized in some tiny functioning part of her mind. The slick wetness conspired her to move more strongly against Wolf, and the thick member no longer seemed as hurtful as it might have been. Soon, the rocking, sliding motion made her hungry for more. She heard Wolf groan as she began to accept him into her hot, welcoming depths. When he eased upward, to capture one of her nipples with his mouth, she moaned, feeling him move more deeply within her.

The moments spun together, and Serena felt her body give away to Wolf's presence within her. He suckled her and held her in his arms, and all she could do was weep with joy and repeat his name over and over again as her brow rested against his head. Very gradually, Wolf began to rock her against him, and Serena felt even more powerful sensations course up through her; heat and raw yearning coaxed her to meet and meld with his rhythm. She felt Wolf lie back on the robe, his hands firm and guiding against her hips. He moved with her strongly now, and she arched, throwing her head back as a powerful series of molten, fusing explosions rocked through her. She felt the heat explode from her very core and surge outward, then move rapidly up her spine into her head. In moments, she floated like a cloud in the sky.

Wolf groaned as he felt her spasms and her arching spine. He absorbed the cry of joy spilling from her lips with gratefulness. He prolonged her pleasure and watched with satisfaction as a blush covered her lovely young skin. And then, after a few motionless seconds, Wolf plunged into her once, twice, three times, before he felt the heat uncurl from his loins and his seed spill powerfully into her waiting, loving body. In those seconds as they melted into oneness, he closed his eyes and lost himself in her scent, her texture and her hands that stroked his belly. More than anything, he prayed that the Great Spirit would grant them a child from this night. A child fashioned from the love of a brave woman's injured heart.

Chapter Ten

"Wolf, come and feel your daughter move inside me." Serena rested on the pillows placed against one of the lodgepoles, her hands across her swollen belly. The winter daylight was gone, and only the firelight in the tepee eased away the darkness and provided a comfortable warmth for them.

Rising from his duty of crushing dried herbs, Wolf walked over to Cante Tinza. Her face mirrored tiredness, and her skin was stretched more tightly across her bones than usual. As he knelt beside her, covering her belly with his hands, he gave her a concerned look. He felt the baby move. He held her exhausted gaze.

"You do too much," he protested as he gently caressed her. "Your eyes are tired." When the baby moved again, Wolf's mouth pulled into a pleased smile.

"*Your* daughter is very much awake and has three times the energy I have right now," Serena teased as she reached up and touched Wolf's cheek.

"In one more moon, you will deliver our daughter into the hands of the old women," he murmured, holding her luminous gaze. How beautiful Cante Tinza had grown since the discovery of her pregnancy. There was an inner glow to her, a joy that radiated like sunlight from within her to all she touched and helped.

Serena had lost track of the months long ago. It had been easy to switch to the cycle of the seasons and move in accordance with nature. "I worry because that's the coldest moon of the winter," she confided, her hands covering Wolf's, which lay protectively against her belly.

"The snow is light this season, and it is not as cold as many others," he soothed. "Besides, our babies are always born strong and healthy."

"I wish you could be with me to deliver our daughter." Serena had known she was pregnant in the third moon after she had shared Wolf's robe. No one had been happier than Wolf over the news, and no one more angry than Deer Woman. Serena wished that the girl would stop being jealous of her, but there was little anyone could do. Once, Deer Woman had disappeared for a moon and no one knew where she had gone. When she came back, she had smiled smugly and said nothing. Even Swift Elk had given up his pursuit of her as a wife because Deer Woman spurned his sincere advances.

"Birth is the responsibility of the women," Wolf told her as he sat down, sliding his arm around her shoulders and drawing her against him. "They have a natural knowing. A man does not give birth, so he should not attend one."

"You help the foals and puppies birth all the time!"

"That," Wolf chided her gently, "is different."

"A baby is no different than a foal."

He smiled and pressed a kiss to her wrinkled brow. "You will be surrounded with the love and care of the birthing women. I will be outside the tepee, praying for you and our child."

She giggled and snuggled her head beneath Wolf's jaw. "I just *know* it's a girl. I've known from the moment I realized I was pregnant."

Wolf nodded. He knew that, too. "She will be beautiful. She will walk in our image, Cante Tinza. You must begin to rest more, woman. If you do not, I will send you to Dreaming Bear and she will see to it you spend your last moon quiet but happy."

Serena smiled up at his fierce countenance, knowing full well Wolf would never send her away from him. Many expectant mothers went to live in a tepee alone to rest and to commune with Mother Earth and remain peaceful. The Lakota believed the nature of the child was directly affected by the surroundings of the mother. If the mother had to endure anger, gossip and many demands upon her time, the baby would be born bad-tempered, whereas if the mother surrounded herself with only moments of peace and tranquillity, the child would be born good-tempered. So, many of the women would spend those nine moons quilling, beading, making blankets, clothes and a cradleboard for their coming baby in the tepee that sat near the edge of the village. Serena had chosen to remain with Wolf, her happiness complete being with him.

"Dreaming Bear wants to become our baby's *hunka* grandmother," she reminded him.

Wolf grunted. He held up his wrist, which showed a recent white scar. "You and I shared our blood with each other. And most of my family has been killed, with the exception of Little Swallow. We are in need of an *unci*, grandmother, who will spoil our two daughters," he agreed.

Laughing quietly, Serena gazed over at their first daughter, Dawn Sky. She was two summers old now, and she no longer slept in her cradleboard, but on her own pallet. Her black hair was barely visible beneath the dark brown fur of the robe under which she slept. Serena held up her wrist, which had been cut for the ceremony that had taken place three days after she agreed to marry Wolf, and stared at the long, thin scar. Her blood had mingled with Wolf's—a promise that they were bound to each other until death.

Wolf reached over, captured her thin wrist and placed a light kiss upon the scar. "We will make Dreaming Bear our *hunka* grandmother soon," he promised with a whisper.

"Good. I don't know what I would have done without her these past few moons, Wolf. Bless her, she watches Dawn Sky most of the time so that I can attend to those who need herb medicine and help you with the doctoring ceremonies."

"Dreaming Bear will make a fine, doting grandmother. Already, she rubs her hands in anticipation, waiting for our daughter to come from your belly."

Laughing softly, Serena leaned up and kissed Wolf. She was never disappointed by the love he managed to convey when their mouths touched and clung to each other. Since her pregnancy, he had become even more helpful, if that was possible. He would not allow her to go with the women to collect the daily wood needed for their cooking fire, nor would he allow her to do many of her expected duties around the tepee. His mouth slid hotly across hers in silent adoration. Since her pregnancy was discovered, he had not loved her, and now, her body ached with the memory of his touch—the fire he brought to life within her. Soon, Serena reminded herself as she drowned in the splendor of his kiss, she would once again share his robe and be able to love him completely.

Easing away from her mouth, Wolf smiled down into her lustrous eyes. "I hope our daughter has green eyes as you do."

Serena sifted her fingers through his thick, loose black hair. "And I hope she has your hair."

"No, I want her to have fire-colored hair such as yours."

"And if she doesn't?"

"I will love her as I love her mother."

Contented, Serena lay against Wolf and closed her eyes. "Do you have to go on that hunting trip tomorrow? Couldn't you stay home?"

He kissed her hair and held her gently in his embrace. "We need every man capable of hunting, to find the last of our meat before the snows come, Cante Tinza." He shifted away from her enough to see the disappointment on her face. "I will carry you in my heart, my woman. The days will pass quickly, and then I will be here once again. Do not look so sad."

"I'm afraid of you leaving," Serena admitted softly, caressing his chest with her hand. The thick elkskin shirt he wore was plain and without much quilling. She touched the wolf claw necklace that hung around his neck. "I'm just afraid."

"I will be safe. No Crow will attack us, if that is what you think."

With a shake of her head, Serena sighed. "No, I just have this terrible feeling, Wolf, and I can't shake it. Something is going to happen. Something terrible." She sat up and shrugged.

"You dream of this?" he asked, concerned.

"No—I, it's nothing I can identify, Wolf. Just this feeling of doom, that's all."

He got to his knees and began to unbraid her fiery-colored hair as he did every night. "Many mothers become frightened just before the birth of their baby. This is natural," he soothed as he caught and held her worried gaze.

"I just wish you didn't have to leave so soon, Wolf."

"We are safe."

"Couldn't you at least leave *some* warriors behind to protect us from attack?"

He smiled as he allowed the thick strands of Cante Tinza's hair to flow through his fingers. "We are deep within our territory, so no Crow will attack us. Last week, our hunters saw *wasicun* miners heading north into the Paha Sapa, away from our village. We are safe, my woman."

"Will you take Kagi with you, then? At least she will alert you if the Crow or the miners stalk the hunting party."

Wolf nodded. "Yes, she will come with us."

Satisfied, Serena felt a bit better. The black wolf had raised her head from where she slept each night at Dawn Sky's side. Kagi was a fine baby-sitter, but Serena also knew that Wolf liked to take her with him on hunts because of her own hunting ability. The wolf had an eerie sense of knowing when their greatest enemy, the Crow, were nearby. She would alert them long before an attack could be initiated against them.

"There she is," Blackjack Kingston snarled. He and his band of miners, twenty in all, hid behind the thickly forested hill that led down to the Lakota village near the river. A light covering of snow had fallen, and Blackjack pulled his buffalo coat a little more tightly around himself. His horse, a huge bay gelding with four white socks, stood quietly beneath his iron hand. His eyes narrowed as he watched Serena make her way down to the river, which was a good quarter mile away from the main village. She was dressed in Lakota clothes and she wore her red hair in braids. It was early afternoon, and the light gray color of the sky indicated that it would soon begin to snow. The wind was sharp and brisk.

"What ya gonna do, boss? Do we ride in shootin' the hell outa dem Injuns?"

Kingston glared at the black-bearded miner to his right, Jake Gunther. "No, you dumb bastard!" Standing up in his stirrups, Kingston kept his voice in a low rasp and told the men who gathered around him in a semicircle, "No shooting! I want that red-haired witch! She's our target. I want all of you to ride pell-mell through the village. Shout, yell, fire your rifles into the air. Create a diversion while I get her."

"But," Jake protested meekly, "what about all those warriors?"

"Deer Woman said they'd be gone this week on a hunting trip." Kingston peered intently down at the village again. "I don't see any bucks. All I see is a couple of doddering old men and women, and the brats."

"I kin get twenty-five dollars for a scalp," Gunther added with a hint, hope in his voice.

"Not this time, you jackass! I want that woman back! I don't want the whole goddamn nation up in arms and comin' to get us. We don't want the Sioux attacking our camp. Understand?"

"Sure, Boss."

Blackjack settled the silver fox cap firmly on his head. His gloved hands gripped the reins more tightly and he snarled, "All right, let's go! Once we get the woman, we leave! No killing! Just scare those Injuns back into their tepees so they leave us alone."

The village dogs began barking loudly, and Serena, who had knelt down between the brown bulrushes to scoop up a kettle of water, raised her head. She heard the thunderous beat of many horses, and she gasped, thinking it was an attack by Crow warriors. Because she was heavy with child, her balance was poor, and she couldn't twist or turn around in a hurry. Just as she straightened, she heard the alarm sounded by the village crier.

"Miners!" he shrilled in a high, wobbly voice. "Miners!"

Gasping, Serena jerked her chin upward. Her eyes widened as she saw at least twenty men on horseback, heavily clothed for the winter, galloping down the hill toward the village. Her heart started pounding in her chest. Instantly, her hand went for the knife she wore in her belt—but it wasn't there. Serena had long ago stopped wearing the belt because of her bulging belly.

She saw the children and women spilling out the tepees with war clubs, spears and anything else they could get their hands on to defend themselves from the forthcoming attack. Serena picked up the kettle and lifted her elkskin skirt to carefully make her way up the slick, icy bank. There was safety in numbers. She had to get back to her tepee and retrieve Wolf's lance that he had left behind.

As Serena made her way up to the top of the bank, she saw three miners split off from the main group. She winced as they started firing their rifles, the sounds echoing harshly through the valley. Screams of frightened children filled the air. She tried to run but the ground was slippery, and she was afraid she'd fall and hurt the baby.

The three riders bore down upon her. Serena was caught out in the open, unarmed, and too far away from the village. Clenching the kettle in her fist, she watched the three miners closing in on her at a gallop. A scream lodged in her throat when she recognized the lead rider. It was Blackjack! With a startled cry, Serena turned to try and escape. He was after her! Her mind spun with questions. How had he found her? How?

Serena ran, but it was nearly impossible to keep her balance. She heard the bay horse thundering down upon her, and at the last moment, she stopped and whirled around. Kingston's narrow face was pale, his blue eyes were pinned on her, and his thin mouth was drawn into a sneer.

The miners jerked their horses to a halt, surrounding Serena. She held up her hand, fearing that one of the sweaty, hard-breathing horses would knock her down and trample her.

"Get up here," Kingston ordered as he dismounted. "You're mine, and you're coming back with me, witch."

"No!" Serena shrieked as he lunged for her. She tried to dodge his hand by stepping back, but she crashed into the side of another horse and rider. Kingston's arm snaked out, and she threw the kettle at him.

"Oww!" he roared, when the kettle struck him in the shoulder.

Gunther leaned down and grabbed one of Serena's long, thick braids. "I got 'er, boss!" he said laughing.

With a whimper, Serena felt herself being pulled against the miner on horseback. Pain radiated through her scalp as he continued to hold her captive with her braid. No! This couldn't be happening! No! She tried to fight, but each time she tried to kick out at Kingston or to claw or scratch him, the miner who had her braid jerked on it, throwing her off balance.

"You Irish witch," Kingston breathed savagely as he grabbed her flailing arm. "You're mine!"

With a cry, Serena realized that she must stop fighting if she was going to save her baby. Kingston's gloved fingers sank deeply into her flesh as he pulled her toward him with a triumphant grin on his mustached face.

"D-don't hurt me," she pleaded. "My baby...my baby..."

"Shut up!" Kingston placed one hand behind her neck and dragged her toward his horse. "Mount up."

Serena shakily climbed into the saddle, one arm stretched protectively across her belly. Kingston quickly mounted behind her. He dug his spurs into the heaving flanks of the gelding, and the horse leaped forward with a grunt, foam dripping from the sides of his open mouth. She clung to the saddle horn, afraid that she was going to fall off. Kingston's arm went around her like an iron band, hauling her against his tall, lean body as they rode at a furious gallop up the hill and away from the village.

Tears froze on Serena's lashes as she saw twenty men on horseback join Kingston. How had he found her? Oh, Great Spirit, she prayed, help me, help me.

Deer Woman watched covertly, pretending to be just as upset as the rest of the village as the miners rode over the hill and disappeared. She hid her smile beneath her hand as she silently said goodbye, once and for all, to Cante Tinza. Kingston had given her many blankets, trading beads and dried buffalo meat for telling him about the red-haired *wasicun*. On the way home from the miners' camp, she had stored all those valuables in an

cave well-known to the Lakota, where she would retrieve
them at a later time. If she had brought them home, everyone would have questioned where she had been, and
Deer Woman wanted no one to know.

Standing at the entrance to her parents' tepee, Deer
Woman saw the distraught faces of the elders and heard
the cries of the youngest children. Kingston had promised not to hurt her people, and he had held to his vow.
Pleased, she walked over to Black Wolf's tepee. Dawn
Sky would now need a new mother, and she planned on
being there when Black Wolf returned from the hunt.
Barely able to contain her joy, Deer Woman ran quickly
between the tepees and people to take her rightful place
as Wolfe's wife.

Kagi began a sad, long howl. Wolf was roused from a
light sleep among the thirty Lakota warriors who had
bedded down for the night. Scowling, he saw the black
female wolf on the hill above them. She howled for-
lornly. That was unlike her. A chill worked its way up his
spine, and he sat up to digest the sense of dread he felt.

Instantly, Wolf thought of Cante Tinza. He knew
without a doubt that Kagi was invisibly bound to her
spirit and sensed her moods no matter how far apart they
were. Throwing off the robe, Wolf stood up.

Tall Crane, who slept nearby, rolled over. "Wolf, what
is it?" he asked thickly.

"I'm going back to the village," he told his friend
grimly, picking up the cottonwood saddle and blanket.

Rubbing his eyes, Tall Crane sat up. "What?"

"Kagi howls. I feel as though something bad has happened. Perhaps to Cante Tinza. I do not know, but I
must find out."

"Well—"

"I must go now. I will see you upon your return," Wolf said. The snow was barely ankle deep, and Wolf knew he could make rapid progress on Wiyaka throughout the night. As he approached Wiyaka, Kagi came bounding off the hill. She wagged her tail fiercely, whining and pacing around him and the horse. The wolf's antics only increased the sense of urgency he felt. Quickly, Wolf mounted the mustang and turned her south toward the village, which lay a day's travel away. Something was terribly wrong, and as he urged the mare into a gallop across the white, wintry meadow beneath the full light of the moon, Wolf had never before felt such dread.

Deer Woman smiled but quickly swallowed the smile as she heard shouts announcing Black Wolf's unexpected arrival. Somehow, he'd found out! But how? Standing up, she waited tensely, gripping the buckskin she worked upon for a new pair of moccasins for Black Wolf. Outside, she could hear several of the elders telling him of Cante Tinza's kidnapping. What would he do? Deer Woman put her quill work aside and smiled over at Dawn Sky, who played without interest with several deer bones. The child had cried endlessly, no matter what she had done to comfort her.

The entrance flap of the tepee was jerked aside. Deer Woman leaped to her feet. "Black Wolf, I greet you."

Wolf glared at her. "What are you doing here?" he demanded, breathing hard. He put the flap back into place. Going over to Dawn Sky, who gave a cry and opened her arms, he picked up his daughter.

"I've come to help, of course," Deer Woman soothed. She came over and patted Dawn Sky's small back as the baby clung to Wolf and sobbed. "Your daughter needed me."

Looking around, Wolf muttered, "I thank you for your help. I intend to leave as soon as I can pack enough food for the journey. Will you look after my daughter while I am away?"

Mouth falling open, Deer Woman stared up at him. "Away? Where?"

Gently, Wolf eased the child from him and gave her to Deer Woman. "I go to rescue Cante Tinza."

"But—"

"She is my wife," he reminded her as he knelt down and pulled the parfleche saddlebags toward him.

"They will kill you if they see you!" Deer Woman cried. She quickly put the child down and moved to Wolf's side. "Don't go, Black Wolf! She is not worth it! Don't you see? Kingston wanted her back. He had claimed her in the first place."

Jerking a look up at Deer Woman's distraught face, Wolf snarled, "Claimed her? He raped her against her will, Deer Woman. That is the full truth of the matter. No, she is my wife. It is my duty to save her."

"What if he has killed her already?" she cried. "All you will be doing is walking into his trap, and he will kill you, too!"

Wolf stood and placed the saddlebags across his shoulder. He took the heavy buffalo robe and draped it across his other arm. Wolf could barely stand the thought of his wife—the woman he loved so fiercely—dead. His voice turned hoarse. "If Kingston has killed her, he will pay with his life."

Tears stung Deer Woman's eyes and she gripped his arm to prevent him from leaving. "You can't go! You have Dawn Sky! What of our people? You are our medicine man. What happens if we need you? Where will you be? Are we so easy to forget in place of that red-haired *wasicun!*"

Angrily, Wolf shook off her hands. "Are you *heyoka,* crazy, Deer Woman? She is my wife! She carries our child in her belly. What kind of husband would I be if I stood by idly and allowed her to be kidnapped? You speak foolishly, girl. Stay and keep my daughter safe." Then, Wolf left.

Deer Woman sobbed. She placed her hand against her mouth to hush her wailing and to dam the tears pouring down her cheeks. Outside, she heard Wolf's horse gallop away, and she knew without a doubt that he rode to his death. Kingston had warned her that if anyone came after the red-haired witch he would kill him.

Serena sat on the edge of the bed, tense and waiting. Kingston's log cabin was one of the largest and finest in the miners' camp. The room was chilly, and she shivered. There was a feather bed and a pine dresser in the small room, and the floor was bare. Her body still ached and throbbed after last night's brutal ride. She gently massaged her belly, praying to the Great Spirit to let her daughter be safe within her. An iron shackle had been placed around her wrist, and the chain fastened to the poster bed. The chain was just long enough for her to get up and walk a few feet.

Lucinda, the negress slave who served Kingston, quietly entered the cold room. She bore a tray of steaming food. The woman was hardly any older than Serena. Her hair was wrapped in brightly colored red cloth, and her dress was made of gingham. She closed the door and quickly made her way over to Serena.

"I brought this for you, Miz Serena." Lucinda placed the tray on the bed. "Now, you gotta eat, no question about it." She placed the tray on the bed beside Serena. "Mah master said to feed you and get you outa those Injun clothes. Ah'll bring the dress he wants you to wear later. Now, eat. Eat!"

Fighting back tears of terror, Serena grabbed Lucinda's long, thin hand. "Please, help me escape, Lucy! Help me!" She saw the girl's round face grow afraid, and her eyes widen.

"Why, Miz Serena, ah cain't do that, you know that. Master Kingston'd have me beat within an inch of mah life with that leather strap he carries. Uh-uh, ah cain't help you as much as I might want to. Jest eat, or Master Kingston will beat me. You know how he is if his orders ain't followed...."

Serena glumly looked down at the feast set before her. Lucy was the cook and housekeeper for Kingston. Of course, he raped her when he felt like it, too. The negress was trembling in front of her, and Serena nodded. "I'll eat," she promised wearily. "I don't want to see him beat you, Lucy."

Rolling her eyes, Lucy whispered, "Praise the Lord! Ah'll be back in jest a little while with your new dress."

Serena stared at the food, not hungry. She worried about losing her baby from the arduous journey. Even more, she wondered what Kingston was going to do with her. Would he rape her even though she was pregnant? With shaking hands, Serena forced herself to eat. She had to eat to keep up her strength, because no matter what, she would defy Kingston just as she had before.

Finally the day was closing, the winter light weak through the mica window. Serena sat, waiting. The hours had dragged by, and she had refused to replace her elkskin dress with the one of calico that lay at the foot of the bed. All the memories of Kingston haunted her. He had always come at night—a candle in his hand as he silently entered her darkened room. He would do the same now.

When darkness was complete, Serena still sat on guard. When she heard the latch to the wooden door move, she gasped softly. Kingston entered, taper in hand, and the light chased away some of the darkness. He wore calf-high black boots, gray trousers and a white shirt with ruffles. The collar was open, revealing the dark hair of his chest.

Serena watched him warily, her stomach knotting with fear. Kingston was more than six feet tall, with swarthy skin and black hair slicked back with bear grease. The clothes he wore, Serena realized, were the finest his considerable gold could buy. He was in his early thirties, and he ruled the miners' camp like a king—his authority undisputed. Blackjack's henchmen were everywhere, shooting anyone who didn't abide by his laws.

Kingston placed the taper on the dresser, turned and rested his hands on his narrow hips.

"Still defying me, witch? Lucinda brought you a dress to wear. Now, I want you out of those smelly Injun clothes."

His voice was raspy, and every nerve in Serena's body sizzled in terror when he spoke. She watched as his blue eyes grew shadowed. He slowly approached her. Although her mouth was dry, Serena dredged up the words she had wanted to ask him since he had kidnapped her. "Why have you done this, Kingston?"

His mouth formed a lethal smile as he leaned nonchalantly against the poster bed. "Why?"

"You nearly killed me and threw me away to die two years ago. And now, after all that time, you came after me. Why?"

He curled back his smiling lips and flashed his yellow teeth with a snarl. He wanted the witch frightened. "As if you don't know," he taunted.

"Know what?" Serena cried, her hands protective across her unborn baby. "What have I done to *you?*"

"Acting was always your best card to play," Kingston sneered. He reached out, grabbing her by her hair. "Pretend no knowledge, will you? How stupid do you think I am? Do you think if you play dumb I'll think you're innocent?" he rasped, his face inches from hers. His hand tightened in her hair. She gave a cry and tried to push him away. "Bitch!" he roared, and forced her down onto the bed on her back. His hands sank into her shoulders, pinning her against the feather mattress.

"Still don't know?" he demanded angrily.

"No!" Serena cried. It was impossible to move. Her breathing was ragged, and so was his. She saw the fury, the crazed wildness that glazed over Kingston's slitted eyes. "What did I do to deserve this?" She could smell the foul odor of whiskey on his breath, and it made her gag.

With a curse, Kingston released her and straightened. "Actress until the end, aren't you, Serena? God help me, but I still find you desirable after all you've done to me and my family." He glared down at her belly. "You're carrying an Injun's brat." With a snort, he said, "I was hoping you'd lose it on the ride here, but you didn't. Well, it doesn't matter. You can stay chained to this bed until the brat's born. Then, I'll give him to one of my negress slaves to wet-nurse. Soon as I can, I'll sell him."

Serena struggled to sit up, a gasp tearing from her. "No! Don't sell my baby! You can't, you can't—"

Kingston smiled a little, pleased with her reaction. "Tears, my dear Serena? Are they real or fake? It doesn't matter." He jabbed his finger at her. "You came back here three nights after my men had dumped you at the river. You came back here for revenge. You set fire to my house, you bitch!" His voice cracked. "You killed my son and my wife, damn you! You're nothing but a vengeful fury in a woman's form." He loomed over her and watched with satisfaction as she lifted her uncuffed arm to try to protect herself.

"I didn't set fire to your house!" Serena cried out. "How could I?"

"You crawled back here because you wanted to get even with me for throwing you out," Kingston growled.

Startled, Serena stared up at him. "But I didn't do it! I swear I didn't do it!"

He stalked to the door. "I'll believe you when hell freezes over, Serena. You fought me from the day I bought you from that damnable Irish slave broker. No matter how much I beat you, you always fought back." Grimly, he looked over at her face, which was carved with terror. "This time, you will pay as never before. No slave of mine escapes." His voice grew hoarse with emotion. "My son is dead because of you. God knows, I loved that boy. He was my life. My life! I had such dreams for Lionel. He was a good boy who was going to inherit all my wealth, all my land someday. But you, you in your vengeance murdered him."

"But I didn't!" Serena wailed. Gulping, she pleaded, "Please, you've got to believe me!"

He snorted violently. "A miner swore he saw you with a torch in your hand. He saw you throw it through my sleeping son's bedroom window!'' His face contorted. ''If I hadn't been away at the time, maybe I could've saved him. My wife, God bless her, tried to save Lionel, but she died in the attempt.''

''I—I'm sorry they died, I really am,'' Serena whispered brokenly, ''but I wasn't the one! The Lakota found me the next morning and took me in. I was with them! I wasn't here. That miner is lying to you!'' she cried hoarsely.

Kingston shook his head. ''No, I believe the miner.'' He glared at her as he placed his hand on the latch of the door. ''You'd best get used to being my slave again. This time, you're going to be kept chained up all the time. I'll wait until after your half-breed brat is born and then you're going to warm my bed every night until I grow tired of you, witch.'' He gave her a twisted smile. ''And when I'm tired of you, I'm going to kill you in just payment for my wife and son's deaths.''

The door slammed shut, and Serena gave a little sob of despair. Kingston was accusing her of killing his wife and son in a house fire! How could he? Serena knew that Kingston constantly cheated the miners, and that more than likely one of them had done it. Her mind swung from thoughts of escaping to thoughts of losing her baby to a slave trader. She decided that, above all else, she had to think about protecting her baby. And what of Wolf? He wouldn't return to the village for at least a week.

Slowly, Serena lay down, trembling badly. She pressed her face into the goose-down pillow, eyes shut. *Wolf.* How much she loved him! What would he do? What *could* he do? Kingston's mining camp was bristling with armed miners who hated the Lakota. There were other Lakota here, but only those who drank the firewater or Indian women who had been stolen on raids and kept prisoner for the miners' insatiable lust. Her heart ached with fear, with loss. Her baby was going to be taken from her! Tears squeezed from beneath Serena's lashes. That just couldn't happen. It just couldn't.

Chapter Eleven

Serena dreaded the coming nightfall. It was her second day in captivity, and Lucy had taken her to another room to wash in a copper tub, and then change into a loose-fitting red robe. A fire was built in Serena's prison room, and she knew as she sat there shackled to the bed that Kingston was going to stalk her in earnest tonight. Lucy had washed and dried her hair and then brushed until it shone with fiery highlights. Although she had lost her appetite, Serena forced herself to eat.

All of her Lakota clothes had been neatly folded and lay on the dresser. Serena wished mightily for their return, for the cotton gown trimmed with white lace at the throat was thin in comparison and didn't keep her warm. Would Kingston rape her tonight? She shuddered in anticipation, worried for the baby she carried. What would he do?

Outside the newly built cabin, she could hear the swearing of miners, the braying of their mules and the ceaseless traffic through the mud and snow of creaky-sounding wagons. Kingston's home sat at the edge of the tent city, two stories tall, lording over his kingdom like a castle.

Later the darkness of the room was driven away by a roaring fire in the fireplace, which kept Serena warmer than before. She worked frantically at the iron cuff that made her already chafed left wrist raw and bloody. She jerked at it constantly, hoping against hope that the heavy chain nailed to the wood of the poster bed would loosen so that she could pull free. Her wrist and forearm were a mass of dark bruises, and her shoulder ached from the constant yanking against the nail that held the iron link in place.

Serena was alerted when she heard the solid thumping of boots echoing eerily along the hallway. The sound was coming toward her door. Gulping, she stopped jerking at the chain and sat very still. The latch moved. Her breath jammed in her throat, her hands automatically covering her baby.

Kingston slowly walked into the room. He held a half-empty bottle of whiskey in his hands. His eyes glittered in the firelight. With the heel of his boot, he quietly shut the door.

"I thought," Kingston said, slurring his words as he walked drunkenly toward her, "I could go to sleep tonight. But I haven't been able to sleep since you came." He stopped, tipped the bottle up to his mouth and took a long swallow. Placing the whiskey container on the dresser, he wiped his mouth with the back of his hand, all the while staring at Serena.

Kingston's eyes finally focused and he walked with deliberation toward her. She sat in terror. He smiled savagely, savoring her fear. "Damn you for being so beautiful," he snarled as he reached out and clamped his hand into her thick, shining hair. "You're a witch. An Irish witch." He saw her wince, cowering as he examined her hair in his large hand. "Your hair reflects you. You're wild. Untamed. I thought I could keep my hands off you until that brat's born, but I can't."

"Please," Serena begged softly, pulling away from his threatening presence, "don't hurt my baby. Don't hurt her, I beg you...."

Kingston studied her upturned face. "You hurt my son. Why shouldn't I hurt your brat?"

She could smell the nauseating odor of whiskey on his breath and tried to move away, but she was trapped between the post of the bed and him. Her heart pounded wildly, and she fought back tears. "I swear, I never came back and set fire to your cabin! I didn't kill your son! I love children! I could never hurt a child, no matter what their color or race!"

He eyed her swollen belly. "I don't believe you," he snarled. He captured her chin between his thumb and index finger. "I'm taking you here and now, witch. I can't stop thinking about you, about what we had. I want it again. I couldn't care less about that brat in your belly. Now, stand up and take off that robe."

Serena jerked her chin out of his grip. She tried to push Kingston away as he advanced upon her. Fighting him with all her strength, she felt him grab the collar of the robe. It ripped sickeningly, and Serena tried to cover her exposed breasts. Out of the corner of her eye, she saw him lift his hand to strike her. The side of her head exploded with light and pain, and she felt herself falling backward into the bed. His groping, hurting hands were all over her, and weakly, she tried to push him away. The taste of blood filled her mouth.

With a shriek, Serena raised her foot and lashed out. Kingston grunted from the blow, which threw him backward off his feet. He crashed to the wooden floor. Serena shakily pulled the robe closed, ignoring the pain radiating up through the left side of her face.

Just as Kingston struggled to his knees, Serena saw the door open. A cry tore from her. Wolf moved silently inside the room, his knife drawn. In one smooth, unbroken motion, he kicked Kingston's legs out from beneath him. Wolf pinned Blackjack to the floor and held a knife to his neck.

"One cry and I will slit your throat," Wolf hissed. He glanced toward the bed. Fury raced through him as he saw blood flowing from Serena's nose and mouth and realized that Kingston had struck her. He pressed his blade against the man's sweaty flesh. "You dared to touch her?"

Kingston's eyes bulged as he felt the sharp knife slit his skin. Blood began to trickle down the side of his neck. His breath was ragged as he stared into the hardened features of the Lakota warrior. "I—I—"

"You are going to die," Wolf said.

"No!" Serena cried. "No more killing, Wolf! He's got the key to my cuff. Get it! Please, get it!"

Wolf hesitated, his stare black and impenetrable. "You touched my wife. No man hurts her and lives to speak of such a foul deed, Kingston. Give me the key she speaks of."

Wolf eased the knife just enough for Kingston to dig frantically into the pocket of his trousers. Then, he took the key from the miner and turned toward her. "Can you free yourself, Cante Tinza?"

Gasping, Serena nodded. She caught the key midair, and, with trembling fingers, unlocked the iron cuff. "Let me get into my dress, Wolf."

"Hurry," he urged. "There is not much time."

Shedding the torn robe, Serena slipped the elkskin dress over her head. By the time she had gotten her moccasins and leggings on, Wolf had locked the miner's wrist in the iron cuff and had placed a gag in his mouth.

Wolf was satisfied that Kingston was no longer a threat. He placed the knife back into the sheath and moved to his wife's side. Gripping her by the arms, he saw the terrible damage to her face.

"He did this to you?"

"Y-yes. Oh, Wolf, you came," and Serena threw her arms around him and sobbed.

Holding her tightly, Wolf glared back toward the miner. "I would never leave you, Cante Tinza. Did he touch you otherwise?"

"N-no, but he was going to rape me." She gulped unsteadily, trying to wipe the tears from her eyes. "If you hadn't come when you did, he would have."

Wolf's mouth thinned. "Cante Tinza, the horses are tied in the woods in back of his house. Kagi waits with them. Move carefully from the house. I will meet you there soon. Now, go."

Serena jerked a look up at Wolf's harsh features, and then over at Kingston, who lay there with unadulterated fear in his eyes. "Wolf, what are you going to do?"

"Something that he has coming to him, my woman. Now go. I do not want you here to see it. Leave."

Gripping his arm, she cried, "Don't kill him! They'll just come after our people again, Wolf."

"I know," he soothed, devoting his attention momentarily to her as he guided her to the door. "I will not kill him."

"Promise?" Serena quavered.

"I vow to allow him to live. Now, quickly follow the hall to the rear door. I have knocked the man who guards that door unconscious. Mount Wiyaka and wait for me. Keep Kagi with you. Do not allow her to show herself."

"A-all right," Serena said. She glanced quickly down the hall and then slipped out the door. What was Wolf going to do to Kingston? Barely able to stand, Serena leaned heavily against the wall and made her way to the door in the dark. She quietly opened the latch, and could see snow beginning to fall. Thick flakes floated silently from the sky. She carefully descended the icy steps, hurrying once she was on the snow-covered ground.

Serena located the hobbled horses amid a forest of pine trees no more than twenty feet away from the rear of the log cabin. Kagi was on a leash that was tied to a nearby pine. The wolf whined and leaped to her feet, wagging her brushy tail wildly in greeting. Serena's hands trembled so badly that she could barely unknot the leash to free Kagi. She whispered to the wolf while she unhobbled the horses. Wiyaka nickered gently in greeting, and Serena climbed unsteadily into the saddle. Wolf had brought along a large bull buffalo robe that not only covered the saddle, but could be brought up around her head to protect her from the freezing cold and snow.

Just as Serena pulled the robe over her head, she saw Wolf leap off the stairs and run silently toward them. She handed him the jaw cord to the other horse. He leaped lithely into the saddle and adjusted his robe over himself.

"We must ride now," he whispered, reaching out and gripping her hand. "If you begin to feel badly as we ride, tell me."

"Y-yes. Oh, Wolf, let's just get out of here!"

"We go home, my woman. Come."

Wolf grew worried. The snow worsened, nearly blizzardlike, and the winds howled around them as they wended their way through the sentinels of pine. The horses stumbled, slid and moved along in the dark at a steady walk. Serena kept falling behind, and he knew that Wiyaka wasn't a lazy walker. He pulled up and waited for her. She was bent forward, her head bowed.

"What is it? The child?" he asked.

Serena bit down on her lip to stop from crying out. "Wolf, I think I'm in labor. It's too early. Too early...."

Wolf couldn't stand the ragged cry of her voice. Dismounting, he approached Wiyaka. "I will ride with you. Are you in much pain?"

"Horrible pain. It started at Kingston's cabin earlier," Serena explained as she lightly touched her belly. "I'm worried I'm going to lose her, Wolf."

He saw the fear in her tear-filled eyes. "No," he rasped. He mounted Wiyaka, and his arm moved gently around Cante Tinza. "I talked to the birthing women, and they said with this kind of ride you may come a few weeks early. They said that if you go into labor, I should find a place to stay and help you birth the child myself."

Exhaustion made her dizzy, and Serena relaxed completely within Wolf's embrace. "I—I'm just so tired, Wolf. I hurt, and all I can do is cry."

"Hush, Cante Tinza, you have gone through much alone. I got here as quickly as I could. I sensed you were in danger when Kagi started howling the first night of our hunting trip."

She shut her eyes, trying to black out the pain from her aching jaw. "I thought I'd never see you again," she sobbed, and pressed her hand to her eyes. "I was so frightened for our baby. Kingston was going to give her to a wet nurse as soon as she was born, and then he was going to sell her to a slave trader. Now, I worry he'll come after us. I can't travel fast, Wolf. I'll slow us down, and—''

"Be still, my woman. Your talk makes you weaker. Conserve yourself. Kingston will not follow us." Wolf guided Wiyaka through the gray dawn of the forest around them. Soon daylight would come, and with it a chance to seek refuge.

Serena twisted a look up at Wolf's hard, shadowed features. She'd never seen him look so cruel as now. "Why won't he?"

"Because he will not be able to walk, much less ride for a number of months."

"What are you saying?"

Wolf stared down at her. "He killed a part of you when he raped you, Cante Tinza. And he was going to rape you again even though you carried our child. Among my people, we do not forgive a man who does this to a woman."

Her eyes widened. "What did you do to him, Wolf?" Serena's words came out in a terrified whisper.

"I gelded him as I would geld any horse." There was satisfaction in his voice. "No longer will he hurt you or any other woman."

"Oh, no," Serena cried, her hand pressed against her mouth.

As they rode Serena dozed between sleep and wakefulness. Each time Wiyaka slipped it jolted her, causing pain to race through her. She tried to keep from crying out, but finally, in her exhaustion, she couldn't help it. The fear of Kingston's men following them was real, even if he was incapacitated. Everything became a nightmare for Serena. Kingston's furious face haunted her each time she closed her eyes. Only Wolf's arms gently holding her kept her from going insane with the pain and terror of their escape.

"We are here," he whispered near her ear.

Serena dazedly raised her head. The snow was falling so heavily it was like a white curtain. The snow-covered pine trees looked like shadows. "Here?" she mumbled.

Wolf dismounted and took Cante Tinza into his arms. "The cave," he told her with a slight, weary smile. "There are many caves in the Paha Sapa. During the winter, when we must hunt, we stay here." He walked carefully through the nearly knee-deep snow toward a huge opening that was partly covered by trees and thick, snow-covered brush.

Much later, Serena sat with her back against the cave wall, wrapped in the thick, warm robe. Her pain came and went like ripples of water through her body. She had lost track of time since contractions began savaging her. She was barely even aware that a warm fire burned in the center of the dry cave.

The cave was huge, and consisted of several rooms. A large store of dried grass that had been picked in the summer fed the two horses, which remained hobbled in the outer room. In the second, more protected room, or cave, there were bladder bags filled with not only dried deer meat, but rich buffalo meat. Cooking utensils were nearby, and Serena watched as Wolf set up housekeeping. It was almost as if they were home in their tepee.

"The stew smells wonderful," she admitted.

Wolf glanced over at her. Cante Tinza's flesh was pale and drawn across her cheekbones and there was darkness beneath her eyes. He worried about her, still angered over the swelling along her left cheek and jaw. "Soon we will eat."

With a slight smile—slight because it hurt to talk due to the blow by Kingston—Serena whispered, "I'm not really hungry."

"I want you to try to eat, my woman, to keep up your strength. Soon our baby will come, and you must be strong." Wolf stirred the kettle suspended over the fire. The draft in the series of caves drew the smoke deep into the underground darkness. He knew that no one would find them. They were safe. Leaving the fire, he laid out several wool blankets. The pallet would become the place to birth their child.

Serena dozed off and on for more than an hour until she felt Wolf pull her gently into his arms. He spoon-fed her the rich buffalo broth that he had flavored with wild onions. She lay in his arms, his back providing comfort from the hard, cool wall of the cave.

"Enough…" she whispered, and closed her eyes, tired beyond belief.

Wolf placed the bowl and spoon aside. He caressed her mussed hair. "You did well," he praised her in a low voice, as he put his arms around her.

"I'm so tired, Wolf, so tired. I want to sleep so badly."

He pressed a kiss to her hair. "Then sleep, my woman, for I will hold you safe."

The slow pound of his heart beneath her ear was soothing, and Serena surrendered to his low voice and the strength of his arms holding her, until she slept despite the labor pains. His large body provided her with a warm haven against the continuous draft.

Wolf felt Cante Tinza slowly relax, and soon her breathing was soft and shallow against his neck. He continued to slowly stroke her matted, damp hair with his fingers. His eyes burned with the fierce fire of anger toward Kingston. He should have killed the *wasicun,* but he had listened to Cante Tinza's pleadings to spare his life. With a sigh, Wolf knew that Kingston, once recovered, would come after them. More than likely, in the spring.

His brows drew down as he caressed her cool cheek. Kingston might be too injured to ride, but he could send his miners after them. Somehow, Kingston knew which band of Lakota Cante Tinza lived with, and he could strike them again. Once she had their baby, they would have to get back to the camp as quickly as possible. Perhaps he should ride ahead to warn the chief so that they could move the camp and not remain a target of Kingston's rage and revenge. He should have killed the *wasicun*. . . .

Wolf rested his mouth against Cante Tinza's hair and closed his eyes. His heart mushroomed with such fierce love for his wife that he wanted to howl like the wolf that lay at her side, proclaiming his love for her to the world. Every once in a while as she slept, she would draw up, like a taut bowstring, and then gradually relax once again. Wolf knew that the labor pains were coming closer and closer together, and that they had become more powerful as the hours of the night moved on toward dawn. He prayed to White Buffalo Calf Woman to make Cante Tinza's birthing swift and easy. He prayed for a sign that his prayer would be granted, for he knew of women who had died in childbirth, and he couldn't lose his red-haired woman. He just couldn't.

Serena awoke to a sharp, tearing pain moving down through the center of her body. Gasping, she tensed, her eyes flying open. She felt, more than saw, Wolf.

"Easy, my woman," he murmured, stroking her hair. "Soon our daughter will come into my hands, into our world."

Serena blinked and realized that gray light was filtering into the chamber. With Wolf's help, she sat up—the pain was too intense and gutting for her to lie on the wool pallet. "Is it daylight?" she whispered in a sleepy voice.

"Three hours ago." Wolf smiled and pointed to the floor near the opening. "Look, White Buffalo Calf Woman has answered my prayer. A mourning dove flew into the cave just as light broke the hold of the night. She paced back and forth, cooing and calling, but did not leave." He smiled down at her from his kneeling position. "This is a very good sign. Your birth will be swift and easy, my woman."

Serena saw the small gray-and-tan mourning dove bob its head back and forth as it walked in a circle at the opening between the cave's first and second room. She gave a small laugh and gazed up into Wolf's face. "She shouldn't be here. They're afraid of humans."

"But—" Wolf gestured "—the bird was sent by White Buffalo Calf Woman."

"How beautiful," Serena whispered. The wonderful sight took her mind off some of her pain.

Wolf caressed her hand. "I prayed for a name."

"You did?" She slipped her hand over Wolf's, the cramplike pain coursing through her abdomen.

"Yes. We shall call our daughter Wakinyela, Mourning Dove."

With a sigh, Serena said, "It's a lovely name, Wolf."

"You approve?"

"You're the medicine man. Why would I dispute what a medicine person would call our baby?"

His laughter was low and rich. "You slept well, nearly half the night. Do you feel rested? Hungry?"

Just being in Wolf's presence buoyed Serena. She realized that her love for him was eternal. Her smile slipped as she held his dark, searching gaze. "Yes, I feel stronger. But I don't want to eat."

Grunting, Wolf stood and faced her. He knelt in front of her. "Early this morning, your water gave way," he said as he pointed to the damp blankets beneath her. "Our daughter will come soon."

"Good," Serena said, closing her eyes as the pain began again. She held her swollen belly with her hands. "I've never felt such awful pain."

"That is why women have the children," Wolf told her as he removed the damp blankets and replaced them with dry ones. "You are stronger than any man. You have the force of spirit within you to tolerate such agony."

"Right now," Serena quavered, "I don't feel very brave."

Wolf placed a rolled buffalo robe behind her back so that she could lie in a partially reclined position. "You are braver than any ten women I have ever known." He picked up her left wrist, which had been chained with the iron cuff, as if showing her an example of her bravery. "You never stopped trying to escape Kingston, did you?" He gazed at the black and blue bruises that mottled her flesh.

"Never. I had to try and get away, Wolf."

"I can tell." He sighed heavily and placed the blanket over her shoulders. "With each pain, I want you to push with all your strength, my woman. That will bring our daughter closer to my waiting hands."

Perspiration was beginning to dot Serena's face. She felt as if she was being ripped in two by the gutting pain. With a nod, she clenched her hands into fists beneath the blanket and did as Wolf instructed. She kept her eyes firmly planted on the mourning dove that cooed and walked back and forth at the cave entrance. It was a miracle, Serena decided as the hours wore on, and her strength threatened to dissolve; each time she wanted to give up, the mourning dove would leap into the air, fly around them in circles and then land back at the entrance. The bird would coo, as if trying to communicate in dove language that she should not give up.

Hair matted against her sweaty flesh, Serena groaned as Wolf eased her into a kneeling position. A small cry tore from her parched lips as the baby bore downward within her. She heard Wolf's soothing voice, low and comforting, and felt his arm around her, steadying her. The agony sliced through Serena and she cried out, throwing back her head and arching her back into a taut, bowlike shape. She felt Wolf's arm tighten around her while blackness danced before her wide, unseeing eyes.

Wolf smiled broadly as his daughter slid into his large, waiting hand. The baby was a healthy pink color, the thick umbilical cord lying across her stomach and she was slowly moving her tiny arms and legs. Placing the baby to one side, Wolf helped his wife to lie back against the robe. With his fingers, he removed the mucus from the baby's nose and mouth.

Serena gasped for breath, her gaze riveted upon the baby in Wolf's hands. With a little cry, she stretched her hands outward to receive her daughter, who was now wrapped in a fawnskin.

"She's beautiful," Serena cried softly, and gazed up into Wolf's face.

"Yes," he agreed, drying off the baby's thick black hair. "Beautiful like her mother."

With a little laugh, Serena stared at the infant in amazement. "She's so tiny. So perfect. Oh, Wolf, she's ours. Ours, beloved...."

Tears stung his eyes as he gently wiped his daughter's arms dry, each of her small fingers perfectly formed. "She has my hair," he murmured proudly. As he cleaned his daughter's face, she opened her eyes for the first time. His smile deepened as he held his wife's luminous gaze. "And she has blue-green eyes."

Words were useless. Serena felt an incredible tiredness overwhelming her. Just then, the mourning dove flew into the air, circled around them and then disappeared out the opening of the cave. Amazed, Serena looked up at Wolf, who cared tenderly for both of them.

"She just flew away."

"It was just as White Buffalo Calf Woman promised," Wolf said thickly, his voice uneven with joy and emotion. As he touched his daughter's drying hair, he whispered, "Wakinyela, we welcome you into our arms and into our hearts."

Serena's vision blurred with her tears of joy. Wolf caressed her hair and leaned down, pressing a kiss to her lips.

"Your tears of happiness are shared with me," he whispered against her lips. As Wolf eased away, he positioned Wakinyela to her milk-swollen breast. "I do not think," Wolf said with a chuckle as he guided his daughter to find the nipple, "that she is going to have an appetite of a bird, my woman."

Serena agreed as the infant made noisy sucking sounds, her tiny bowlike mouth moving strongly as she latched on to the nipple that would give her sustenance. Wolf knelt over both of them, his arm around Serena's shoulders, and his other hand—almost half the size of Wakinyela—positioned against his daughter.

Serena closed her eyes and rested her head tiredly against Wolf. Her mind was spongy with fatigue, but the worry of what would happen to them ate away at her like a living thing. Kingston thought she had killed his son, and he would never cease trying to get his revenge.

As much as Serena wanted to talk to Wolf of her worries, she could not. She ached for Kingston's loss of his son. No child should ever be placed between adults who hated or feared one another. More than anything, Serena wanted Wakinyela to be raised in peace, with the fierce love of Wolf and herself surrounding her.

Chapter Twelve

"Cante Tinza is to blame for us having to move! My hands turn blue from the cold. It is her fault!" Deer Woman whined to her parents. Everywhere she looked, families were busy taking down their tepees and packing the horses and dogs alike to proceed to another wintering ground far away from the Dried Willow region, in case of attack by miners hunting for Cante Tinza or Wolf.

"Do not complain," Swift Elk chided as he helped her roll up a buffalo robe. "We would do this no matter who had been kidnapped by the *wasicuns*. This is not Cante Tinza's fault."

Glaring at the brave, Deer Woman watched with envy as several older women, who had gone over to Black Wolf's tepee earlier, did the packing there that normally would be done by the wife. Two days ago, Wolf had ridden in on his buffalo runner through the knee-deep snow, his wife and new baby in his arms.

"I'd like to know how she got free," Deer Woman muttered defiantly, throwing the robe onto the packhorse and tying it with numb fingers. Her breath came out in white clouds as she spoke. The dawn was a pale pink color along the horizon. Steam rose off the river like a curtain, even though ice covered nearly half of the blue water. The Lakota people were heavily bundled against the icy chill of the clear morning. It was so cold that Deer Woman had heard the snap and pop of trees at night as they buckled from the plunging temperature.

Swift Elk followed her back to the pile of lodgepoles that had been taken down. "I hear Black Wolf gelded the man who took her."

"What?" Deer Woman jerked to a halt, and her mouth fell open. "I did not hear that!"

"It was the same *wasicun* who held her prisoner before." With a grin, Swift Elk picked up the first lodgepole, which had been scraped smooth of bark. He carried it to a horse that would drag the poles. "Perhaps that is gossip. If you are so curious, Deer Woman, why don't you go to Black Wolf and ask him yourself?"

"She is going to bring nothing but death and unhappiness to our people!" Deer Woman stood there with her hands placed petulantly on her hips. "Who's to say the *wasicun* won't come after her again when the snow melts? We are in danger no matter where we move!"

Swift Elk shook his head. "The chief moves us far away. The *wasicuns* won't find us."

Jerking up one of the poles, Deer Woman snapped, "Are you so blinded by that *wasicun*'s red hair that you have not thought of the horse soldiers? There is talk that the horse soldiers will ride into an Indian camp if there is any *wasicun*, child or woman, among the tribe."

"Stop screeching like a wounded owl," Swift Elk muttered with a frown. "We have a treaty with the *wasicuns*. The horse soldiers have better things to do than hunt each tribe searching for a *wasicun*. Besides, Cante Tinza stays of her own choice. She has never been our prisoner."

Jealousy ate at Deer Woman. "Treaty!" she spit angrily. "The *wasicuns* break our treaty with them whenever it suits them and you know that! They want the gold that lies in our streams and rivers. You are blind like an old man, Swift Elk!"

How could her carefully laid plan have gone so wrong? Deer Woman wondered. Kingston was gelded. Would that frighten him into staying away? Deer Woman prayed that it did not, for the miner was a man as ruthless and vengeful as she'd ever seen.

Luck had been on her side when she heard several drunken miners talking about Kingston's family dying in the fire. She had entered the camp beneath a trade blanket, and pretended to be one of the Indians who lived there and drank the firewater. She had eavesdropped behind one of the canvas tents and heard the miners discussing the fire. Then, the plan had formed in her mind. She told Kingston that Cante Tinza had bragged about setting fire to his cabin herself in order to get revenge against him for raping her earlier. Deer Woman knew it was a lie, but she was frantic to rid herself of the *wasicun*.

Clinging to what little hope was left, Deer Woman didn't know what else could be done. Nearly everyone in the village had gone to greet Wolf and his *wasicun* wife shortly after their arrival. Talk raged about the beauty of their daughter, Wakinyela, who had black hair and blue-green eyes.

If only Kingston would come after Cante Tinza again....

Wolf stirred drowsily. His arm was wrapped around Cante Tinza, who lay naked against him. The buffalo robe kept them more than warm, for it was the moon of the green leaves, when all things blossomed beneath the returning sunlight and warmth. Cante Tinza slept deeply beside him, and he gently eased her onto her back. Outside the tepee, the snort of horses—the first sounds of the camp coming awake—caught his attention.

Wolf inhaled deeply as he pressed his face into her thick, rich hair, which had been recently cleansed with soapweed and then rinsed with bergamot-scented water. Rising on one elbow, Wolf checked on their children, who slept nearby. Dawn Sky, who would soon be three summers old, slept with only a few strands of her black hair visible above the robe. Wakinyela lay in the cradleboard that Cante Tinza had made for her before she was kidnapped by Kingston. Between the children lay Kagi, who had instinctively become their guardian.

His brows moved downward for a moment as he transferred his attention to his wife's tranquil features. In the five moons since her release from Kingston, she had been unusually tense and edgy. Her sleep was broken, disturbed by bad dreams. Wolf caressed her unmarred brow and marveled at her beauty—the ripe color of her parted lips, the cover of copper stars thrown across her cheeks and nose....

He felt himself becoming hard with need of her, and his mouth curved slightly as he allowed his fingers to trail from the slender length of her neck downward to cup one of her milk-filled breasts. Normally, her breasts were small, but Wakinyela, who had the hunger of six wolf pups combined, had swelled them to nearly twice their size. Wolf marveled at their rounded perfection and beauty. He realized that some of the terrible scars put there by Kingston were still receding, and he hoped, over time, that the scars would become less of an embarrassment and shame to his wife.

His heart swelled with such fierce love for Cante Tinza that he felt his eyes fill with tears of gratitude. Each day was a gift to them, he realized as he watched her slowly begin to pull from the wings of sleep. With his thumb, he caressed the hardening nipple, and he smiled as he heard her moan softly with pleasure. Outside, Wolf could hear the melodic song of a nearby meadowlark, always a harbinger of good news. Sliding his hand across her rounded belly, he splayed his dark fingers against her lustrous flesh. In several more summers, after she finished nursing Wakinyela, Wolf wanted to create another child from their love. She was a good mother, a loving one in the tradition of Lakota ways.

Serena pulled from sleep as heated ribbons of longing flowed through her lower body. She smiled softly as she felt Wolf's large, callused hand slide downward to the juncture of her thighs, and she opened them to his knowing exploration. Slowly opening her eyes, Serena drowned in his dark, gleaming gaze as he lay above her. His hair was an ebony curtain, loose and hanging across his broad shoulders. As he caressed her, discovering her moistness, she moaned again and pressed herself against his body.

Wolf leaned down and captured Cante Tinza's parted lips, tasting the yielding softness of her as with his fingers he continued his grazing touch against her swollen womanhood. Her moan was caught as he hungrily slid his mouth against hers and silently communicated how much he wanted her, how much he loved her. Soon the children would wake on their own, but he wanted to love his wife before that time arrived. As he eased his mouth from her smiling lips, he felt her hands range across his shoulders and back.

Teething one of her nipples, Wolf could taste the sweetness of the milk that she carried for his daughter. Cante Tinza's fingers dug frantically into his back, and he smiled to himself as he gently moved to cover her, to bury himself deeply within her welcoming depths. As he lifted his head and placed his hands around her hair, his fingers buried in the strands, he met and held her luminous eyes. She opened her thighs, arching slightly to receive him, all of him, into her.

Wolf bit back a groan and thrust his fingers into her red hair as she pulled him within her slick, heated depths. Her hands moved across his hips, and her legs entwined to capture his so that all he could do was lie there in the scalding beauty of her. As she rocked her hips, his lips drew away from his teeth, and his hands clenched slowly into fists that held her fiery-colored hair.

Wolf became lost in the hotness of Cante Tinza, the strength and love of her as she met, matched and challenged his rhythm. He had awakened with the intent of pleasing his wife first, but she had other ideas. Helplessly snared within her unselfish and loving gesture to give him pleasure this morning before their children awoke, Wolf surrendered to her generosity and beauty. Very quickly, he tensed against her, his world anchoring to a halt of intense feeling as her damp, soft body cajoled the essence out of him and into her. Moments later, Wolf relaxed and buried his head beside hers, breathing raggedly. He kept most of his weight off her as he lay captured by her loving form.

Perspiration dotted Serena's face as she lay there with Wolf blanketing her. She smiled and, with her eyes closed, ran her hands gently up and down his back and hips. "I love you," she whispered, and kissed his damp cheek. Serena wasn't disappointed as Wolf lifted his head, slid his mouth reverently across her lips and kissed her deeply for a long, long time. She absorbed his power, his undying love for her. Since returning to the camp, Serena had seen a change in Wolf. He was more attentive, if possible, more on guard for her safety than before. And he revealed his feelings toward her openly, and without apology.

Serena sighed happily as Wolf moved to one side and positioned her on top of him. He smiled at her and brought the robe across her shoulders. With her hands, she caressed his brow and then moved her fingers through his silky black hair. "It seems as though you share our daughter's appetite—only in a different way," she teased him with a softened laugh.

Wolf's brows moved upward and his mouth pulled into a lazy smile. He reached up and tangled his fingers through her hair, which lay pooled across his chest. "At least I left the milk for our daughter."

Giggling, Serena luxuriated beneath Wolf's adoring caresses. "That's true," she breathed, and leaned down to touch her lips to his mouth. His mouth was strong, chiseled and, often, not smiling. When he dealt with his patients or with tribal business, he never smiled. But in the privacy of their tepee, his mouth rarely moved into that hard, unyielding line. Running her tongue lightly across his flat lower lip, she felt him grip her hips firmly and move her provocatively against him.

"So, even now," she breathed, "you want more."

He felt himself growing hard once again beneath the heat and teasing of her tongue, and from her sinuous body rubbing against his own. Although the children had been aware of them loving each other sometimes during the darkness, Wolf knew that Dawn Sky would awaken very shortly. She always climbed into their arms, snuggling down between them, and Wolf didn't want to be aroused then. "You are at fault," he told her archly.

"Me?" Serena slowly eased off Wolf because she saw Dawn Sky stirring. She shrugged her deerskin dress over her head and shoulders. The front of the dress had been specially designed so that she could unfasten the top to feed Wakinyela.

With a chuckle, Wolf sat up. He put on his breech-clout and then brought the elk comb from the parfleche against the wall of the tepee. "Yes, you." He turned Cante Tinza around so that she knelt with her back to him. His thighs bracketed her slender body as he began to brush the snarls out of her hair. This was something he enjoyed doing each morning. The moments with his wife were precious and far between. The tribe was beginning to gather foodstuffs for the coming year, and in groups of five or ten the women often ranged over the hills gathering wild onions, bulbs and other herbs used in cooking. He saw Cante Tinza only at night, after Father Sun had slid beneath the horizon.

Serena sighed and relaxed, her hands resting on Wolf's curved, muscular thighs. She enjoyed rubbing her hands across his athletic legs and feeling them tense beneath her ministrations. "I love being pampered like this," she admitted quietly as Wolf's fingers moved gently across her scalp.

"A wife deserves respect," Wolf told her darkly, and he leaned over and placed a kiss on the side of her neck to prove his point.

"I never saw a white man respect his wife like this," she admitted.

"*Wasicuns* keep their women like slaves," Wolf growled. He asked her to turn so that he could begin to braid her hair. Before he did, he reached for his knife. "I want two lengths of your hair."

Serena looked at him. "Why?"

Wolf smiled. "I had a dream last night. I saw a strand of your red hair braided with a strand of my black hair. I saw a pair of hands take our hair and braid them into one, and then make it into a circle." A pleased expression lingered on his face as he held her curious gaze. "I want to make such a necklace for each of us to wear. It will have great power because it was given to me in my dream. The braided hair we wear will symbolize our undying love for each other. Nothing can break the circle that binds us."

Serena nodded. "What a beautiful dream," she murmured as Wolf took the hair he needed from her head. She watched him lay the long strands beside the robe. Her hair was halfway down her back, and Wolf's was just as long.

"You will cut strands from mine when you comb and braid my hair," he directed, tying off her braids. Today, he decorated her braids with eagle fluff, feathers taken from beneath the tail of the mighty bird. The eagle feathers proclaimed her bravery, and Wolf gave a grunt of satisfaction when he had finished.

"You go to hunt bulbs today?" he asked.

"Yes. This morning I'm going to help Little Swallow and several other wives tan those new buffalo hides. Later today I will hunt wild onion with them."

"I will care for our children this afternoon, then," Wolf told her. He didn't want their children away with Cante Tinza. If Kingston tried to attack or capture her again, Wolf was afraid that the *wasicun* would kill them out of hatred. Instead, he cared for the children in camp when she had to forage the hills and meadows with the women for wood or food.

Serena turned around between his thighs and faced him with a smile. She saw Dawn Sky stir and sit up, rubbing her puffy eyes with small fists. "Our daughter awakens," she warned as she took the comb and began to run the teeth through his silky black hair.

With a grunt, Wolf saw Dawn Sky rise, toddle over to the entrance and go outside. She would relieve herself, and come right back in to snuggle in his arms as Cante Tinza brushed his hair. A few minutes later, Dawn Sky returned. She turned to make sure the flap was secure, and then with a laugh, launched herself into Wolf's open and waiting arms.

Serena moved aside as Dawn Sky fell into Wolf's arms with a giggle. He made snuffling bear sounds against his daughter's chest and in her mussed hair. The laughter and giggles heightened in the tepee when Serena laughed with them. Those joyous sounds always woke Wakinyela, so Serena hurried to finish braiding Wolf's hair before the baby began to fuss, wanting her first meal of the day.

"Here," Serena told Wolf, "*you* comb and braid our daughter's hair. Wakinyela is already awake."

Wolf took Dawn Sky into his arms and settled her in his lap. The little girl sat primly, her hands folded expectantly in her lap as she awaited his combing of her hair. He watched with pleasure as Cante Tinza went over to their other daughter, picked her up out of the cradleboard and changed her fawnskin diaper. As he brushed Dawn Sky's thin, shining black hair into place, Wolf had never felt happier or more fulfilled.

He watched as Cante Tinza loosened the fastener on her dress, revealing her smooth, white breast heavy with milk. Wakinyela's small hands moved rapidly, eager as she was to suckle the dusky nipple. His smile deepened as he watched his daughter's mouth move noisily, tiny rivulets of milk spilling from the corners of her mouth as Cante Tinza held her against her breast.

"Wakinyela always reminds me of a starving wolf pup," he said, chuckling as he gently braided Dawn Sky's hair.

"You'd think," Serena said, gazing down at her daughter with a tender look, "that she was starving to death!"

"Perhaps, someday when she is older, she may earn a wolf name," he said smugly.

With a laugh, Serena looked up. "I wouldn't doubt that at all." As children grew older, their names changed, depending upon their personalities, or their experiences. Serena had found out that Tall Crane had been called Eagle Boy as a youth, but one day, when he was washing down at the river after taking part in a sweat lodge, a great blue heron came and landed no more than six feet away from him. A number of men, including Wolf, had seen the surprising event occur. And then the heron had remained there, preening herself in the ankle-deep water. She pulled out three huge wing feathers, which fell into the water and flowed downstream to where Tall Crane knelt on the bank. Everyone agreed that the heron had come to announce to him that she was now his spirit guide. To this day, Tall Crane wore those three gray-blue feathers in his hair.

The suckling sounds of Wakinyela mingled with the outside activity of the awakening camp around them. Serena watched as Wolf dressed their daughter. Her hair was in neat little braids, and he had fastened red trade beads to the end of each of them because red was Dawn Sky's favorite color. He then pulled a clean pair of beaded moccasins from another parfleche. Dawn Sky lay on her back, waving her legs back and forth in the air. This was a game Wolf played with his daughter every morning. He would take the moccasin and pretend that it was an eagle swooping down to capture her little foot. Dawn Sky would frantically move her legs around, giggling and shaking with laughter as Wolf dived again and again with the moccasin until he captured each wayward foot.

"Who do you go to pick wild onion with?" Wolf wanted to know, capturing one of Dawn Sky's feet. The little girl shrieked with delight as he pretended his fingers were *iktomi*, the spider, walking up her leg to tickle her ribs.

"Little Swallow, Dreaming Bear and, I believe, Deer Woman. Why?"

Frowning, Wolf kissed his daughter's foot and then tied the moccasin snugly into place. "Deer Woman?"

"Yes."

"She is jealous of you. I sometimes see the looks she gives you, and it makes me uncomfortable when you must be around her."

With a shrug, Serena said, "I keep praying that over time she will understand that we love each other, Wolf, and stop wishing that you were her husband."

When Wolf finished dressing his daughter, he lifted her into a standing position and smoothed down the deerskin dress that barely grazed her thin little ankles. Dawn Sky moved over to her mother to watch Wakinyela feed. Wolf stood and rearranged his breechclout and placed moccasins on his feet. The day would be warm, and he wasn't going to put the leggings on unless he had to ride a horse.

Placing several sticks of wood over the coals of the fire, Wolf reached over and picked up Dawn Sky's doll, which had been made by Dreaming Bear, her *hunka* grandmother. He gave it to his daughter. The girl imitated her mother by placing the doll to her own chest, rocking and holding it, just as Cante Tinza fed Wakinyela at her breast. With a smile, Wolf returned his attention to the fire. Dawn Sky had her own parfleche, which contained a woman's work bag, a small tent, tent poles and several wooden horses. All these things were made so that Dawn Sky could begin to imitate her mother's duties, so that she grew up understanding her responsibilities not only as a woman but as a member of the tribe. Tall Crane, who had asked to become their daughters' *hunka* uncle, had carved the three wooden horses out of sacred cottonwood. Often, he would take Dawn Sky on a horseback ride, and she would sit proudly, grip the mane and smile.

The serenity of the tepee filled Wolf with such a sense of utter tranquility and joy that he found it hard to speak. The giggles of Dawn Sky mingled with the noisy suckling sounds of Wakinyela. Kagi, who always slept with the children as their guard, came over and placed her cold nose against his shoulder. He petted the wolf absently, and returned to preparing their morning meal. Normally, Cante Tinza would prepare their food, but he wanted her to enjoy feeding their daughter and not be pressed by such obligations. Later on, when Wakinyela was able to take her first steps, he would relinquish this task to his wife.

"The place you go to find the wild onion is near the swamp?" he asked over his shoulder.

"Yes. This is a new place to me."

"Be careful," he warned. "There is a bulb known as *psin hubloka,* that resembles the wild onion but is very poisonous. I have seen families die because young wives without proper instructions had picked the *psin hubloka* thinking it was wild onion. The wives would cut it up and serve it in stew and all who ate of it would die. And their deaths were tortured and long. Let Dreaming Bear show you these bulbs so you may know the difference."

The sun was warm without being hot on Serena as she dug with a pointed stick into the soft, rich red earth of the Paha Sapa. Not far away was Dreaming Bear, whose silver hair vividly contrasted with the green meadow that flowed into a swamp at one end. Little Swallow had gathered pondweed, the thickened rootstock that could be eaten either raw or cooked, while they dug the wild onion bulbs. Absently, Serena touched the braided necklace of hair around her throat. Earlier, Wolf had surprised her with the present. He'd placed it around her throat and braided the hair closed. She had then braided closed his hair necklace around his much larger, thicker neck.

Deer Woman worked off by herself, refusing to remain near the three of them. She hadn't spoken a word since riding out with them hours earlier. Serena sighed unhappily. Every time the young woman looked up, she glared at Serena, as if it were Serena's fault she was alive and breathing.

The meadow was oval and rolling, and as Serena straightened, her hand pressed against her lower back, which ached from remaining in that posture far too long, she gazed upon the unending beauty before her eyes. The dark blue sky was cobbled with puffy white clouds, and the spearlike spires of thousands of pine trees surrounded the meadow and scented the air with their fragrance. The grass was a rich, vibrant green, waving beneath the inconstant breeze. The horses hobbled at the other end of the meadow eagerly ate the succulent food. Meadow flowers bloomed in many bright shades of yellow, blue, pink and red, reminding Serena of a scattered rainbow.

"Listen!" Little Swallow called out as she straightened, her brows drawn into a frown. "Do you hear that?" She turned to the other women.

"What?" Serena asked, her heart picking up in beat, fear snaking through her.

Little Swallow raised her hand, listening intently. "Horses! Many horses are coming our way."

Deer Woman was the first to run toward their own horses at the far end of the meadow. Serena hurried over to Dreaming Bear, who had a bad limp and could not move hastily. As she gripped her by one arm Little Swallow came running over to assist in getting the old woman to her horse as quickly as possible.

Now, Serena heard the sound—a rumbling reverberation through the air. It reminded her of the great buffalo hunts that had taken place late last year, in which the beasts created a thunderous vibration that shook the ground and the air. As they hurried at a fast walk, Dreaming Bear puffing between them, she asked, "What is it? Buffalo?"

"Horses. Many horses," Little Swallow gasped. "Maybe Crow."

Fear struck Serena. They were near their summer encampment of Gray Buffalo Horn, and there was always the risk of Crow warriors suddenly attacking them. Serena gripped Dreaming Bear's arm more firmly. The old woman was short and fat, and was easily tired by any sudden activity. Ahead, Serena saw that Deer Woman had already unhobbled and mounted her horse.

"Why doesn't she release our horses?" Serena cried.

Little Swallow shook her head in anger "That girl is selfish! She thinks of no one but herself. Look! She rides off! Wait until we get back to camp. I will tell Chief Badger Mouth of her cowardice. She should have stayed and helped us!"

The air trembled now. Serena gasped as she saw the horsemen appear out of the pine forest near the swamp. "Oh, no!"

Little Swallow jerked a look over her shoulder. "Horse soldiers!"

"Aiyeee!" Dreaming Bear shrilled. "Let me go! Save yourselves!"

"No," Serena said with a gulp. They broke into a run, nearly dragging the old woman between them. Gasping for air, nearly to the horses, Serena rasped, "What will they do? Will they kill us?"

Little Swallow released Dreaming Bear and fell to her knees to release the first horse. "I do not know! We are at peace with them. But look how they ride!"

Rifle shots filled the air. Serena gave a cry and boosted Dreaming Bear up on her bay more. The horse soldiers were bearing down on them—the sound of a bugle echoing throughout the meadow as they drew closer and closer.

"Hurry! Hurry!" Serena cried. She quickly unhobbled Little Swallow's gray gelding.

"Get to Wiyaka!" Little Swallow ordered, holding back as Dreaming Bear set her horse to a swift gallop into the pines.

The hobbles were new and stiff. Frantically, Serena tore at the leather, trying to release Wiyaka's front legs.

She saw the horse soldiers coming over the rise, no more than a quarter mile away.

"Go!" she cried to Little Swallow. "Save yourself! Save yourself!"

Bullets began to zing around them, lifting geysers of dirt into the air. Wiyaka whinnied plaintively and moved jerkily; the sound of rifles caused the horse to panic.

"No!" Little Swallow rode around the horse, her hand outstretched. "Take my hand, Cante Tinza! Take it! Ride with me!"

Serena realized that if they both rode the same horse, they could never outrun the horse soldiers. "No! Go! Go!" Serena yelled, and she stood up and slapped the rump of the horse. The animal leaped forward, startled and terrorized by the rifles. Little Swallow nearly fell off as the horse bolted at a dead run toward the safety of the pines. She lurched forward, hands flying to the mane and clinging to it as the animal disappeared among the timber.

With a shattering feeling, Serena knew she could not escape. She stood here holding Wiyaka's jaw cord, waiting for bullets to tear into her body, waiting for her death. Tears came to her eyes. How she loved Wolf and her children. *Oh, Great Spirit, keep them safe. Keep them safe....*

A horse soldier bore down upon her. She could see the leader clearly, a young man with blond hair and a drooping blond mustache. Only once before had she seen Army soldiers, and that was on her journey to the Dakota Territory. They had shadowed the wagon trains to try to prevent Indians from attacking them. This soldier rode a bay horse with foam streaming from its open mouth, and its hide glistened with sweat. Directly behind him was another horse soldier in a dark blue wool uniform decorated with yellow piping, who carried a red and white flag. Behind him were at least thirty men, riding in columns of two.

Shutting her eyes, Serena awaited her fate. At least the other three women had got away. Little Swallow would tell Wolf what had happened. They would find her body lying in the meadow, she was sure, because she had heard stories of horse soldiers killing, scalping and leaving the body to be eaten by buzzards.

"Company, halt!"

Serena jerked open her eyes. The soldier with blond hair had raised his gloved hand. His face was round and his cheeks were bright red. Although he was only in his middle twenties, his blue eyes looked old. Serena held his gaze defiantly when she realized they weren't going to kill her. They were going to take her prisoner. The entire company surrounded her atop dancing and snorting horses. She stood there stiffly as the man who was in charge rode slowly up to her.

"Are you Miss Serena Rogan?" he demanded.

How long it was since she'd heard that name. "Yes."

The officer smiled a little and saluted her. "Ma'am, I'm Captain Jason Anderson. We were told a white woman had been captured by the Injuns, a woman with red hair. That's you." His smile increased and he tipped his hat to her. "Ma'am, we're here to rescue you. We'll take you back to the fort and you can leave the hellish prison you must have endured at the hands of these redskins." He spurred his horse forward, holding out his hand to her. "Welcome home, Miss Rogan. You're among your own kind now. We'll take you back to the fort, get you out of those filthy Injun clothes and see to it that you're cared for properly."

Chapter Thirteen

"I don't want to go to the fort!" Serena cried out angrily as she stood tensely in front of the captain. "I want to go home. Home to my husband and baby."

Captain Anderson held on to his patience. "Ma'am, I've seen women captured by the redskins before. They all say that. You have got to understand something: you have to go home to your own kind. You're a white woman, and you should be living in white society."

Serena whirled around and jabbed her finger in the direction of the village that lay an hour east of the meadow. "I am married, Captain! I have a baby daughter. I refuse to go with you. My people are the Lakota, not you!"

Anderson tightened his mouth and looked around the meadow. "Miss Rogan, I don't have time to sit here and argue with you. Please get on your horse and come with us. You've been a prisoner of the Sioux far too long. You just don't know it."

Her mouth fell open, and she took a step back. "I don't want to go with you!" she screamed.

"Sergeant Blake," Anderson snapped, "get Miss Rogan on her horse. Right now!"

With a cry, Serena tried to dodge the tall, skinny sergeant. He grabbed her by the arm.

"Be gentle with her," Anderson boomed.

"Yes, sir."

Serena felt the sergeant's hand instantly ease its talonlike grip on her arm. He guided her toward Wiyaka.

"Mount up," the sergeant growled.

Wildly, Serena looked around as she mounted the black mare. The jaw cord was ripped from her hands by the sergeant. He glared up at her.

"You're gonna follow behind my horse."

Escape, her heart cried. But Serena was surrounded by the troop of cavalry. There was no escape. Frantically, she tried to think. Captain Anderson gave the signal with his hand, the bugler sounded the notes, and the whole troop turned around. Sergeant Blake rode beside the captain, and Serena trailed them, unable to guide her horse. Even if she wanted to escape, Serena thought, it couldn't be now. No, if she did get away, they would only follow her back to the camp. She feared they would shoot and kill her people—perhaps her children. No, she couldn't try escape right now.

Trembling, with tears in her eyes, Serena tried to think clearly. Wolf had decided to go deep into the Paha Sapa with the children this afternoon, to hunt certain herbs. Did anyone know that? Would Wolf, once he found out, come after her?

The captain ordered the troop into a slow canter across the rolling meadow, heading due south. All Serena could do was ride along. She was a prisoner of her own kind. She would have to pick and choose the time when she could escape, but first she had to find out how and why the U.S. Army had found her. Where were they taking her? Back to Kingston? A shiver wound up her spine, and she bit hard on her lower lip to keep from crying out.

Near dusk, Anderson called the troop to a halt. They had met a military wagon train on the grassy plain, and camp would be made. Serena saw the open stares of the men as she was escorted by Anderson to a tent that had recently been set up by several soldiers. Her swollen breasts ached from the long, hard ride. She thought of Wakinyela, and knew that Dreaming Bear would take her to another mother to be nursed. At least her daughter wouldn't die in her absence.

Anderson smiled down at Serena and guided her toward the tent. "I want to be the first to welcome you home, Miss Rogan. I've asked my men to give you all the possible amenities we can, few that they are. The tent is yours for the night. I've managed to round up a washbasin and water, and there's even a cot with blankets for you to sleep on. Unfortunately, I don't have any women's clothing for you, or you could change out of that rag you're wearing." He opened the flap of the tent. "There's even a comb and brush with a mirror we've managed to find for you."

Serena turned and looked up into Anderson's badly sunburned face. He was fair skinned, and his long blond hair rested against the collar of his uniform.

"Please, Captain, we have to talk. Thank you for the tent, but it doesn't mean anything to me."

Anderson sighed and placed his hands on his hips. "Miss Rogan, I know you want to go back, but think, will you? You've been a prisoner for more than two years among those savages who stole you from—"

"I wasn't a prisoner!" Serena tried to steady her voice. "Oh, please, you don't understand, captain? I didn't want to have to tell you all the horrible, sordid details, but I wasn't a captive." She launched into the story of how she'd come to America in the first place, how Kingston had kept her a prisoner and then dumped her for dead along the river. She saw Anderson's face grow dark as she finished the story.

"Look," Anderson said, "it was Mr. Kingston who notified the fort that there was a white woman, you, who had been taken prisoner. According to him, you were his washerwoman, and you had gone to the river to wash clothes and were jumped by a bunch of Sioux warriors. He said he tried to get you back last winter, but that a medicine man by the name of Black Wolf came and recaptured you."

"My husband rescued me from that evil man," Serena hissed. "If it hadn't been for Wolf, I would have died. Kingston is lying to you! Can't you see that?"

Pushing the hat back on his head, Anderson moved uncomfortably. "Miss Rogan, I've got to tell you, Mr. Kingston is highly regarded by the commander of our fort. I was at that dinner when Mr. Kingston made an emotional and sincere plea to have you rescued."

"He's lying!" she cried.

"I don't know, ma'am."

"Then you think I'm lying?"

He shrugged and looked down at his dusty black boots. "Ma'am, I've been out here on the frontier for seven years. I've seen many women stolen by Injuns, and their behavior is just like yours. I guess what I'm trying to say is that if you live with those thievin' redskins long enough, you get so you believe you're a part of their life. But you aren't. You're a white woman. You deserve your freedom, and that's what we're going to give you."

"Then let me go right now," Serena quavered, "because if I'm as free as you say, Captain, I'm going to march right out of here, mount my horse and go back to my husband and daughter!''

Sadly, Anderson said, ''No, ma'am. The commander has given orders to have you sent back east on a military wagon train that's heading for reassignment in Ohio. If you have relatives, we'll gladly send them word that you're alive and well, and see to it that you get back to them.''

Bitterly, Serena glared up at the officer. ''I have no one in America, Captain. My family died in Ireland. I'm the only survivor.''

''Then, the commander has already made arrangements for you to be sent to a God-fearing Dutch family that has a farm along the Ohio River.''

''I don't want to go there!''

''You don't have a choice, Miss Rogan. We know from experience that it takes about two years to get a woman who's been held captive by Injuns to finally get comfortable staying with her own kind again. Frederick and Camille Gent have agreed to take you in and offer you employment so that you can get back on your feet.''

''I'll be a prisoner,'' Serena whispered hoarsely.

Anderson rubbed his jaw that needed to be shaved. ''Not if you voluntarily stay, ma'am. But if you try to escape, that's a different story.''

Fighting back tears, Serena looked out over the camp. The horses had been unsaddled and picketed along a rope strung between elm trees. At least fifteen tents had been pitched, and seventeen wagons had been filled with various military supplies. She wiped her tears away with the back of her hand and held Anderson's gaze.

''Doesn't it bother you that I've been torn from my baby? She's only five months old. She needs me! How can you do this? How can you rip a baby from its mother?''

"I have my orders," Anderson muttered.

"But my baby!"

"It's a half-breed," he snarled.

Shocked, Serena studied his hardened features. "That baby is *human!*" she shrieked, and launched herself at the officer, her fists pummeling his face, shoulders and chest.

Wolf stood tensely as Tall Crane and Little Swallow finished telling him of Cante Tinza's capture by the horse soldiers. He had gotten back at dusk, only to be surrounded by tearful relatives. Holding Wakinyela in his arms, he finally sat down in his sister's tepee. Dreaming Bear held Dawn Sky, both of them looking mournful.

Little Swallow served the evening meal to everyone in the tepee. Among them was Chief Badger Mouth.

"What will you do?" Badger Mouth demanded after they finished eating.

Wolf gave Wakinyela to Dreaming Bear, who would take her and Dawn Sky back to his tepee for the night to sleep. When the children had left, he grimly met the chief's narrowed eyes.

"I will find her and bring her home."

"Little Swallow doesn't know where the horse soldiers come from. There are many forts in the area."

He heard the warning in the chief's voice. Wolf unconsciously touched the braided-hair necklace around his neck. Fury warred with grief as he thought of Cante Tinza's capture. He knew she would fight to escape— there was no question. "I don't know where they are taking her," Wolf admitted in a low, unsteady voice, "but I will find out."

"You would leave our people without a medicine man?"

Wolf snapped a look at the old chief. His conscience railed him over the question. Wolf knew his duties were first and foremost to his people. Grimly, he said, "You are right—I should not leave—but my daughters need their mother. And I need my wife." He lifted his head and held Badger Mouth's accusing look. "If your wife were captured by the horse soldiers, would you not go after her? Would you not forsake your duties to do this?"

"It is not the same and you know that!" Badger Mouth raised his hand toward the top of the tepee. The firelight danced off his grizzled hair. "There are any number of capable warriors who could lead in my absence to go after my wife. There are no other medicine men."

"You have any number of women who know of herbs," Wolf said.

"I do not want you running after that *wasicun*," the chief said flatly.

Anger blinded Wolf and he rose to his feet. "*Wasicun?* Is that what you call my wife? The woman who saved the lives of many of our women and children?"

Badger Mouth held Wolf's glare. "Let her go. She is white. She belongs to the whites, not to us. Not to you."

Fury raged through Wolf but he tempered it. "I know you have never favored Cante Tinza's presence in our camp. You and several others. But that does not matter. She is my wife, and I will track her down and find her."

Badger Mouth spit into the fire. "And for how long will you do this? What if they have sent her far away?"

"Then I will do whatever I can to find her, no matter where they have taken her."

"She is lost to you!" the chief said in a thundering voice. "Release her!"

"Never!" Wolf turned on his heel and left the tepee, breathing hard. Overhead, the night sky was a blanket of stars. He halted and looked up at them. The pain in his chest was so great that it felt as if his heart were being torn from his body. The stars reminded him of the copper stars across Cante Tinza's cheeks and nose. Closing his eyes, he saw her face, and choked back a sob. He loved her with his life. Who had done this to them? Who?

As he walked back to his tepee in the darkness, Wolf sensed that Kingston had done this to him in revenge. Was Cante Tinza going to be taken back to Kingston's camp? It was the first place he would look. Right now, he had to prepare for a long, hard journey. There was much to do. If Kingston was behind her capture, Wolf knew that he would brutally beat her and probably kill her for what Wolf had done to him.

"Black Wolf! Wait! Wait!"

Wolf halted and turned. He saw Deer Woman running toward him.

"Where do you go in such a hurry?" she asked, stopping in front of him.

"I go to find my wife," he snapped. "Where else do you think?" Wolf strode on.

"Stop!" Deer Woman reached out and gripped his arm. "Why don't you let her go? She goes back to her own kind, Black Wolf. Didn't you realize that she would do this someday?"

He jerked his arm out of her grasp. "Are you *heyoka*, girl? Cante Tinza was taken against her will." His mouth turned down. "And according to Little Swallow, if you had not run like a coward when the horse soldiers were coming, she would be here with us this very night."

Startled, Deer Woman felt her mouth fall open. "Coward? You call me a coward?"

"I do," Wolf rasped. "Little Swallow said you should have stayed and unhobbled the other three horses before riding off. Instead, you abandoned the other women. My wife stayed behind to help Dreaming Bear. The woman is old, and she cannot run." He saw Deer Woman's face turn haughty, her chin rise, and her eyes blaze with anger. Wolf didn't care. It was time she learned what responsibility toward other tribal members meant.

"You ran," he said. "My wife and my sister did not run. They kept Dreaming Bear safe."

Angrily, Deer Woman rattled, "You are the *heyoka* one, Black Wolf! You fool yourself into thinking that this *wasicun really* loves you! Her skin is white! Ours is red! You were blinded by the color of her hair, her skin, that is all!"

Blindly, Wolf gripped her by the shoulders and gave her a shake. "Lies fall easily from your mouth, girl. Keep your lips sealed, for you do not know of what you speak. I love Cante Tinza with my *life*. I will give it, if necessary, to find her once again."

Wolf released Deer Woman, and she gave a cry and stepped away from him. "You go after her?" she screeched, her voice echoing through the darkened camp.

Breathing raggedly, Wolf stared at her. "Even now, you do not understand. You have blind eyes, girl. You always will." Wolf turned to leave, but he felt her fingers dig into his arm.

"You will never find her!" Deer Woman sobbed hysterically.

"I will or I will die in the effort," he snarled.

"No!" She gave him a sly smile. "I *know* you will not find her! I told Kingston last summer that the *wasicun* was here with us. *He* wanted her!"

Wolf stared at Deer Woman in shock. "You what?"

She released his arm and stepped away, smiling through her tears. "Yes, I went to him! Where did you think I had gone for a month, Black Wolf? I went to Kingston and told him." She wiped the tears from her eyes. "I love you! I have always loved you, and yet you only had eyes for that *wasicun!* Why can you not love me? I am a Lakota woman. Am I not pleasing to your eyes?"

Wolf held himself in tight control as he stared down into her shadowed features. He saw the wildness in Deer Woman's eyes, and heard the unsteadiness in her voice. She was babbling.

"Did you go to Kingston this time?" he asked in a dangerously low voice.

"No. I was praying to the Great Spirit that the *wasicun* would be taken away, and now she has been. Oh, Black Wolf, don't you see? This is the way it should be. You should marry your own kind—"

Gripping Deer Woman's arm, he jerked her to him. She gave a little cry as her hand came to rest against his chest. "You see this?" he snarled as he held up his wrist in front of her eyes. "Look at that knife scar, Deer Woman, and look at it well. I took a ceremonial vow when my wrist was cut and placed against Cante Tinza's wrist. Our blood mingled and joined. Only death can separate us, girl. Death!"

Deer Woman gave a little moan and tried to break out of his grip, but it was impossible. "She is nothing like us! Nothing!" she shrieked.

With a hiss, Wolf released her. "Nothing?" he demanded hoarsely. "Girl, you are as prejudiced as the *wasicuns!*" He held up his wrist. "You forget one thing. When our flesh is cut, no matter what our skin color, we all bleed red. *That* makes us connected, girl. Connected!" Whirling around, Wolf left her standing in the middle of the camp. He wanted to kill Deer Woman for what she'd done. It all made sense to Wolf now. Kingston had been behind this with her help.

As he entered his tepee, he saw that his children slept. Dreaming Bear had unbraided her hair and was combing it. She nodded to him, her eyes sad.

"You heard?" he asked tightly as he walked quickly over to the saddlebags.

"Yes. The girl has shamed herself in the eyes of all of us."

Wolf packed dried deer meat and pemmican. "I go after Cante Tinza. Will you care for our children until we return? Tall Crane has already promised that he will live here with them and be a father to them."

Placing the elk comb in her lap, Dreaming Bear gave another nod. "You are like a grandson to me, Black Wolf. I will pray daily for your safe return with Cante Tinza."

"I don't know where they've taken her," he muttered. "Perhaps to Kingston's camp. I will look there first."

"This could take a long time."

"Yes." He glanced up at the old woman's heavily lined face and sad expression. "I do not have a choice. And I do not want one."

"Your children will be safe with Tall Crane and me. We are their blood relatives by ceremony. We will love them as you and your wife love them."

Grateful, Wolf went over to his two sleeping children. Getting down on his knees, he gazed at Wakinyela, who slept in the cradleboard fashioned by Cante Tinza's hands. Barely touching his daughter's silky black hair, Wolf pressed a kiss to her tiny brow. Next, he went to Dawn Sky, who lay atop her robe, sleeping soundly.

He touched Dawn Sky's smooth hair. "If we do not return," he said softly, "tell them of our love for them, Dreaming Bear. Do not let them forget their mother, for she saved Dawn Sky's life that day by nearly giving her own."

"I won't, my grandson. Go now, and may the Great Spirit guide your heart to her."

Wolf got to his feet, saddlebags in hand. Kagi followed, wagging her tail. "I will take Cante Tinza's wolf with me. She may pick up her scent when I cannot."

With a slight nod, Dreaming Bear offered, "Kagi sees into the invisible worlds. She will be your guide, and she will warn you when enemies are near."

Wolf took one more look at his sleeping children and felt a lump form in his throat. How must Cante Tinza feel this night? He knew deep in his heart that she must be crying herself to sleep with loneliness, fear and uncertainty. Without a word, he turned away and slipped out of the tepee. His vision was blinded by falling tears as he headed in the general direction of the horse herd, which was guarded by Lakota warriors. The wolf trotted alertly at his side.

"Now, you're not goin' anywhere, little lady," Sergeant Blake admonished. He placed the ropes around Serena's wrists and then guided her to the covered wagon. "I've lost enough sleep over you tryin' to escape the past two days. And I ain't gonna have the captain chewin' my ears off about it. Today, you ride in the back of this here wagon. Now, up you go.''

Serena moved into the wagon filled with horse blankets and bullhide-covered saddles. Sergeant Blake chewed on a wad of tobacco, which made the side of his cheek stick out like a chipmunk's hiding nuts. He tied the rope to the side of the wagon.

''Now, if ya wanna tend to womanly things, you jest let me know. There's water nearby. All ya gotta do is ask fer it. We'll be stoppin' about noon and I'll bring ya a plate of beans and biscuits.''

Sitting down, Serena watched the sergeant clamber out of the wagon and walk away. This was the third day of her captivity, and they were moving farther and farther south across the plains, leaving the Paha Sapa far behind. Every jolt of the wagon reminded her that her daughter needed her milk. Exhausted, Serena drew up her knees and rested her head against them.

According to the captain, they would be arriving at a fort by evening. Serena had tried each night to escape, only to be caught and brought back to camp. The ropes on her wrists were rough, chafing her skin. What would they do with her at the fort? According to Captain Anderson, she would be taken care of by the officers' wives. The next morning, she would be leaving on another military wagon train bound for Ohio.

Her tears were endless. They sprang to her eyes each time she thought of her baby daughter. Her heart felt ripped apart when she thought of Wolf. She loved her family fiercely, and her anger over her return to white civilization made her want to escape even more. Who did these people think they were? She was a prisoner now as never before. Once Anderson had almost let her go. She had almost persuaded him because of her baby daughter, but in the end, his prejudice toward Indians won out. Didn't white men have *any* heart, any feelings for humans—no matter what their color? Serena was convinced they were all monsters. She hated them for what they were doing to her.

"Welcome, Miss Rogan. I'm Adelaide Comstock, the commander's wife."

Serena stared out of the wagon at a woman in her thirties dressed in a fine cotton dress. Her hair was braided and rolled into a bun on top of her hand. She held a parasol that matched the dark blue of her dress. She smiled up at Serena. Beside her was a younger woman, who stared at Serena with an open mouth.

"Come, come. I want you to get a bath. Some of the ladies of the post have donated some clothes for you. I'm sure something will fit. Come down out of there, now."

Serena moved slowly—her wrists still bound. Sergeant Blake stood nearby.

"Now, Mrs. Comstock, she's wantin' to escape," the sergeant warned.

Adelaide looked Serena Rogan up and down. She was positively filthy in the hide dress, and her braided hair needed not only to be washed, but combed. When she saw the dark stains across the top of Serena's dress, Adelaide frowned. What on earth had caused that? she wondered. Not wanting to touch the woman, she stepped back.

"Escort Miss Rogan into the bath quarters, Sergeant. Have two of the negress laundry women bathe and dress her. Then, have her brought over to our quarters for tea."

"Yes, ma'am!" Blake gripped Serena by the arm and led her across the flat, hard-packed earth inside the fort.

Adelaide turned to Rebecca Standing, one of the lieutenants' wives. "Filthy, isn't she?"

"Lord above, Mrs. Comstock, she looks wild and angry."

"And did you see the hide dress across her bosom? I wonder why it's so wet looking."

With a tremble, Rebecca, who carried a parasol in her gloved hands, said, "Surely the good captain will fill us in."

"Of course," Adelaide said as she swept off the wooden porch and picked up her skirt. She spotted the blond-haired officer in the livery area.

"Captain Anderson?" she called gaily.

Anderson turned. He tipped his hat. "Mrs. Comstock, Mrs. Standing."

Adelaide moved into the shade, not wanting her skin to burn or tan. "Captain, tell me about Miss Rogan. She looks very unhappy—and dirty."

"Well," he said, "she doesn't want to be here, ma'am. She tried to escape several times."

"My, my. Doesn't she realize she's very fortunate to be among us?"

"I don't think so, ma'am."

"Er, Captain, what are those stains across the woman's bosom?"

Flushing, Anderson avoided their inquiring gazes. "Uh...well, apparently Miss Rogan had a baby five months ago by one of those heathen savages."

"Oh, dear," Adelaide whispered. "Of all things. How terrible!"

"She's a soiled woman," Rebecca whispered. "Imagine, being forced to have a baby by one of those filthy redskins."

Adelaide frowned. "Whether she knows it or not, she's well rid of the brat. It's nothing but a half-breed. Miss Rogan would be scorned by good townspeople if she had come back with the baby. It's just as well she left it behind."

"I don't think she feels that way," Anderson warned them diplomatically. "Miss Rogan swears that she chose to live with the redskins. The man who told us about her, Mr. Kingston, had a different story."

"Well," Adelaide said dramatically, "everyone in these parts knows Blackjack Kingston. He's a man of honor. His word is good enough for me."

Rebecca shook her head. "Miss Rogan is soiled goods. What man would ever want her for a wife? She's been living with a heathen redskin and had his brat."

"If she's smart," Adelaide said, "she'll keep that ugly little secret to herself."

"I'm just glad she's not staying here," Rebecca said as she opened her parasol and stepped into the hot sunlight. "Why, she's a fallen woman, Mrs. Comstock. All the soldiers would do is follow her around."

With a laugh, Adelaide agreed. "Miss Rogan is only staying overnight. We'll treat her with courtesy by having a tea party in her honor. I'm sure she'll appreciate tea after the past three days of traveling. Come, I want to make sure Millie has everything set up properly."

Chapter Fourteen

"Miss Serena Rogan, I want you to meet the God-fearing people who have so kindly volunteered to take you in for the next year," Major John Hale said frankly. Hale had met the military wagon train at the Ohio border three weeks ago. He stood gripping Serena's arm as two farm people approached. "I'd like you to meet Frederick and Camille Gent. They are known in these parts for their generosity toward others."

Serena stood apprehensively as the Gents came forward to meet her. Her hands were tightly knotted in the skirt of her yellow calico dress. The shoes on her feet hurt; in fact, she had refused to wear them throughout the trip except for now.

Her gaze moved to the short thickset man, who had a graying beard and small, close-set blue eyes. Gent must be in his forties, Serena guessed. He carried a pitchfork in his wide, thick, callused hands. He wore a black hat with a brim, a dark blue shirt with the sleeves rolled up on his hairy arms, and black trousers held up by suspenders. Behind him, wearing a dark green cotton dress, was Camille, who stood with her head bowed. She was thin faced, nervous looking, and appeared to be much younger than he—perhaps in her early twenties. Serena's senses shouted in alarm, and she took a step back against Hale.

Gent's face was round, his flesh sunburned, his cheeks blazing bright red. There was something about the man that frightened Serena, and she felt panic deep within her. When would her nightmare existence cease? On the wagon train, she had had to be guarded twenty-four hours a day because many of the soldiers thought she was nothing more than a soiled dove after word leaked out that she had lived with the Sioux and had a baby by one of them. The men either hated her and spurned her with noxious glances, or felt she was bedding material and had no respect for her at all. The three-month battle to save herself from being raped once again had finally ended. Or had it?

Gent shook hands with the major and then looked down at Serena. "Welcome to our humble Ohio farm, Miss Rogan." He turned and waited until his small, short wife drew abreast of him. "This is my wife, Mrs. Gent."

Serena nodded warily to the couple. Gent's face didn't change. Camille smiled slightly and did a bob curtsy.

Serena wondered if the chains that bound her feet would finally be taken off. The army had tired of her escape attempts and had treated her like a prisoner, placing chains around her ankles to prevent her from slipping away.

"I must warn you," Hale told them severely, "that Miss Rogan does not want to remain in the civilized world. She'd rather go back to those savages."

"Because my baby is back there!" Serena flared at the officer.

Camille gasped; her hands flew to her mouth, and her eyes were wide with shock.

Serena jerked her head in the woman's direction. She saw the censure in her eyes, just as she'd seen it in those of everyone who knew she'd had a baby by an Indian.

"God help you," Gent murmured apologetically, and he shook his shaggy head.

"And I don't believe in your God, either!" Serena added in a whisper. "I was taught unselfishness, caring and generosity by the Lakota people. All I've gotten since my recapture is chains and guards and people looking down upon me as if I'm some sort of monster because I had a child by the man I love. A man who is *still* my husband!"

Major Hale nudged Serena forward. "She's all yours, Mr. Gent. I would strongly advise you keep her in chains until you're *very* sure she doesn't want to go back to those savages. She's like a lot of the women we've gotten back from them—they take the good Lord's name in vain and spurn the white society. You're going to have your hands full, I warn you."

Gent slid a glance up and down Serena. There was disgust mirrored in his features. "I can assure you, Major, that Miss Rogan will learn once again that our Lord is her savior. Nightly reading of the Bible will teach her that."

Serena glared at the farmer. "I can't read, and if I did, I would refuse to read your Bible!"

"God help us," Camille whispered in a frightened voice.

Hale cleared his throat. "In the months she has been with us, she has been very angry and upset, Mr. Gent. Miss Rogan will say just about anything to make us let her go."

Gent nodded. "I understand, Major. In the Netherlands we didn't spare the rod to spoil the child. I think what Miss Rogan needs is a strong, guiding hand to bring her back to the ways of our Lord and to her people.''

Hale tipped his hat in Camille's direction. "We must continue our journey eastward, so if you'll excuse me?'' Hale handed Frederick an envelope. "And here is the promised money for keeping Miss Rogan until she understands that she's a white woman, not an Indian.''

With a gasp, Serena eyed the envelope passing between their hands. "Whose money is that?'' she demanded.

"From your benefactor, Mr. Kingston," Hale replied.

"What?"

"Of course. Didn't they tell you? He had gone to the nearest fort and given a reward of one thousand dollars for your return to us. The man is incredibly generous. He said he did it out of a guilty conscience because he'd brought you from Ireland to be his washerwoman. Of course, after you were captured—"

"I wasn't captured!" Serena cried and stamped her foot. "You know that!"

Hale drew himself up, giving her a bored look. He glanced over at the Gents, apology in his tone. "Miss Rogan claims Mr. Kingston raped her and beat her. Then he threw her out into the wilds to die. Of course, the money you hold, Mr. Gent, is Mr. Kingston's generous reward for Miss Rogan's return to us. I don't see how Miss Rogan could be telling the truth. Mr. Kingston is a fine, upstanding citizen in the Dakota Territory."

Gent fingered the envelope with a slight smile. "She's gotten away from the Lord, Major. Don't worry. In a year's time, Miss Rogan will have come back to us. I won't disappoint Mr. Kingston." He waved the envelope in the air. Then, glancing over at Serena, he said, "Come with us, girl. And no more back talk. I won't put up with it from my wife, and I certainly won't put up with it from you."

Serena glared at the short, thickly muscular farmer. "Get these chains off me."

Gent smiled as he watched the officer move back to the wagon and mount his horse. "Not until you can prove to me that you won't run away." He pointed somberly at the envelope in his hand. "A fine, respected man paid good money to see you come back to us. By the Lord's will, I'll carry out Mr. Kingston's wishes. Camille?"

She hurried over to her husband. "Yes, dear?"

"Go down to the barn. Fix a place in the first stall, the brood mare's stall. Put fresh straw in there."

Camille gave her husband a startled look. She knew better than to ask why, for he was a man with a short temper. Long ago, he'd taught her not to ask such silly questions.

"Of course, dear," she said, and she hurried down the slight incline toward their cabin, which was surrounded with fields of corn, wheat and grass.

Gent grinned a little as he gestured for Serena to move ahead of him. "So, you like being a savage, do you? Well, you shouldn't mind staying out in the barn, then, with all the animals. The Injuns I've seen are a drunken lot, caught up in the devil's ways by drinking firewater."

Serena moved ahead, awkward in the leather shoes on her feet, the chains forcing her to take small, mincing steps. She hated the shoes, and swore to get rid of them as soon as she could.

Looking around as the sun hovered on the horizon, Serena studied her new prison. Gent's farm wasn't big, but it had a few milk cows, six workhorses and a pen of chickens. The house sat in the middle of a large cleared area. The September air was filled with the fragrance that came with the change of seasons, and Serena inhaled the scents deeply into her lungs. As it did so often, her mind revolved back to her tribe, to Wolf. The camp would be moving back toward the Dried Willow constellation at this time, preparing once again for the coming winter.

As she walked down the incline toward the cabin, which had a porch, she saw chickens industriously scratching into the rich black soil of the yard, hunting for insects. There were several sheep in another pen, whose wool was used to make clothes. The place was clean and neat; there were no broken windows, and no doors hung at awkward angles from leather straps. Serena saw that the barn was a fairly large one-story structure made of boards that had weathered gray from many harsh winters.

"Now," Gent told her as she walked a few steps ahead of him, "we'll treat you like you want to be treated. If you act like a savage, I will beat it out of you with my belt. If you act like a lady," he added with disgust, "which I doubt you will, then you will be treated as such. My father raised me with discipline and sternness. It makes no difference if you're a woman or not. If you don't do as I order, you will be punished."

His threats made her skin crawl, and Serena clamped her mouth shut. As they entered the gloomy interior of the barn, she saw Camille standing expectantly at the door to what would be Serena's stall. She could smell the new-mown hay drying above the stalls.

"It's ready, dear."

"Good." Gent grunted. "Go get her another dress. You're about the same size. This one she's wearing stinks. She needs a bath." He picked up one of Serena's braids.

She jerked away from him, nearly falling over the chains.

"From now on," Gent growled, "you wear your hair in a style becoming a lady, not a squaw."

"I will wear my hair the way I want!" Serena whispered angrily. "You cannot *make* me change my hair!"

With a slight smile, Gent shrugged. "Have it your way. When I come out here tomorrow morning to show you your duties, your hair had better be looking like my wife's or you'll get your first beating with my leather strap." He touched the thick belt around his waist and tapped it with his fingers as if it were a good friend. "It's your choice."

"You're no different from any other white," Serena spit, backing away until she could go no farther, the stall wall halting her retreat. "All you know are threats and violence! My husband is a medicine man, the most gentle person I know. He *never* laid a hand on me, *never* threatened me. You don't respect women," she rattled, her voice dangerously off-key, "you use violence to keep us in line. Is it any wonder I want to go home? My home isn't with you! It never will be!"

Serena's voice echoed eerily through the barn. She saw Gent's face grow flushed, and saw him tense. He curled his large, stubby fingers into fists at his sides.

"I don't take back talk from any woman," he shouted, and he grabbed her by the arm and shoved her roughly.

Serena fell into the fresh straw that had been spread on the hard dirt floor. She saw Gent's bulblike nose grow bright red, its blood vessels looking like blue spiderwebs across the surface of his skin as he charged toward her like a crazed bull. She muffled a cry when she saw him unbuckling his belt as he approached. She tried to protect herself from his unexpected attack by curling up into a tight ball and placing her arms over her head.

As the strap struck her across the arms, back and legs, Serena bit down hard on her lower lip, tasting blood. She refused to cry out, to beg for mercy. Pain stung her flesh, radiating outward. He was hitting her as hard as he could, and she cringed with each snap of the leather belt biting into her tender flesh. Anger warred with pain. Tears squeezed from beneath her tightly shut eyes. She endured—as she had endured under Kingston's hand. Finally, Gent moved away, his breathing ragged.

"When my wife returns," he rasped as he slid the belt back through the loops of his trousers, "you will strip down, you will wash and you will unbraid that hair of yours. You will look like a white woman or else."

"You've *got* to follow my husband's orders!" Camille begged urgently as she stood just inside the stall, her voice in a whisper. "It's been a month, Serena, and you just can't go on taking these beatings. Give up!"

Serena looked at the woman, who was a timid mouse in her husband's shadow. Her eyes softened. "Please, let me go, Cammy. You *know* I belong back with my people, my husband. I know you're childless, but you're a woman. You must know how much I miss my baby." She stood there with her hands outstretched, the end of the six-foot length of chain still bolted to the stall wall. "You have the key. You could unlock these chains and let me go."

With a shudder, Cammy shook her head. "Oh, no, Serena. Please, don't ask me that! You know Frederick would beat me within an inch of my life if I helped you escape." She twisted her hands and said, "Give up. Stop braiding your hair. Try to learn to read the Bible. When I married Frederick, he was a kind man, but when we came to America he changed. He became so worried about us making it here that he started losing his temper all the time. At first I tried to fight back, like you, but Lord help me, it only made it worse.''

Ashamed, Camille wrung her hands and looked down at her feet. "The worst of it was that I finally got pregnant. We were so happy. I'd been afraid I was barren, and he wanted at least eight children. A drunk Indian came by one day, and he chased me around the farm. I was screaming and yelling for help, but Frederick was in town getting our monthly supplies. The Indian finally left, disappeared into the woods. I started bleeding shortly after that.''

Touching her wrinkled brow, Camille whispered in a painful tone, "I lost my baby, Serena. Frederick came home that night and found me passed out on the floor, bleeding. The doc came out two days later and told us I'd lost the baby. Frederick has hated Injuns ever since.'' She touched her flat stomach with her work-worn hand. "He hasn't hit me since, but he's got all this rage bottled up inside himself. I know he's grieving, and he blames Injuns for what happened.''

Serena stared openmouthed at the nervous woman. Cammy's hands were never still, and she was so thin that it was pitiful. "I'm so sorry you lost your child. How awful it must be for you, Cammy. I—I didn't know.''

"That's why you got to do as Frederick orders. He sees those braids of yours and he remembers what happened—how I lost my baby. You just can't defy him. I'm afraid he's going to kill you, and you don't deserve that. You must bow to him. Men are stronger and smarter than we are. It's our place to be their servants. God has ordained it so.''

Serena couldn't even be angry with Cammy, who lived in abject fear of her overbearing husband. "I understand," she quavered, "better than you know." She knew that neither of the Gents believed that Kingston was the villain he was. Serena stood there on her bare, callused feet, her blue gingham dress too thin for the chilly October nights she spent in the barn. Darkness was falling, and she knew Cammy had to get back to the cabin or else Frederick would roar her name from the porch.

"Please, stop braiding your hair!" Cammy pleaded. "He beats you every morning. You can't keep defying him."

Serena hung her head. Braiding her hair was the only act of freedom she had left. In every other way, Gent kept her a prisoner.

"And start learning to read the Bible! If you'd just do those two things, he'd let you stay inside the house at night. It's warmer there. I don't want you to freeze to death out here. Winter's coming on. You've got to save yourself!"

With a shake of her head, Serena held Cammy's frightened stare. "You don't understand," she told her wearily. "My husband's people are a humble people. They understand the importance of helping one another, working together and using love, not violence, to get people to do things."

"But you can't keep living in a dreamworld. You aren't going back." Cammy pointed to Serena's chains. "Do you want to wear those forever?"

"Kingston paid your husband enough money for a year. After that, he has to let me go. Why would he continue to feed me or keep me after that?"

With a moan, Cammy looked around, afraid that her husband might unexpectedly come out and overhear their conversation. "Frederick will keep you until you surrender! If it takes five years, he'll do it. He's a stubborn man and his word is his bond. If Mr. Kingston gave him that money to straighten you out, he'll do it until his last breath.''

Serena stared in shock at the woman. "What are you saying?"

"Frederick will decide when or if you ever leave us."

"Then I'm nothing more than a slave," Serena rattled. The drenching reality washed through her, chilling her. She wrapped her arms around herself.

"At least you have a roof over your head and something to eat. It's better than those niggers down south have."

"You and I are both slaves," Serena told her fervently. "Slaves to Frederick. White men look at white women as beasts of burden, that's all. They take their pleasure with us when it pleases them, and then they throw us aside when they don't want us."

"Lord, don't speak that way! If Frederick hears you saying such things, he'll beat you to death!"

Defiantly, Serena rasped, "I'd rather die than stay here under his hand."

With a little moan, Cammy left the stall and shut the door. She ran down the aisle, her skirt rustling as she left.

Serena sat with her head bowed. She touched the braided black and red hair that still remained around her throat. When Camille had started to cut it off, Serena had pushed her away. No one was going to take the necklace Wolf had made from their hair. No one.

Tears stung Serena's eyes. The past month had been a different kind of hell. Wolf would never be able to find her. He would be in terrible danger if he tried to leave his tribe's territory. He could be killed either by whites, who were jumpy and nervous about Indians, or by another tribe's warriors. Serena knew that this time Wolf would not come after her. He would choose to stay with his people, to raise their two children. It was up to her to escape—to make her way back to him and their daughters.

Heart aching with loneliness for her family, Serena lay down and brought the thin wool blanket over her shoulders. The October nights were cold, and sometimes she awoke near dawn, shivering. How she missed her daughters and Wolf! Her dreams at night replayed her happy years with the Lakota, especially the birth of Wakinyela and the tenderness of Wolf as he cared for her in the cave afterward. Wolf's words and ideas were carried forever in her heart.

As she lay there with her knees drawn up toward her body, Serena's mind gyrated. Frederick Gent seemed to have a sixth sense about her desire to escape. During the day, no matter if she was on the porch churning butter, in the barn milking the cows or in the kitchen helping Cammy make bread, he purposely kept the end of her chain bolted to a nearby wall.

Without a doubt, Frederick Gent considered Serena the devil's own spawn. He forced Cammy to come out and read to her from the Bible each night after the day's work had been done. Serena knew that Gent hated her defiance. Little by little, he was wearing her down. The Dutchman was rigid, opinionated and unyielding. He came out to the barn each morning to see if she had unbraided her hair. If her hair was braided, he beat her with his belt.

Serena felt sorry for Cammy, who was a child compared to Frederick. He had married her when she was fifteen years old in the Netherlands. He had brought her to America five years ago and they had worked side by side to create their farm out of the thick Ohio woodlands. Cammy had looked grief-stricken as she shared the loss of her baby with her. Serena's heart ached for her, for she understood what loss of a child did to a person.

Some mornings when Cammy came out with hot porridge and a thick slice of bread, Serena knew the woman had been cruelly raped by her husband. Cammy's dark brown eyes would show the animal fright, and her hands would be shaking nervously. The bond they shared, Serena thought, was one of misery at the hands of a white man.

"So, you think you can talk my wife into letting you escape?"

Serena heard Gent's thunderous voice. She was barely awake, and the man's tone was hard and angry against her ears. Lifting her lashes, she realized with a start that Frederick was leaning over her, his face red with fury. Her eyes flew open as he forced her on her back and closed his fingers around her throat. In his other hand he held a knife.

With a snarl, Gent straddled Serena. His weight was suffocating as his fingers dug into the sides of her neck to hold her still. Serena struggled to fight him off. She saw him put down the knife and ball his fist. The side of her head exploded with pain and light.

"You evil woman," he breathed raggedly, grabbing the knife. "You frightened my wife, you threatened her, and now I'm going to make *sure* you start bending to my will."

Groggily, Serena opened her eyes as far as the swollen lids would allow. She lay limply beneath him, and she felt one of her braids being lifted. The smile on Gent's face showed his glee as he took the knife and began to saw through her hair at the top of the braid. Trying to lift her hand, and unable to do so, Serena made a mewling sound.

"Nooo..."

"It's time you gave up your savagery," he snarled, and cut the second braid away from the side of her head. "And this is going, too," he said as he placed the knife against her throat and cut through the hair necklace. "No more defiance, girl. You think you're a slave? Well, I'll show you slavery." He got off her and put the knife into a sheath on his belt. "Get up!" he roared.

Dazed, Serena weakly struggled to obey his order. The pain in her head was excruciating. She heard Gent roaring at her like a wounded bull, his voice buffeting her ears. Blood flowed from her nose and mouth. She saw him lean down. His hand was like a hurtful talon against her arm as he hauled her upright. If he hadn't pushed her against the side of the stall, Serena would have crumpled. Gent took the key and unlocked the chain from the wall.

"Get going!" he snarled, and pushed her toward the open stall door.

Serena tripped and fell to her hands and knees. Gent snarled her name and raised his booted foot to kick at her. Serena wasn't able to move fast enough to dodge the coming blow to her ribs. The wind was knocked out of her as she slammed against the hard-packed floor of the aisle.

"Get up or I'll kick you all the way to the cabin!" he roared.

In pain, Serena slowly got to her hands and knees. Through her tears of agony, she saw Cammy standing at the entrance to the barn, her hands pressed against her mouth, her eyes wide with terror. Serena stood with her feet wide apart to keep from falling once again. As she hobbled toward the entrance, she saw Cammy's stricken features more closely. Both her eyes were blackened, and the side of her face was swollen. Serena realized that Cammy had shared their conversation from the night before with Frederick, but she couldn't be angry with the woman. She was nothing but a frightened shadow of herself.

Once they were in the cabin, Frederick made Serena go to a windowless room. He shoved her into the small, cramped place. There were several blankets on the floor and a Bible. Serena turned, expecting him to strike her again.

"Now, you're staying in here," Gent told her, his eyes narrowing. "In the dark, where you belong. Every evening my wife will come in and teach you to read the Bible. You will get down on your knees and pray with her for forgiveness from the Lord for your unclean thoughts. If you don't do it, I'll beat you within an inch of your life until you surrender your soul to the Lord. I'm tired of you defying me. I'm the man of this house. I don't want to hear any more about the Injuns. You aren't going back—ever. You either surrender or you will remain here for as long as it takes to break your spirit and embrace the Lord as your God." He shook his finger at her, sputtering. "No more talk about the Great Spirit! This is the devil in disguise! I will not allow you to sully my wife's mind. Understand?"

The door was slammed shut, and Serena was left in complete darkness. Tears formed and fell as she realized that all her hair had been cut off. But worse, she realized as she frantically felt around her neck for the hair necklace—it was gone, too. Anguish fused with anger and then terror. Serena ached physically, but the blow to her spirit, to her hope of ever getting away from Gent, was far worse. Despair settled around her like a suffocating cloak.

As Serena lay sobbing quietly, rolled up into a ball, she felt her hope shatter. She had fought through five months, never giving up hope. Now her braids had been destroyed, and so had the necklace Wolf had made with his own hands. Serena retreated deep within herself, deep into the memories of her days with the Lakota. They had respected her, loved her and treated like a human being, not like some animal to be whipped and beaten.

The darkness that surrounded her began to invade her heart and mind. She felt broken beneath the weight of Gent's power over her. Her last physical reminders of her life with Wolf were gone, destroyed. Her hair was so short that it would take a year before it touched her shoulders once again. The darkness of reality began to flow through her as never before. For so long, Serena had told herself that someday she would be able to escape. She knew Wolf would never come after her because the distance was too great. And besides that, it would be impossible for him to find her.

Tears trickled hotly down Serena's cheeks as she lay on the cold floor, sobbing. She tried to grasp on to straws of hope, but there were none left to grasp. Her baby daughter would never see her again, never have memory of her or of the love she held for her. Dawn Sky would remember her. Would she cry because she was lost to them? And then there was Wolf. Moaning, Serena cried harder. Wolf would remember her always, just as she would *never* forget him. Gent might be able to break her spirit, but he could never reach inside her heart and destroy the love she held for Wolf—not ever.

Chapter Fifteen

"Girl, get that milking done," Frederick ordered.

Serena winced inwardly as Gent moved by her carrying two pails of milk. The mid-June warmth, fragrant with the scent of growing grass and flowers, blew through the aisle of the barn.

As Serena sat milking, Cammy came by to retrieve the pail from her. "Hurry," she whispered urgently, "Frederick wants us to get that butter churned. He's leaving for town tomorrow and wants to sell it there."

With almost mechanical movements, Serena removed the pail and placed an empty one beneath the cow. She handed the pail filled with milk to Cammy, who scurried away with a tight, nervous smile.

The fragrance of the grass stirred Serena's senses as she methodically began the milking once again. Why did it all smell so wonderful? Her mind sluggishly began to look back over the past nine months she had spent with the Gents. In October, Frederick had placed her in the dark, windowless room. She had remained there for five months. Her only reprieve was Cammy coming in nightly to teach her to read from the Bible.

The beatings stopped because her hair, now barely midway down her neck, could no longer be braided. Serena's hands trembled as she milked the patient cow. Lately, her dreams, vivid and colorful, had returned. When Frederick kept her locked up in the room, deprived of light and exercise, she had stopped dreaming. It was as if her entire world had shattered and dissolved. She was left with such a vast feeling of numbness and emptiness that she could do little more than functional things such as get up, complete her toilet, take a sponge bath from a basin of water once a week and look forward to Cammy's nightly company.

The unspoken fear of Frederick coming into the room with his belt was always there, so Cammy had refused to talk to her about anything other than reading. When winter came she had nearly frozen to death in the unheated room. She would sit bundled in blankets, listening to her teeth chatter, sitting with her arms wrapped around her knees, feeling empty and lost.

Patting the cow affectionately, Serena stood up. She wore ill-fitting shoes that pinched her feet because Frederick had ordered her to dress like a lady once he was satisfied her spirit was broken. No longer did she wear the chains.

Placing the pail aside, Serena untied the cow and led her out of the barn. Serena lifted her face to absorb that wonderful sensation of sunlight bathing her body. She released the cow into the pasture, locked the gate and then stood with her hands resting on the weathered boards. All around her, life abounded with such dazzling color, fragrance and drama that Serena closed her eyes and hungrily allowed it to embrace her.

A sadness moved through her, and memories of the past, of Wolf and her baby daughter, touched her hibernating heart. It was one of the few times Serena had remembered them since her release from the dark room in the cabin. Her hands tightened on the wood; if Frederick caught her daydreaming like this, he'd put her back into that room as he had before, as punishment.

What was it about today? Serena opened her eyes and scanned the wooded horizon that embraced the farm. To the west, she saw huge white clouds billowing upward, indicating that a powerful thunderstorm would surely strike the farm within the next hour. The wind moved hotly across Serena's skirt, shifting the material against her legs.

Serena stood there mesmerized. From some hidden, forgotten corner of her mind and heart, she recalled the first storm she'd weathered with Wolf. The scene came back vividly, gripping her, as if it were more real than where she was now, standing at the gate to the cow pasture.

She had been out with Wolf in the late afternoon, collecting herbs in a flower-laden meadow in the Paha Sapa. He had come over to her, touched her shoulder and told her to look up at Father Sky. Serena had straightened, aware of Wolf's powerful presence at her side. He was smiling, and his dark eyes were dancing with delight as he pointed to the approaching storm.

He placed his hand on her shoulder again, his voice flowing through her as he told her about the mighty thunder beings—invisible spirit helpers to Father Sky, giants that trod the vastness above Mother Earth. The thunder beings would gather the many cloud spirits, then shape and combine them into a massive thunderstorm. They would then walk and guide these storms across Father Sky, hurling down bolts of lightning onto Mother Earth.

Wolf had leaned close, his lips near her ear as he told her that Father Sky loved Mother Earth, that the rain and lightning were his way of making love to her, showing to her his reverence. The lightning fed Mother Earth, and the rain quenched her thirst. When the storm broke, and the lightning forks danced around them, Wolf had pulled Serena into the safety of a small, nearby cave. He had placed her between his legs with her back to him. They had watched the rain fall furiously, soaked up quickly by Mother Earth. Serena had leaned against his damp body, feeling his heat, feeling his love for her. She remembered Wolf's head against her own, his mouth pressing small kisses against the damp hair at her temple, his hands caressing her arms.

With a little cry, the emotions from that lost memory deluged Serena and made her slowly sink to the earth. She pressed her hand against her eyes, not only seeing that memory, but feeling it. For the past seven months, she'd felt nothing. Nothing!

The thunder rumbled, and Serena lifted her chin and opened her eyes. Tears rolled down her cheeks as she watched the storm move with frightening speed toward the farm. The memories were flooding back from somewhere deep within her, like a caldron boiling over. She did not think of finding shelter. She could only remain kneeling on the rich, warm earth, her hand on the gate, staring up at the storm in awe. Serena saw several bolts of lightning fork downward, striking the woods. She felt the thunder vibrate through her, paying homage to what was occurring within her.

With a shaking hand, Serena barely touched her breast. Her heart was beating frantically, as if it knew something she was only beginning to become aware of. Overwhelmed by the memories of her years spent with Wolf and the Lakota, Serena could do nothing but feel, sob, and remain crouched on the ground in the path of the storm. The wind began to pick up, whipping around her, ruffling the short, shorn hair that hung lifelessly around her face.

When had she forgotten her life with Wolf? *When?* The word caromed through her, in the same way the thunder rolled and growled across the sky. The sun was blotted out by the approaching clouds, and Serena realized with a gasp that after all those moments spent in darkness she had almost ceased to exist. Now her breathing became ragged as she felt the first stirrings of anger—of outrage—at what Frederick had done to her. Her hand tightened around the wood of the gate and she felt slivers press into her flesh.

Staring wildly up at the dark, roiling mass of clouds now covering more than half of Father Sky, Serena realized that Frederick had kept her a prisoner in many ways. He had brainwashed her. The wind was cooler, and was slapping against her in gusts now. So many memories of her love for Wolf came back, a trickle at first, but now a rushing river moving through her. How could she have forgotten him? And Wakinyela! Her daughter! The baby created out of their love for each other. Her hands pressed hard against her breast, Serena bowed her head, sobbing in earnest.

Her senses were coming alive once more. She smelled the fragrance of rain in the air as it caressed Mother Earth. A new strength flowed through Serena, and she shakily got to her feet. Her skirt was plastered against her body as she stood in the face of the storm. Slowly lifting her hands skyward, she remembered Wolf telling her that those who possessed thunder-being medicine could feel the tingling in their fingertips as they reached toward the sky.

The rain began. At first, there were large plops exploding against the dry, parched earth. Then smaller drops, but more rapid, soaking into her hair and the dress she was wearing. The rain was cooling against her face as she lifted it to the sky, reminding her that life goes on, that it is a never-ending cycle. Standing within the fury of the storm, drenched to the skin, Serena allowed the cleansing rain to further heal her.

For half an hour, Serena stood there as the world around her darkened, the lightning danced close to the farm, and the thunder split and rolled through the dark, angry halls of clouds. Wolf had thunder-being medicine. Serena knew that with her heart and soul. Once she had seen him give a rain ceremony. He had lifted the pipe he carried to Father Sky, chanting and singing. An hour later, she watched in amazement as the thunder beings approached with a storm that brought badly needed water to the tribe.

The storm was her friend, Serena realized humbly. It was a symbol of her reawakening, of her coming out of the depths of hopeless despair. She had been cruelly subjugated, just like an animal, into living and thinking a certain way—Frederick Gent's way. The water trickled down across her face, and her lips formed a soft smile. She was alive! Alive!

As she turned and looked toward the cabin, Serena understood that she was not only alive, but free. Free to decide what to do with her life. Gent could not keep her any longer, she realized with a feeling of euphoria. She could go home...home to Wolf, to the Lakota people, where she belonged. Serena didn't want to remain in a white world where men treated women like animals. Her husband and her children were in the Dakota Territory, and, Great Spirit willing, she would return there.

Serena moved at last back into the barn, unaware that her clothes were wet and clinging to her body. Her steps grew hurried as she crossed the muddy barnyard to the porch of the cabin. It was as if her mind had escaped a huge, dark trap from the past nine months of her life, and she thought not only of escape, but of having the courage to make her way back to Wolf and her children.

Opening the cabin door, Serena hurried to her room. She had only a few meager items to pack, and no money at all. But that didn't matter.

"Where have you been?" Frederick demanded as he moved to the entrance of her room, barring any escape.

"Getting soaked by the thunder beings," Serena replied over her shoulder. She took a shawl that she'd made, placed her other dress into the folds and rolled it up into a bundle.

"Thunder beings?" Gent scowled. "What's this? You weren't ever to mention any of those Injun words again, girl."

Serena turned, her eyes narrowed and somber. "I'm leaving, Frederick."

"What?"

She tensed and saw his face turn red, an indication of his temper. "I'm going home, and you can't stop me short of shooting me in the back. I'm going home to my husband and my daughters. Now, stand aside."

Camille peeked around her husband, her face white. "Serena! You can't go! That's crazy!"

Serena's stomach was tied into a knot because she knew what Gent was capable of doing to her. She slowly approached him. He was tense and hunched over, as if he were going to attack her.

"You foolish woman," he growled, "you're going nowhere. You *owe* us a year of your time. You have to work off—"

"Kingston paid you to keep me. Consider the three months as a reward. Now, get out of my way!" Serena shrieked. She ducked beneath his arms and escaped into the living room of the cabin.

"Hold it!" Gent roared. He turned and grabbed Serena by the arm. "The devil's got your tongue again, girl. What you need is to get him beat out of you. Camille! Get my belt! Now!"

Serena lurched away from Frederick, slipping her hand out of his grasp. She knew without a doubt that if she didn't get away Gent would place her in leg irons once again and bolt the chain to a wall. Worse, he'd throw her into that dark, windowless room. Desperation fueled Serena's bid for freedom. But she tripped over the hem of her skirt, and fell to the wooden floor.

"Come here!" Frederick bawled, leaning over to grip her by the shoulder.

With a scream, Serena rolled away from him. She lost her bundle, but that no longer mattered. Leaping to her feet, she ran for the front door. The rain was pummeling the roof of the house, and she could hear the wind rising to almost a humanlike howl. Lightning bolts struck so close to the cabin that she flinched. But they didn't make Serena detour from her race toward the door. She heard Frederick's heavy, booted feet thunking across the floor behind her.

Just as she reached the door, it was flung open. There stood Wolf in his deerskin shirt and leggings, his black, braided hair hanging down his chest. Serena stopped short, her eyes widening enormously. She heard Gent give a shout of surprise. Camille screamed.

Serena felt dizzy as she stared at Wolf, who filled the doorway with his powerful presence. Was she seeing things? Was her desperation so great that she imagined him in the doorway? His face was thinner, leaner and harder looking. His mouth was a single line, curved in at the corners, as if he was experiencing pain. In his right hand was a rifle, and water was dripping from its barrel onto the floor.

She saw Wolf raise the rifle and aim it past her at Gent.

"Drop the belt," Wolf ordered the huge, red-faced *wasicun.*

Frederick's mouth fell open, and he allowed the thick leather belt to fall from his hand.

"Wolf?" Serena's voice was shaken, unsure.

Without looking at her, he held out his left hand in her direction. "Come, Cante Tinza."

Rattled, Serena stared in disbelief. Frederick's face was turning a plum color, and the blue spiderweb lines on his nose were standing out against his red flesh. Camille had her hands across her mouth, and her eyes were huge with fear as she stood frozen at the doorway. Serena's gaze moved back to Wolf, to his tall, overwhelming presence. "Y-you're real?" She had spoken Lakota without realizing it, the language slipping from her lips with such ease.

Wolf's mouth barely lifted at the corners, his gaze never leaving Gent. "I am, Cante Tinza. I am not some ghost. Was this *wasicun* going to hurt you?"

"Yes. I—I was trying to leave."

"Leave?"

"Yes," Serena rasped, tears filling her eyes. "Oh, Wolf, I was going to come home. I was going to try and make it back to you and Wakinyela and Dawn Sky."

The corners of his mouth deepened. "Then come, we must go. I have two horses out front. What of this *wasicun?* Does he have a rifle?"

"Yes."

"Then get it. Take any food that you think we can use and bring it along. I will hold the *wasicuns* here while you do that."

With a bare nod, Serena hurried out of the room and ran to the kitchen. Hands shaking badly, she stuffed three loaves of freshly baked bread into an unused flour sack. Canned goods would break, so she left them. Fortunately, Frederick liked smoked ham and bacon, so she put several pounds of each into the sack. Her heart kept hammering. And her head kept saying, *Wolf is here, Wolf is here.* But how?

Serena retrieved the rifle and several boxes of bullets from the Gents' bedroom and then ran to the living room, being careful to stay away from Frederick, who was breathing raggedly and curling his fists as if he wanted to kill Wolf.

"I'm ready."

Wolf nodded. "My two best buffalo runners are with me. You mount Wiyaka. I will come then."

"Don't hurt them, Wolf."

"Did they hurt you?"

Serena had seen enough violence. "He did, but it isn't his fault. He, and later, she tried to convert me to their religion and make me stay in the *wasicun* world."

Wolf eyed the belt on the floor, and glared into the man's purple face. "Tell him not to follow us. If he does, I will kill him."

Serena went to stand next to Wolf. She still couldn't believe he was here. Perhaps her mind was making it up, as it had those many months in the darkness of that one room.

Gulping, she switched back to English. "Frederick, Wolf says not to follow us. If you do, he'll kill you."

Camille gave a frightened cry and fainted.

Frederick turned around and looked down at his wife, who lay on the floor, her flesh pasty in color. Angrily, he turned toward them. "You'll *never* get away with this! I'll have the local militia come after you! They'll find you and kill this redskin!" he said as he pointed angrily at Wolf.

Joy flowed through Serena as she realized Wolf would protect her no matter who came after them. They were in great danger, but if Wolf had been able to track her down and find her, then she knew that they could also return safely to the Paha Sapa.

"Don't follow us," she pleaded. "I don't belong here, Frederick. Don't you understand that?"

He glared at her. "You're a white woman! You ain't no Injun! You skin's white!"

Swallowing hard, Serena lifted her left wrist that bore the long, thin white scar from the ceremony that had made her one with Wolf. "Do you see this, Frederick?"

"Yes. What of it?" he snapped irritably.

"Many years ago, Wolf cut my wrist and his own. Our blood mingled." She looked up at Wolf's harsh profile, tears in her eyes, her voice raspy. "What you don't want to understand is that I love this man with all my heart— with my life, if necessary. I'm going home to my children, Frederick, and to live with them and my husband."

"The devil's got you, girl!" he roared.

Serena smiled slightly as she moved to Wolf. She could smell the dampness of the deerskin he wore, and his male scent. It stirred her senses and touched her heart as nothing else ever could. "Frederick, did you know that the Lakota don't have a devil or hell in their belief? The Great Spirit is a loving presence, not one to be feared like your God. No, I believe in goodness, in respect and love toward others. I don't need your devil. And as for hell, you put me in one by keeping me a prisoner in that room for so many months." Anger tinged her voice. "I hope you rot in your hell, Frederick. You're a cruel man with no heart." She turned and left.

The rain was beginning to cease, the worst of the storm having passed eastward, leaving everything cleansed in its path. Serena gave a cry of joy as she saw Kagi tied with a rope to the saddle of Wiyaka. The wolf whined and leaped happily toward her. She leaned down, hugging the wolf and crying. Untying Kagi, Serena mounted Wiyaka, who also nickered her own kind of greeting to her.

Wolf backed out of the door, his rifle still trained on Gent. He glanced over his shoulder. Cante Tinza had brought the dark bay gelding up to the porch and held the jaw cord out to him. He saw hope burning in her eyes, and he lithely leaped into the saddle. Taking the jaw cord from her fingers, he kept his gaze trained on the door to make sure Gent didn't come charging out.

"We ride west, into the woods," he told her. Wolf desperately wanted to embrace Cante Tinza, to taste the sweetness of her lips, but he didn't dare. They were in great danger, and he knew they must ride long and hard to leave Gent and the militia behind. Her hair was cut off, which angered him. Who had done this to her? Probably the *wasicun*. Bridling his anger, he dug his heels into his gelding.

For three hours they traveled nonstop deep into the woodlands of Ohio. The sun had come back out. Wolf looked up and pointed to Father Sky. "Look."

Serena followed his hand. Above them, bright and beautiful, was a rainbow. "A good sign?"

"Yes," he agreed. "We stop."

The horses were tired, their flanks heaving from the galloping and trotting they'd done hours on end. Serena dismounted. Her legs felt rubbery because she hadn't ridden a horse in nearly a year. She leaned against Wiyaka for a moment and watched as Wolf dismounted.

Wolf came around and eased between the two horses. "Come here, my wife." He opened his arms and saw her lips draw into a heart-melting smile. With a groan, he took her weight, his arms going tightly around her.

"Oh, Wolf," Serena sobbed. She buried her head against his chest, holding him as tightly as she could with her womanly strength. "I missed you. I missed you so much!"

He kissed her damp hair, her flushed cheek and finally sought and found her waiting lips. Crushing her mouth against his, he drank deeply of her, feeling her heat, her taste. She was shaking badly in his arms, and he laughed huskily as he tore his mouth from her wet, full lips. There was such joy in her green eyes, joy that danced in eyes with flecks of sunlight deep within them.

"You are my life," he whispered against her mouth. "My life, my heart. I could not let you be taken from me, Cante Tinza. I could not."

With a muffled sound, Serena clung to Wolf, kissing him repeatedly with wild abandon. His mouth was strong and cherishing against hers. "I feel as if I'm dreaming," she said with a little laugh, near hysteria. "All those months in that dark, cold room—I thought I was going crazy. I dreamed you were there with me. I remember talking to you. Oh, I talked out loud so much that first month or two...."

He framed her face with his hands and saw the haunted look in her eyes. "What do you speak of, my heart? What dark room?"

With a sob, Serena closed her eyes and absorbed Wolf's strength. His hands, callused and large, felt steadying to her unstable emotional state. "Frederick cut off my braids and cut off my necklace made of our hair," she choked out. "He threw me into a dark room. I don't know for how long. I only know it was months. It was so dark, and I was so cold. I was so lonely. At first, all I remember is my mind going crazy. I'd be sitting on the floor wrapped in my blankets and I'd see you appear to me. I'd talk to you. I'd cry. I was so worried for our babies, for you."

Closing his eyes, Wolf felt her pain. He rested his brow against her hair. "The *wasicun* tortured you." Now he wished he had killed the man. Cante Tinza was a woman who blossomed out on the land because she was close to Mother Earth. Wolf couldn't begin to imagine her being kept in a dark room for months. Gently, he began to caress her short hair, which was badly in need of being combed. Her tears ripped at him as he began to realize the cruelty she'd endured.

"I—I gave up, Wolf. I surrendered," she babbled. "After a while, my mind seemed to snap. I felt empty. I had no memory of you, or of our daughters. It was then that Frederick took off my leg irons and let me walk freely around his farm."

"Leg irons?" His eyes narrowed with fury.

"Y-yes. The Army put me in them after they captured me. Oh, Wolf, I tried to escape so many times. Once, I got a half a day away from the Army wagon train, but they found me. I was so close to escaping." Serena closed her eyes and whispered, "They put me in chains just like Kingston had. I wore them until this spring, when Frederick finally let me out of the room."

Grimly, Wolf caressed her cheeks with his thumbs, taking her tears away. "Kingston is dead."

Shaken, Serena gazed up to his hard, lined face. "Dead?"

With a slight smile, pleasure in his voice, Wolf said, "The day after the Army captured you, I rode into Kingston's mining camp. I found him asleep in his bed. I held a knife to his throat and he told me everything." Touching Cante Tinza's wrinkled brow, he smoothed it with his fingers. "Kingston told the Army of your whereabouts with us. He lied and told them that we had captured you. He gave them money to give to a family who would keep you for a year to make sure you stayed with *wasicuns*."

"But—how did you know *where* I was?"

"Kingston's black woman showed me a letter he had written to this man named Gent. I could not read it, but she read it for me. She came from Kentucky and knew where Ohio was, and where this area near the river was."

Serena shut her eyes and collapsed against Wolf's strong, steadying body. His arms were tight and protective around her as she sagged against him. "I don't see how you got here."

Wolf smiled faintly as he ran his hand gently up and down her damp back. "Kagi was my eyes and ears. She often alerted me to *wasicun* patrols. I also had to avoid other tribes, and she kept me safe from them. She will do the same on our way home. We will ask her to keep us out of the way of our enemies."

Sniffing, Serena eased away from Wolf just enough to gaze up into his dark, warm eyes. "It will be so dangerous. The Army will come after me, Wolf."

"Yes, but if we are careful, we can avoid them."

The future looked hopeless to Serena. "Frederick could notify the Army post near the Paha Sapa. They could come and get me again. I would put the tribe into more danger."

Wolf shook his head. "Let us live each day as it arrives, Cante Tinza. When we make camp tonight, all I want to do is hold my wife in my arms. I want to hear the strong, brave beat of her heart against my heart. More than anything, I want to show you how much I love you, how much I have missed you."

Chapter Sixteen

Near dusk, they stopped for the night. They had headed in a northwesterly direction, and to avoid detection they remained within the embrace of the thick woodlands that carpeted Ohio. Wolf had cautioned Cante Tinza not to speak as they rode for fear of being overheard by a dog that might bark an alarm. The horses were wet, and their heads hung as Serena unsaddled them and then placed hobbles on them so that they could forage for grass.

Wolf dug a deep hole, placed dried grass and small sticks into it and with flint sparks started a fire. An hour earlier he had spotted a rabbit and had killed it with an arrow. They worked quietly in unison. What little smoke was created by the fire was quickly dispersed as it rose and spread upward through the branches of the beech and oak trees surrounding them. Even with darkness coming, the firelight would be hidden because of the depth of the hole.

Serena fell into her tasks, just as if she were home again with the Lakota tribe. Joy thrummed through her as she looked up from skinning the rabbit to see Wolf walking silently around the camp. He gathered wood and then went to a nearby stream and got water. Kagi remained steadfastly at her side, her yellow eyes bright with silent happiness that Serena was back.

The rabbit was quartered and roasted over the fire. They sat cross-legged, their knees barely touching, as they ate the sumptuous meal. Earlier, Wolf had decided that their camp was relatively safe as Kagi hadn't sounded any alarm. If humans were within three miles of them, she would have been stiffly alert.

"Would you like to have your deerskin dress back?" he asked, gesturing to the cotton one she wore.

"Yes."

Wolf smiled and eased to his moccasined feet. Going to the bulging parfleche saddlebags, he pulled out one of her dresses. Cante Tinza looked less strained now. Wolf hurt for her, for all that she had suffered through with the *wasicuns*. Yet as he handed her the dress and he saw her eyes alight with joy, his heart almost burst with fierce, unfettered love for her. He watched as she eagerly unrolled the deerskin dress.

"Little Swallow made me bring your work dress. She also packed a pair of your moccasins." He watched Cante Tinza move her fingertips across the smooth, soft hide. How many nights had he dreamed of her running her hands across him?

Tears flooded into Serena's eyes as she gazed up at Wolf's darkly shadowed features. The light of a quarter moon broke the darkness enough to reveal the bare outline of his face. "I've missed everyone so much, Wolf."

He heard the quaver in her voice and knelt in front of her, gently threading his fingers through her hair. He could tell that someone had carelessly hacked it off because it hung in uneven lengths halfway down her neck. He saw the pain in her face as he caressed her red hair. Leaning down, he barely grazed her lips.

"Your hair will grow back," he reassured her in a whisper. He felt the softness of her lips meet and meld with his. His hands framed her face and he felt Cante Tinza shudder. "Come here," he said thickly, and pulled her into his arms to hold her tightly. She began to cry, her face pressed against his shirt, her fingers clutching at the soft deerskin across his chest. All Wolf could do was hold her, and stroke her head, shoulders and back to help her release the horror of her many moons of imprisonment. His mouth turned down with anger, and rage tunneled through him at the humiliation Cante Tinza had had to endure. To treat a woman with so little respect was beyond his comprehension. Didn't *wasicuns* realize that it was the women who carried their beloved children? The children who were their future? Their hope? More important, didn't they realize that women were just as sacred as any man, perhaps more so? They gave their blood once a moon to Mother Earth, and that was something men wished that they could do, but could not. All a man could do was symbolically cut his arms and allow the blood to drip from his fingertips and have it absorbed by the Mother Earth.

Much later Cante Tinza's weeping ceased. The fire had gone out, and only the thin, washed-out moonlight covered the wooded region. Easing her away from him just enough to lift her chin so that he could look into her eyes, Wolf smiled gently.

"Dawn Sky and Wakinyela are safe and with Dreaming Bear."

Sniffing, Serena nodded and tried to wipe away the tears with her fingers. "I'm glad. I—I miss them so much, Wolf."

"We both do," he agreed quietly, caressing her shoulders. "It has been nine moons since I last saw them, too."

He saw her face reflect his pain, and he shook his head. "I had to find you, Cante Tinza."

"But the tribe doesn't have a medicine person," she whispered.

"The chief reminded me of my responsibility," Wolf told her. "But I told him I had a responsibility toward my wife, too." He grazed her cheek and held her sad eyes. "Dreaming Bear knows of herbs, and she will do her best to help those who become sick in my absence."

"Wakinyela will be walking by now," Serena said softly, looking into the darkness and feeling the pain well up through her. "Do you know that for many moons I forgot about my family, about you?"

"If someone had kept me in a dark room as you were, I would have gone *heyoka,* crazy," Wolf confided. He held her gaze. "You were like a bear hibernating for that time. You drew deep within yourself and you went into the other realms just as the bear does when it goes into its cave for the cold moons."

"That thunderstorm," Serena whispered. "Something happened, Wolf. Something awakened in me. I was sitting there milking the cow and I felt it. I heard it. I took the cow out to the pasture and I remember seeing the thunder beings creating this storm. All the memories, all the feelings about you and my babies suddenly came flooding back to me."

He smiled and reached into the parfleche saddlebag. "The bear within you, which was hibernating, awoke. That is why the memories came back to you." He withdrew the elk bone comb. "Let me care for your hair, my woman."

"Oh, no, Wolf. It's terrible looking." Serena pulled away, her fingers trembling across the hacked-off strands. "I—I saw myself in the pond one day. I look ugly!"

Patiently, Wolf captured her hands and placed them in her lap. "No more protests," he chided her gently, and began to ease the comb through the copper-colored strands. "Do not deny me a pleasure I have missed for so long. I do not care if your hair is short or long. It is the woman who wears this hair that I love."

Sniffing, Serena closed her eyes, absorbing his touch like a starving person. "I had forgotten how wonderful this could be," she quavered.

"Because you thought you had been abandoned and saw no escape from that *wasicun.*"

She gazed up at his face and saw the hardness melt away from his features; the corners of his mouth drew upward, and his eyes glinted with happiness. "I never thought you'd come, Wolf," Serena admitted, ashamed of herself. "I didn't see how you could find me. It must have been so dangerous coming here."

"Yes, and it will be dangerous going home. But with Kagi's eyes, ears and nose, we will be safe."

"And you said Kingston is dead?"

"Yes."

"Do you think Frederick will try and tell the fort near the Paha Sapa that I'm there? I fear they will come and get me again, Wolf."

He sat back, satisfied. Cante Tinza's hair now looked softer and tamed, the strands gleaming dully in the moonlight. The worry and anxiety in her eyes was real, and he reached over and captured her hand. "Chief Badger Mouth made a decision," he told her somberly. "Before I left, he agreed that our tribe should leave the Paha Sapa."

Gasping, Serena's eyes widened. "Leave? Where will we go?"

"To Canada. The horse soldiers cannot cross the border to chase us and kill us if we live in that country." Wolf pointed north. "As soon as we return, and as soon as we can travel, the chief will lead us north to that country."

"But will the Canadians leave us alone?"

Wolf nodded. "Already, other Lakota tribes have moved up there, and they live in peace. The *wasicuns* there respect the Lakota and do not bother them." His hand tightened around hers. "You will finally be safe, Cante Tinza. No *wasicun* will come and drag you off again."

It sounded too good to be true. Serena gripped Wolf's hand. "This is like a dream. I'm afraid I'll wake up and find myself back at their farm," she said shuddering.

Wolf understood. The night air was warm and fragrant with life. It was the moon when berries were ripe. He reached forward and began to unbutton her dress.

"I have prayed endlessly to the Great Spirit for your safety—to find you alive," he told her in an unsteady voice. "You are my woman. You hold my heart in your hands, Cante Tinza." Wolf saw the desire grow in her eyes as he continued to ease the buttons from the fabric. "Tonight is the first night I will share my robe with you once again. I want to hold you in my arms. I want to share my love with you." His hands stilled on the fabric, and the dress parted to reveal the chemise she wore beneath it. "I know you feel unsure because you are like a wild horse that is suddenly set free after being hobbled and held prisoner." He settled his hands against her long, slender neck, his thumbs stroking her soft flesh. "Guide me. Tell me how much you want from me. If it does not feel right to you, then stop me."

Serena closed her eyes as Wolf's low, vibrant voice flowed through her. His touch was evoking, stirring not only her heart to life, but her body as well. His fingers moved slowly down her neck, following her collarbones and easing the dress away from her shoulders. Serena felt the dress pool around her hips. Words choked up in her throat, and she opened her eyes and smiled tremulously up into his eyes.

"I love you with all my heart and soul. How can I tell you to stop when all I've dreamed of is being with you, beloved?" Serena reached over and caressed Wolf's cheek, and his eyes grew dark with desire. A soft gasp formed as she felt Wolf's hands gently curve around her breasts. He held her as if she were a delicate vessel that might break. As Serena surrendered to him and moved into his arms, she felt fragile.

Wolf had laid out the robe earlier. It was a summer buffalo robe, the hairs short and smooth, unlike the hairy, thick robes used during the cold moons. With an understanding nod, he guided Cante Tinza to the robe, where he continued to undress her. The dress was removed and placed on the ground in a heap. Next went the white cotton chemise and petticoat. The moonlight bathed her ivory-colored body as she knelt between his legs, her long, slender hands resting upon her curved thighs.

Wolf's smile deepened as she helped him slip the deerskin shirt over his head. The pleasure, the wanting of him, shone clearly in her dark green eyes as she tentatively ran her hands across his chest.

"You are so beautiful," Serena whispered unsteadily, feeling his heat, his power beneath the taut flesh of his chest. Courage radiated from within Wolf, Serena realized humbly, for Wolf was a man of conviction and loyalty.

She saw his eyes grow velvet with desire for her as he removed his leggings and breechclout. They knelt naked in front of each other. Serena felt no shame in gazing at Wolf. She leaned over and began to untie and then unbraid his hair. The ebony strands fell around his shoulders and framed his face. With trembling fingers, she closed her eyes and kneaded his scalp, refamiliarizing herself with him all over again. His hair was thick and luxuriant. As she moved her hands down to the taut muscles of his shoulders and chest, coals of longing flared to life within her once again.

How cold and desolate she had been, Serena realized as Wolf caressed her breasts, his thumbs grazing her hardening nipples. When he slid his hand around her waist and drew her into his arms, she sighed in anticipation. His lips closed over her nipple, and she gave a small cry of exultation as she felt hot, tremoring bolts jaggedly racing through her. She surrendered to his caresses, feeling and absorbing his love in every fiber of her being. How she had needed Wolf's touch!

Serena felt herself being placed on the robe, the warmth of the fur against her back. As Wolf's hands drifted down and across her body, as he reacquainted himself with every curve of her, she sighed and closed her eyes. His hands were teasing and strong at the same time. She felt him hesitate as his hands ranged down her legs to her ankles.

Wolf scowled as he saw for the first time the scars caused by the leg irons Cante Tinza had had to wear on her small ankles. He brushed his fingertips across the scarred flesh. He felt unadulterated rage. Once again, she had borne the anger of the *wasicuns* against her as a woman, a woman who was courageous in the face of overwhelming odds. Leaning down, he kissed those scars, wanting to take the pain away from her, to erase the memory of her imprisonment.

Later Wolf moved to her side to mold his body against the length of hers. He slid his arm beneath her neck, and splayed his other hand across her rounded belly. He saw the unsureness and shame in her eyes over his discovery of the scars that marked her ankles. Gently, he moved his hand across her abdomen.

"I pray that before we reach home you carry our next child within you, my woman." When he leaned down to caress her lips he felt her fire for him returning. As Wolf eased from her moist lips, he whispered, "A child who will be born in freedom, who will never have to endure what you have gone through."

His words vibrated through Serena, and with a small cry she lifted her arms and placed them around Wolf's shoulders. He had never judged her. He had never shamed her. All he saw was her beauty, despite the scars she bore. Drowning in the splendor of his strong, cherishing mouth, she felt his hand drift downward toward her thighs, and she opened herself to him, inviting his exploration of her.

Her moan drowned in his mouth as he continued to caress her. When he moved across her, settling his weight against her, Serena had never before felt as joyous or as powerful as a woman. As Wolf moved slowly into her, she arched her back to accept him. The wet slickness of her melted and joined his rigid thrust.

Wolf stilled himself and placed his hands against Cante Tinza's face. She was scalding him with her fire, yet he didn't want to move just yet. He simply wanted to savor her.

"Look at me," he whispered raggedly. Her lashes lifted to reveal drowsy green eyes that were flecked with sunlight. As her lips parted, Wolf groaned. "We are one, Cante Tinza. We will always be one. Time and distance do not separate us—ever."

She smiled tremulously and felt him thrust slowly, deeply, into her. The hardness of his body, the tautness of him as a man, had never been more apparent, and yet she felt herself adjusting, surrendering in so many beautiful ways to him. With each slow thrust, the pleasure built a hundredfold within her. Wolf's hands framed her face, his mouth captured hers, and she moaned as he began not only to fill her fully with his presence, but to give back so much of what had been taken from her.

In those moments before the shattering pleasure exploded throughout her, Serena understood what real love between a man and a woman meant. It wasn't about a man subjugating a woman, it was about a man blending with a woman to become one. Wolf understood their symmetry.

Later, they lay quietly in each other's arms, the robe drawn over them. Serena was exhausted, and very quickly fell asleep in Wolf's protective embrace. The feeling of safety had never been more intense. For the first time in months, she dreamed of seeing her babies and of seeing the Lakota people who had shaped her life with love and respect, not cruelty, prejudice or imprisonment.

The leaves of the Paha Sapa were turning brilliant shades of orange, yellow and red as Serena rode with Wolf at her side. The dark green of the pines was a vivid contrast to the colors of the trees that were now shedding their leaves. She traded a happy look with him as they rode at an easy gallop across the meadow that she knew would bring them to the camp. It had taken them three moons to return, and Serena could hardly wait to see her children.

Kagi raced ahead and disappeared over the last rise. At the top of the knoll, they reined their horses to a halt. Serena gasped. There, spread out along a river, was their camp. Wolf pointed to his tepee, which had a black wolf painted on the exterior above the entrance.

Heart pounding, Serena saw Dreaming Bear walking Wakinyela outside their tepee. She turned to Wolf, tears in her eyes. "She's walking."

He smiled. "Very well, too." His smile deepened as he reached over and gripped her hand. "Let's greet our family."

The last mile down the long, sloping hill was breathtaking. Serena heard the camp crier announcing their arrival in his high, falsetto voice, his shrill Lakota words bringing the daily work to a halt. She saw groups of women working over tanned buffalo hides and elderly women at the community cooking pots, all look up. But her eyes were on Wakinyela, her daughter.

Dreaming Bear gave a warbling cry of welcome and leaned down to point to the riders approaching from the east and to whisper into Wakinyela's ear. The little girl wore a buckskin dress and moccasins, her black hair in tiny braids adorned with eagle feather fluff.

Serena urged Wiyaka at a faster gallop, the wind tearing past her. The mare seemed to understand her urgency and began to stretch her stride, her hooves creating a thundering sound as they struck the dry, hard ground. Little Swallow came running toward her, hand raised in the air. At her side was Dawn Sky. How she had grown, Serena thought, sadness moving through her. In the full year Serena had been gone, Dawn Sky had become a beautiful little girl, so tall and straight like Wolf.

"*Ina! Ina!*" Wakinyela cried, her arms stretched outward, toddling forward.

With a cry, Serena pulled the horse to a halt and fairly flew out of the saddle. She ran toward her daughter, who had her tiny arms stretched toward her. Wakinyela's eyes were so green that they took Serena's breath away in amazement. As she knelt to receive her daughter's embrace, Serena sobbed. *Ina* meant mother. As Wakinyela's arms closed around her neck, Serena stood holding her baby tightly against her. Dreaming Bear had taught the child the word *mother,* and had obviously not let Wakinyela forget about her, even though she'd been missing from her life for so long.

Serena felt pats of welcome on her shoulders and back, and heard the excited and happy Lakota voices as people began to surround her. She smiled through her tears, reaching out with her one hand to greet them in return. Dawn Sky came up and threw her arms around Serena's legs. Kneeling, Serena gathered her other daughter into her arms. The three of them silently embraced, and Serena wept.

Gradually, she heard Wolf's voice, low and husky, intrude into the excited chatter and laughter that surrounded her. She looked up to see him standing at her side. With a smile, she eased to her full height and handed Wakinyela to him. Their daughter gave a cry and hugged her father. Serena pressed kiss after kiss on Dawn Sky's round face and ran her hands across her black, braided hair.

"How beautiful you've become," Serena whispered as she knelt before Dawn Sky.

"Dreaming Bear said you'd return, *Ina*," she cried, sniffing. "The tepee has been so empty without you and *Ahtay*, Father."

"I know, I know," Serena soothed. She held the sobbing little girl tightly.

Little Swallow touched Serena's shoulder. "Welcome home, my sister."

"It's so good to be here," Serena quavered, smiling up at Wolf's sister.

"Your children have been very good in your absence." Little Swallow patted Dawn Sky's head affectionately. "We are so glad you have come back to us." She gave her brother a worried look. "We were so afraid that Wolf might die in trying to find you."

"I almost did," Wolf joked as he held Wakinyela in his arms, "but Kagi saved me many times."

The entire village now surrounded them. Serena was thrilled when Wakinyela wanted to return to her arms. Dawn Sky hung near her, her small hand tightly wrapped in Serena's dress, afraid to let go of her. The younger boys who had yet to become warriors rode their horses around and around the camp, yipping and yelling their welcome. The dogs barked. The older warriors and their wives all came forward with kind words of welcome.

Throughout it all, Serena looked for Deer Woman. Wolf had told her that she'd been responsible for alerting Kingston in the first place, and that she had lied to make Kingston think that Serena had set his cabin on fire, killing his wife and son. As the crowd began to dissipate and everyone returned to their duties, Little Swallow walked with Serena and Wakinyela to Wolf's tepee.

In a low voice that no one could hear, Serena asked her sister-in-law, "Where is Deer Woman?"

Little Swallow went into the tepee. Once inside, she said, "Deer Woman has been banished from the tribe. She was going through the village stirring up trouble. She tried to turn all of us against you, to blame you for Wolf's absence. Chief Badger Mouth was very upset that Wolf left to find you. He was worried because without Wolf, without his medicine, some of our people could have died. Tall Crane, who is Wolf's *hunka* brother, came forward with the truth. Wolf had told him before he left that Deer Woman was responsible for your being captured the first time, by Kingston."

Serena set Wakinyela down, and the little girl promptly grabbed onto her skirt. "What did the chief do?"

Little Swallow smiled grimly. "He banished her from the tribe."

"How long ago?"

"It happened a moon after Wolf left."

"Where did she go?"

With a shrug, Little Swallow said, "Who knows? The girl only stirs up trouble. She does not want to be a part of us."

Touching her throat, Serena whispered, "I've never before heard of someone being banished."

"Sometimes it must be done for the good of all, Cante Tinza. Do not look ashamed or feel bad for the girl. The feelings she had were not right. They turned bad—and it was her choice. She did not have to stir up more trouble."

"But where would she go?"

"Probably to one of the forts or to a mining camp."

"Oh, no...." Serena closed her eyes. "Only Lakota who drink are in those camps, Little Swallow. The women I saw—" she drew in a ragged breath "—are soiled doves who make their living lying with the miners."

"That is her choice," Little Swallow said gently as she laid her hand on Serena's shoulder. "Now that you are back, we will break camp and begin our journey north to Canada. I was praying that you would return soon. I understand it is a two-moon journey to that country. We should get there before the worst of the cold moons arrive."

Serena nodded. So much was happening so quickly. She smiled down at Wakinyela, who had decided to sit at her feet and play with the short fringe on her dress. "Thank you for taking care of our children," she said brokenly, and gave Little Swallow a long hug.

Blushing, Little Swallow drew away and smiled. "They are good children. Tall Crane has been a good *hunka* uncle. Dreaming Bear has done most of the work, and they love their hunka grandmother."

Wolf entered the tepee and nodded to his sister. "Not much has changed since I left." He touched his sister's face. "You have lost some weight?"

"Some."

Serena smiled up at Wolf as he placed his arm around her. "We have good news for you, Little Swallow."

"Oh?" Her brows lifted and she smiled. "A good surprise?"

"The best," Serena murmured, gazing lovingly up at her husband, who stood proudly at her side. "Wolf? Do you want to tell her?"

He nodded. "Cante Tinza carries our second child in her belly."

With a gasp of delight, Little Swallow clapped her hands together. "Oh! This is great news! May I tell the people?"

With a laugh, Serena nodded. "Of course."

With a shy touch of Serena's belly, Little Swallow asked, "Do you feel it is a boy or a girl?"

"A boy."

"Yes?"

Wolf smiled, pleased. "We have two daughters. Now, they will teach their brother that women are strong and courageous, like their mother." He gazed down at his wife and saw the utter joy in her eyes. Their lives would never be easy, but at least by moving into Canada, they would be safe from the horse soldiers and miners, who now raped and plundered their sacred land. Most of all, Cante Tinza would be safe from further threats.

He caressed her hair, knowing that for her life would take on happier times. She had a brave heart and an even stronger soul, which endured, and he knew the Great Spirit always rewarded those who had the courage to walk with their fears and move forward. Silently, Wolf promised his wife that he would make up for all the pain and loneliness she had undergone. As a medicine man, he knew the power of love was the strongest emotion given to human beings. And his love would heal her, just as her love would heal him.

* * * * *